FINAL SHOT

A Psych 'n' Roll Mystery

by **Ira Kalina**

PRAISE FOR IRA KALINA'S THRILLER
FINAL SHOT

"A great read from a first-time author. Kalina's first work of fiction blew me away. It's a tour-de-force-hold-on-for-dear-life-page-turner. I read the last 150 pages in one sitting... taut, expertly crafted scenes with dialogue that sounds like real people talking. And the story moves rapidly, as if fired from a proverbial cannon. Read *Final Shot...* it's good, old-fashioned fun."

–John Edmondson, *Derry News*

"*Final Shot* ably balance[s] character development and back-story... the action moves briskly.... fast-paced... buoyed by a likable hero."

–*Kirkus Reviews*

"*Final Shot...* Mystery, music, money, and murder... Ira Kalina has created an edgy crime thriller with a solid underpinning of psychological insight in his first novel about a rock 'n' roll-loving psychologist turned radio star caught up in a decades-old Nazi vendetta. Trust me, you'll be holding your breath for Ike Miller's next Psych 'n' Roll adventure."

–Bridget McKenna, author
The Little Book of Self-Editing

"*Final Shot* is quite a feat, at once a genre novel—mystery/thriller—and a breaker of conventions. Well written, fast-paced, the novel features a unique protagonist, Dr Ike, psychologist, radio rock n' roll maven, former basketball star, he's a man with a heart and a lotta moves who must face a personal challenge that is connected with the darkest historical tragedy of the 20th century, the Holocaust."

–Peter Pitzele, author *Our Fathers' Wells*

ISBN: 1481896814
ISBN-13: 9781481896818
Library of Congress Control Number: 2013900341
CreateSpace Independent Publishing Platform
North Charleston, South Carolina

Author's Note

"Final Shot" is a work of fiction. Names, characters, places and events either are a product of the author's imagination or are fictitious and any resemblence to actual persons living or dead, business establishments, events, or locales is purely coincidental.

For

David and Noah

<u>PART I</u>

CHAPTER ONE

THE BLESSED

October 2010

Every time Baruch Gittlestein would drive his van into Manhattan, he'd worry. Then again, Gittlestein would worry whether or not he was driving. Everything and anything could jumble his almost ninety-year-old brain. Most notably it was the little things. Like the garbage at the entrance to the Brooklyn Bridge incline, or the omnipresent pothole he'd dubbed the *dybbuk* that cratered the center of the access ramp. Baruch was always hypervigilant about traffic merging from the side and tailing from behind, so he checked his mirrors repeatedly. The quick back and forth from mirror to windshield and windshield to mirror made his sidelocks jitter against his bearded face and his right foot bounce on the brake pedal as if he suffered from a restless leg. His agitation was so pronounced that the old white van mimicked the movement of the elderly Hasid's body.

Arriving on the bridge, Baruch's angst propelled him up from his seat when he heard horn salvos coming at him from behind. His black fedora smashed against the van's ceiling. His heart beat furiously and his stomach turned. He checked his mirror again and he saw the irritated face of an overweight, middle-aged woman with orange-red hair. He watched her pound the wheel of her Land Rover.

Impatient drivers are the devil, Baruch thought. And then, *did this cow really think that orange hair makes her look young?*

That was Baruch Gittlestein.

He'd make the tiniest item into a huge story — a *gantseh magilla* was the Yiddish expression. Whenever he thought someone had flashed him a dirty look, or if he observed something off-kilter he'd ruminate about it, turn it around, and blow it up until another agony entered his mind. Gittlestein could never push aside the small stuff, no matter how much he prayed, no matter how much the rabbi and his fellow congregants tried to reassure him, not even after the powerful drugs and electroshock therapy the doctors had prescribed. His only peace came from his discussions with his friend, Otto Sperber, a fellow Auschwitz survivor and famous psychoanalyst. Otto understood his fears and never labeled them as paranoia. Despite Dr. Sperber's reassurances, it was the smallest, sometimes the microscopic that would fuel Baruch's obsessions: Like a deadly flu virus from a handshake, or a melanoma caused by too much exposure to the sun. The world was a dangerous place. Baruch would worry in a never-ending loop, and before he knew it the doctors would send electricity through his temples and he'd awake with "the zipping and zapping" as his only memory.

"It is hard to believe you are the Blessed when they did that to you," Otto Sperber had told him.

And wasn't that the truth and his burden?

After the war, and in devotion to *Hashem*, he'd changed his name from Benjamin to Baruch. He believed his survival had been a divine intervention, a blessing. But in all the years since, the blessing had turned into a nightmare and the Blessed had become the Cursed. How could he be blessed when so many of the little things were against him?

In the garment district now he drove in a circle, street to avenue, avenue to street, automobiles in line like the cattle cars on the tracks of Poland. He felt the crawling sensation in his stomach. The voices became louder. They told him the woman — the fat one with the dyed hair — was a threat after all. The chorus warned him to be cautious, that danger was near. He looked in the mirrors to check if she was behind him. He scanned the midtown streets. And as he turned his head to the right, he saw something. Right there, a parking spot in front of Hirsch the furrier's shop, of all places. Baruch despised Hirsch, a *gonif* who overcharged for storage. Because Baruch refused to be ripped off, he'd kept his coat with its mink trim in his bedroom closet during the summer. He was wearing it now. The cloth moth-eaten, the tiny holes an abomination.

Baruch wanted to avoid Hirsch and prayed that Hirsch wouldn't see him. But he had to bring a package to the big post office for the rabbi, and a parking spot in this neighborhood was a gift from *Hashem*. He backed the van into the space and collided with a gray Mercedes. The elderly Hasid exhaled a deep, long breath and inched the vehicle forward. He turned the motor off and retrieved the parcel from the floor behind his seat. He stiffly rolled his long body from the van and onto the street where, even though it was Sunday, streams of people walked briskly by, shops were open for business, and the smell of Middle Eastern food, another one of the little things, infiltrated the air.

And there, shouting and pointing, was Hirsch the furrier.

"You bastard, Gittlestein. You dented my fender!"

They were a mutual detestation society, these two. Baruch knew that Hirsch could never forgive him for rejecting his services. And, now, Hirsch accused Baruch of purposely colliding with the Mercedes. "I know it is so," Hirsch said. "I know this the way I know mink and fox and raccoon."

Simon Hirsch was a diminutive man, round like the actor Mickey Rooney, and Baruch towered over him. "You called me a bastard. You are a bastard, a Nazi lover. I should take an axe to your *farstunkinah* Nazi car. You couldn't buy a Chevrolet, a Cadillac? You had to buy a German car? What is wrong with you?"

They were face-to-face—more accurately, face-to-chest—when Hirsch threw his hands up into the air, shook his head, and moaned, "*Oy*, please go away." He turned and retreated into his shop.

Baruch was about to charge after the furrier, but as he pivoted toward the store he dropped the rabbi's package. Another little thing, but one that made him lose interest in continuing the confrontation with his *gonif* nemesis. Instead, he flashed his middle finger in Hirsch's direction, picked up the package, and moved on toward the post office.

The massive Corinthian structure on Eighth Avenue that was the main post office in New York City reminded Baruch of the Reichstag. As an architecture student during the years before everything changed, he'd abhorred the work of Albert Speer, who'd combined the Gothic with Roman designs to create the Third Reich's garish, mythical structures. America had been a safe haven, but a building like this made him think that Nazism lived in the hearts of the powerful in New York and Washington. Even the famous and seemingly benign saying engraved above the entrance, "Neither snow nor rain nor heat nor gloom of night stays these couriers from the swift completion of their appointed rounds," made him think of how the Nazi bastards tried to fool the world with their "Arbeit Macht Frei" propaganda. He loathed everything about the building, but the worst were the high, wide steps—steps that put pressure on his arthritic ankles and knees. *Couldn't the schmucks who designed this place have foreseen that an old person might have to drop off a letter?* He thought every time he came here.

Baruch *kvetched* his way to the top of the staircase and walked the columned hallway. The lines were light, but at the window for overseas packages he encountered a long queue. Baruch shuffled his feet to the end of the line and placed the rabbi's Jerusalem-destined parcel on the marble floor. Waiting was another one of the tiny things that brought the voices on. They were distant at first, only a whisper. But soon they rose in a crescendo because the line remained frozen in place. The voices warned him to stay alert. That today was the day it would finally happen.

Baruch never remembered that delusions like this one had occurred hundreds of times. Even if he did, it wouldn't have changed a thing. He began to perspire. His hands trembled. "Please, God, keep me safe," he repeated in Hebrew over and over again. His prayers were accompanied by, what the pious called *shukling*: rocking, half turning left to right, right to left, his head shaking, his knees bending while he fingered the knotted strings of his *tsitses*. He began to calm down, the feeling reinforced by the movement of the line. He was now third. Not good yet, but better. He retreated again to his praying.

The customer behind him tapped his shoulder. "Hey, would you keep it down?"

Baruch turned to see a young man, late twenties or early thirties. He had piercing brown eyes and a scar that traversed his chin. He wore jeans and a navy exercise jacket and looked at Baruch with a phony smile. There was something else. His voice had a familiar ring.

The chorus in Baruch's head shouted now: *You must go! You must run!*

"What's wrong with you?" the man asked.

Baruch looked at him again and thought he saw the sneer he'd observed countless times coming from another man, a man who'd sent Baruch's pregnant wife to the gas, a man who was now supposed to be dead.

This wasn't one of the tiny things.

This was it. What he'd feared for over sixty years.

You must go! You must run!

He cried out, "They have come for me." He shouted it again and then once more. His voice echoed through the cavernous building.

People were unmoved by his outburst — drug addicts and the mentally ill were frequent visitors to this post office. A security guard approached Baruch. "Please, sir, you must calm down or you'll have to leave."

With his flailing arms and long legs that made him look like a giant Hasidic praying mantis, Baruch ran — leaving the rabbi's package on the floor — through the exit and onto the long and steep stairs. He lost his balance. His black hat fell to the ground and he tumbled the last few steps onto the sidewalk. A Con Edison worker and a cop rushed to his aid. Despite the possibility he'd seriously injured himself, Baruch rose with the legs of a pummeled boxer, grabbed the fedora, pushed the helpers away, and took off for his van.

Pumped up with adrenaline, he fled despite a twisted ankle and injury to his arthritic knee. And when he saw a fat woman with phony red hair, perhaps one of hundreds, or maybe even thousands, that walked the city's street on that day, the symptoms of his final heart attack exploded from his left arm into his chest. He stumbled, put his hands to his throat, and fell in front of Hirsch the furrier's shop.

Just before he made his transition to a better world, Baruch Gittlestein heard his furrier nemesis cry out, "*Gey en drerd arein.*" It was a contemptuous phrase. Taken as a whole, it meant drop dead. But word-for-word it translated to "go lay in the dirt." Tomorrow the *gonif* furrier would get his wish — a burial for Gittlestein which hundreds of men in black hats and black coats would attend.

Hirsch would not be among them.

CHAPTER TWO

BEFORE THE PAIN

A Big Apple Sunday morning. Early October. Sunny. Mild. Spectacular.

Ike Miller, dressed in his college team warm-up suit and black, high-top basketball shoes, stood on the foul line of a Hell's Kitchen Playground court. The sounds of traffic from Eleventh Avenue and the West Side Highway rushed by like intermittent gusts of wind, but Ike remained focused on the front of the rim, one of countless hoops he'd targeted since he first played the game as an eight-year old. Ike stretched his six-foot-one frame upward, raised the basketball over his head and with a bend of the knees and flick of his right wrist launched it toward the basket. The instant the ball left his hand, he knew its trajectory was off to the left. He watched, ticked off at himself, as it clanked off the iron cylinder, ricocheted against the backboard, fell to the ground, and bounced its way to the chain-link fence behind the basket.

In hoops-talk, Ike Miller had just thrown a brick.

Hooting and whistling came out of nowhere. Ike, having arrived at an empty playground, nearly jumped out of his Nikes. He turned to see a group of mid-to-late-teen boys elbowing and jostling each other as they pointed at him from the center court circle. The tallest of them approached.

"Dude, you'd have better luck if you crossed yourself before taking a free throw. Don't you know that?"

Ike, being Jewish, had never engaged in that particular ritual. "What's your name?" he asked.

"None of your business."

"I'm Ike," he said.

The kid stared at him.

"Why won't you tell me your name?" Ike asked.

"What the fuck you doing here?"

"It's a public court. I can play here just like anyone else," Ike said, disturbed as to where this was going.

"It's our court. Fuck off."

It was obvious to Ike, a credentialed shrink. The boy was showing his friends how tough he was. Still, there was something frail, even poignant, in the dark brown eyes, partially obscured by the hood of his red sweat-shirt. Despite the boy's machismo, Ike felt for him.

A voice bellowed from the other end of the court. "Hey, hey, hey. What's happening here? Antwanne, I can't believe you're picking a fight again. I told you to cut that crap out."

Antwanne lowered his head and stepped away from Ike. The rest of the kids backed up as well. Whoever had just reprimanded Antwanne was coming Ike's way.

"Sorry about that. They get a bit territorial," he said and extended his hand. "My name's Jamal." Jamal was dressed in New York Knicks warm-up pants and sweat-shirt, sleeves pushed up to his elbow. A whistle hung from his neck. "Hey, don't I know you from somewhere?" he asked.

Ike noticed that Jamal was looking him over very closely. "Maybe from radio and TV. Ever hear of a show called *Psych 'n' Roll*?"

Jamal laughed. "*Psych 'n' Roll*, huh? Interesting name. Never watched, never listened. But you're about my age. You ever play high school ball in Brooklyn?"

It was Jamal's laugh, a deep "ha, ha," that triggered the recall. Jamal had been a legendary high school and playground basketball player. At seventeen he'd com-peted with and against Ike on the courts of Manhattan Beach in Brooklyn. They were pick-up game teammates the first time Ike dunked a basketball. "Jamal Jamison? What do you know?" Ike said smiling and shaking his head.

"Yeah. And you?"

"Ike. Ike Miller."

Jamal's eyes sparkled. "Ike Miller? No fucking way. What's happening my man?" He offered a fist bump and Ike met it. "How you been after all these years?"

"Great. Like I said I have this radio show and I'm still playing ball."

Jamal nodded his head. A smile grew on his face as if he'd just remembered something special. "You know that dunk Ike, I'll never forget it. How excited you were. It was like you lost your virginity. Amazing, man."

"Yeah. That's exactly how I felt."

"So what brings you to this part of town?" Jamal asked.

"Just looking for a game," Ike said.

"You look like you're in pretty good shape. Although the way you threw up that free throw wasn't the way I remember you."

Ike laughed. "First one of the day. Takes a while to get all the parts moving right."

"I know what you mean," Jamal nodded. "So if you want a game, play with us. One of our guys is out sick this morning."

"Shit" and "fuck" bounced around the nine boys. But Jamal's stern look ended that quickly.

"I have to ask you something," Ike said.

"Shoot."

"I've never seen a court like this in town, new bleachers, state-of-the-art scoreboard with a digital clock, rims and nets in great shape, perfectly lined greentop in ace condition. What's up with that?"

"Antwanne, start a layup line at the other end. I'm gonna talk to my old buddy here." Jamal gestured to Ike that they take a short stroll.

"These kids," Jamal pointed his head toward the layup drill. "They all got a story, and it's not *Father Knows Best*, if you know what I'm saying."

Ike nodded.

"I work for the Garden—"

"As in Madison Square?"

"Director of community relations," Jamal smiled and nodded. "The powers that be on Thirty-Third

Street had sympathy for an old broken-down hoopster and hired me."

"Community Relations, huh? I think we announce your clinics on our radio station," Ike said.

"How do you like that?" Jamal said. "Well, that's how I met these kids. They weren't happy when they got me as their coach. They were hoping for Melo or Amar'e. But it turned out it was the best thing for all of us. Anyway, you asked about this place. You remember when we played we could play anywhere. Courts in Brooklyn, no matter how tough the neighborhood, were always in good condition."

"True. And we played no matter the weather," Ike said.

"Damn straight. I think you played with me once after a snowstorm. We got shovels, cleaned up the place and rumbled all afternoon."

Ike nodded and smiled.

Jamal glanced at his boys and shouted, "Guys, reverse it now."

Ike watched as Jamal's kids worked the left side of the basket. A couple of boys dunked, but all of them had perfect layup form.

"So this court," Jamal continued, "was a mess. Baskets hung by broken bolts. Blacktop was buckled and cracked. Back in the day we had to shovel snow but at least we had courts that weren't obstacle courses."

"What got it done?" Ike asked.

"Garden promised if the boys stayed in school, got decent grades, and stayed out of trouble they'd fix it."

"Did more than that," Ike said, gesturing to the clock and the line of bleachers.

"I tell you Ike. When a corporation like the Garden wants something done, they do it right. Not like the military. Not like our government. But that's talk for another time."

Ike zeroed in on his old teammate. His right forearm was inked with marine tattoos: an eagle perched on an anchor, a rifle sight with "one shot, one kill" inscribed above it, and the famous marine motto, "Semper Fi."

"You sound pissed off about your service," Ike said.

"I was a sniper. Did too much killing, and for what? When I came back I made it my business to do some good. Got the job at the Garden and then I met these boys."

"One of your tatts says marksman."

The hearty laugh emerged again. "Yeah. Did better with my sniper rifle than the round ball."

"But I remember you had a sweet shot," Ike said.

"Thanks. But 'D' was my thing. That's what I was known for at Western Kentucky."

It was the first Ike had heard that Jamal played college ball, and he was glad about it, having once had a glimpse into his old teammate's hardships at home. Ike recalled that one of the things they both had in common was an absent father. But Jamal had very little money and often had to leave games to babysit his younger brothers and sisters.

"Shutting down opponents makes you a winner. When your shot's not working it's good defense that gets you through," Ike said.

"Right. That's what I'm trying to teach these kids." Jamal pointed to his boys. "But you know how it is. Everyone wants to be a scorer, a shooter. Especially

Antwanne. But I've been working with him and I think he's starting to get it."

Ike could tell that Jamal's crew was getting antsy because they'd stopped the drill and were pushing and shoving and laughing at something that sounded like a good-natured rank-out fest.

"Let's play. You ready to show these boys your stuff?"

Ike nodded.

Jamal called everyone to gather round. "My friend, Ike, here is gonna scrimmage with us. Now if you think he's a pushover, I've got to warn you. Not only was he all-city from Madison High back in the day, but he played in the NCAA finals." He turned to Ike. "That was something. Great game. Heartbreaking. It's amazing what hoops can do to you." He turned back to his boys. "Anyway, I want you all to get up for some good competition and to play tough 'D'. Whoever guards Ike, hmm, let's see, Antwanne, I want that to be you. Young man, you better stay close to him because my friend here don't shoot no blanks."

Four boys approached Ike. They were members of the second unit. Benny, a stocky kid and the shortest of the crew, sported a buzz haircut. His uniform was a decaled red t-shirt that announced Hell's Kitchen Devils, with a logo of Satan dribbling a flaming basketball. Ike and Benny bumped fists. The rest of his mates introduced themselves: Dominique, a kid about Ike's height with watery, light blue eyes; Sol, who wore his silky black hair long and tied in a ponytail that hung through the back of his Yankees cap; and Bruce whose arms and neck were covered in an eclectic display of tattoos that would put his coach's inkwork to shame. Unlike Benny, the rest of Ike's teammates had long and lean bodies.

Antwanne's team, the starting five, wore contrasting black t-shirts with just the word "Devils" in red. His mates were Bull, a handle in contrast to his reed-thin appearance; Reggie, who must have spent a good deal of time in the weight room, his milk chocolate physique as cut as a young Stallone; Rabbit, a short boy with a jittery demeanor; and Junior—at eighteen, the oldest of the crew.

Jamal was both coach and game ref. The latter fit in with Ike's memory of his old friend, as he'd been the Manhattan Beach court arbiter, breaking up fights and making sure games he played in, despite the tough competition, stayed civil.

Referee Jamal called both teams to the center court for a jump ball. Ike's team gave him the honor. He went up against Antwanne, whose young legs launched him higher than Ike's did. Antwanne tapped the ball behind him toward Rabbit. But Benny anticipated the move and corralled the basketball.

The game was on.

From the start Antwanne acted like he was out to prove himself superior to his older opponent. He pushed against Ike's body, hand-checked and fouled him often, and gave him very little space to maneuver with or without the ball. Ike was used to it. Opponents used these tactics once they learned about Ike's hoops resume. Playground basketball was always like that. Egos ruled. But in the end, smart play, whether in the schoolyard, park, or in the arena, usually won. It would take a little time. And Ike was willing to bide it, knowing full well he hadn't yet warmed up. The result was that Ike's first shot missed as badly as his clanked free throw.

"Don't shoot no blanks huh? What a bunch of…" But before he could finish Jamal stared him down and Antwanne canned the trash talk.

Play was ragged with only zeros showing on the digital scoreboard. But as the morning sun rose higher in the Manhattan sky and warmed the air and asphalt, the boys and Ike warmed up as well. It was as if a switch was flipped and everything about playing this wonderful city game fell into place. With Antwanne leading the way the starting five built up an early advantage. Ike's young adversary moved like a hoops Baryshnikov. On one play, he spun and twirled around Ike and, rather than force his way to the basket, passed to Bull on the foul line. Bull held the ball over his head and waited for Rabbit to cut to the hole for an easy layup.

Back the other way, Sol found Dominique unguarded in the corner. He made his defender pay by swishing the open shot. "You've been working on it. Way to go, Dominique!" Jamal shouted from the midcourt circle.

Unfamiliar with his teammates, Ike had his lapses. One of them led to a turnover as Antwanne and Junior double-teamed him just over the center court line. Antwanne pilfered the ball, dribbled once, and threw a perfect basket-level pass that led to Bull's emphatic dunk. It rattled the backboard and had everyone, including a few spectators who'd happened onto the bleachers, shouting, body slamming, and high-fiving.

Though Jamal had been Ike's cred patron, he'd yet to show hoops action that matched his old friend's words. Finally, when Ike's darting hands returned Antwanne's favor by swiping the ball on his headlong drive to the basket, and then chest-passed full court to Benny for an easy layup, Ike heard a different kind of hooting and whistling from when he'd first arrived. He followed that play with a rebound of Rabbit's failed long-ranged shot and sent an outlet pass to Dominique who then zipped the ball back to Ike who'd galloped to his sweet spot just behind the elbow on the three-point line. There, he launched a high arcing jumper that barely touched the metal chains on its way through. It was that shot, the pureness and beauty of the flight of the ball as it spun its way to the goal that had always brought him the crowd's adulation, their cries of *IKIE! IKIE! IKIE!* in those heady college days. The exhilaration that came from success and the communal love that followed was a feeling he tried to retrieve every time he stepped onto a court after that last play in the NCAA championship. Now it was all about what had happened before the pain. Before the game Jamal had only a few moments ago called heartbreaking. It was why Ike pursued these weekend games. All for the carefree bliss that was always his before the shit hit the fan—a phrase he often used whenever he described the drama of that weekend.

And on this weekend, it came down to this: less than ten seconds left and the score tied. Fifteen feet from the hoop, Benny and Sol set a double pick that Ike ran behind. Bruce hit him with a quick pass. Ike rose from the

asphalt and at the apex of his jump flicked his wrist. He
watched the grooved leather ball trace a high, curved
path that softly found its target. And as the digital clock
displayed quadruple zeroes and its game-over horn
blared, the Hell's Kitchen Devils surrounded him. This
time as members of both teams fist-bumped and high-
fived one another, Ike felt he was at home and not some
intruder on an alien tribe's sacred ground.

Jamal strolled over. "Man, you still got it. Loved
watching you out there. Tell me something. You played
great. You're in great shape, and your team won. So
what's the hurt, my man?"

Ike felt a throbbing pain in his knee. The right leg
was telling him not to go where Jamal had just gone—
a place he had avoided in the weeks and months, and
years after that last game. No matter how many times
he'd repeated the weekend hoops ritual, nobody had
ever noticed or, if they had, ever asked. But now that
Jamal had, Ike couldn't block the pain in his knee, or
the vivid scene of those final seconds in the championship game on that terrible weekend. He couldn't stop
the crushing grief that had been its outcome. Because
Ike didn't want to burden this man he'd known when
they were kids not much older than the boys he played
with today, Ike stuffed his emotions—stuffed them
hard.

"You okay?" Jamal asked.

"Yeah," Ike lied. "Just my knee. I'm sure you know
what I'm saying."

Jamal nodded. "Don't I ever. Got my own repaired
ACL to prove it," he said as he pointed to the center of
his leg. "But, listen, you take care now. And by the way,

if you ever get to the Garden, look me up. If you want to see a Knicks game or a concert, I can arrange it. So if you need anything just come on by."

Ike felt good about the offer. There was something solid about his old teammate and he was glad he'd lucked out and reconnected with him today, a truly spectacular autumn Sunday in the Big Apple.

"Thanks," Ike said. "I might just take you up on that."

CHAPTER THREE

IS IT SAFE HERE?

Every Monday Hymie Safier would go food shopping with Stephanie, his live-in girlfriend. Hymie was a Holocaust survivor who rejected the stereotype of the Jewish refugee who was only comfortable among his own kind. Save for the *landsman* group of Feldstein, Sperber, Gittlestein, and Miller—the last two should rest in peace, especially Baruch, who'd suffered so much and whose funeral Hymie had attended in the morning—most of his friends and associates were in the construction trades, not the most Jewish of professions. Here on Staten Island his connections were more with the mob than the synagogue. Hymie had made a fortune building houses and the money continued to flow in. His company, Safier Building Associates, built most of the two-family houses in Staten Island, a borough that Hymie considered the least Jewish place in New

York City and that always seemed as if it belonged more to Jersey than the Big Apple.

Hymie was also physically different from the others in his survivor's group. He was a tall and heavy man. Only Baruch Gittlestein had matched him in height. The rest, Hymie would quip, were matzo munchkins. Hymie was bigger in other ways as well. He'd fill up the room with his larger-than-life personality, he was the one who'd always crack one-liners and tell funny stories. He was beginning one now.

"Stephanie, my dear, do you know how Staten Island got its name?"

Stephanie, overly made-up and bordering on anorexia, rolled her eyes. "How, Hymie?"

"Vell," (whenever he told this or any other Yiddish joke he exaggerated his already thick Jewish accent) "ven Columbus came into the Hudson River mit the Nina, the Pinta, and the Santa Maria, a couple of Jews ver mit him. So you know vat heppended?"

"No dear, tell me."

"Vell, one Jew points and says to the other, 'You see the land over dere?' The second Jew looks and answers 'Yes,' and the first Jew says 'Vell, is stat an island?'"

Stephanie shot him a blank stare.

"That's it. That's how it got its name. 'Is stat an island.' You know, Staten Island."

"Very funny," Stephanie said. "But, my dear man, not to criticize, but Columbus, and I know because I'm Italian, didn't discover Staten Island. I think it was Henry Hudson. You know, the Hudson River was named after him."

"Hudson, Columbus, who cares? It's a joke," Hymie said, shaking his head.

"Okay. Are you going to help me with the groceries?" Stephanie asked.

Hymie gave her a stern look. His generation of men never did the kitchen work. That was for the women. Estelle, his wife of fifty years, a survivor too, died from emphysema. She'd been a heavy smoker. She never asked him to help in the kitchen. She knew her role, not like the modern women of today, like the one in front of him. He had to constantly put this one in her place. Hymie was no dope. He was fully aware that his money was why Stephanie was with him. But he stayed with her anyway, because when a man gets into his eighties it's not so good to be alone. Besides, she gave him excellent blowjobs. Could you imagine that at his age he could enjoy such a thing? That was another way he was different from the other survivors. At least he thought so.

"I'm going to read the paper."

Though he was not the introspective type, Hymie needed some time not only to check out the news but to be alone to think about his friend's death and its meaning to him. Their survivor's group was getting smaller. He wondered who would be the next to go.

He headed for the great room.

By Staten Island standards the house that Hymie and Stephanie lived in was palatial: five bedrooms, a living room, the great room (Hymie would say, "What is so great about it?") with a stone fireplace, a kitchen the biggest and best chefs in the world would die for, all constructed and decorated with items that were world class in material and design. It had been the home of his marriage and family. He had raised three children, William and David, a doctor and a lawyer, and Marilyn, a cantor, something wonderful but hard for him to believe. *Yentl* had sure made its mark, he would tell everyone he met. He had six grandchildren and Marilyn was pregnant with her third child. His only sorrow was that Estelle was not here to see this. He had tried to get her to stop smoking, but she never could. From his wife's illness, he'd learned about the malignancy of addictions—that when a person was hooked it didn't matter what the physical threat was. The day she died she'd smoked a pack of these killers. Now only the house remained with its comforts and its memories of Estelle and the children.

A house this large had its detractions. The cost to heat and cool it was getting astronomical. For a man his age, the many steps he had to negotiate could be trying on his arthritic joints, especially when he had to descend the stairs to the garage two stories below. The biggest problem was that it was nearly impossible to hear if an intruder entered the house. He had installed state-of-the-art alarm systems, cameras with monitors, and intercoms. Half the time the electronics didn't work and it was too complicated for his brain to comprehend the instructions, and he'd gotten tired of calling the company for service whenever it went on the fritz. Certainly Stephanie hadn't the patience or desire to learn how to fix it, and she had too many of her own things to do to wait around for service. Besides, she never worried about intruders. She was a daughter of a mobster. Her only worry had been the feds, and they'd need a warrant to get in.

Hymie, as always, joked with her. He made a pun to match the situation. "Stephanie, do you think it's safe here?"

She looked at him as if to say, "What the hell are you talking about?"

"Safier, safe here. You know 'safe here' is my name, Safier..."

Stephanie made a face that said, "What are you, some kind of moron?" but only said, "Darling don't you know that if you have to explain a joke, it really isn't funny."

Hymie laughed anyway and thought the problem with little Stephanie was that she grew up a IAP, an Italian American Princess, in a household rolling in money from the carting business (or the fall-on-the-floor euphemism "environmental services"), until the feds broke up their extortion racket. Anyway, Stephanie was too busy doing her nails to hear anything that could make her feel unsafe here. And Hymie, who still loved to get blowjobs, denied his vulnerability even though he was occasionally concerned about the broken security system.

And that was how the thugs got into the house. Stephanie was putting some purple color on her fingers, the alarm system didn't work, and Hymie, with his failing hearing and the distraction of thinking about Baruch's death, didn't hear a thing. By the time Hymie was aware of an intruder in the great room it was too late to get up from his chair and retrieve the shotgun he kept in the closet ten feet from where he was sitting, just for this exact purpose. The thug had powerful hands and held the old man by the neck. Stephanie was already tied to a chair with duct tape over her mouth.

The second man, the one who had subdued Stephanie, came into the great room carrying her and the chair. He was younger and more muscular than the first man, and had an air of authority about him that the first man didn't possess. He had a slash scar that traversed the chin of his triangular face. He stared at Hymie through cold, brown eyes. He placed Stephanie—mouth sealed with duct tape and eyes bulging in fright—opposite Hymie, then turned and drove his fist into Hymie's forehead. Hymie took the jab. He'd learn to absorb blows, figuratively and literally, many times throughout his life. He'd been an excellent amateur boxer before the Nazis invaded Poland. He waited for a chance now to show this young *bulvan* that he still had something left.

"Tough old Jew, are you?" the intruder asked sarcastically.

Hymie wondered how he knew he was Jewish. Maybe he'd noticed the mezuzahs on the doors or the menorahs on the dining room breakfront. The thug mentioning that Hymie was a Jew, inflamed him even more, and it spurred him out of his chair. With a right hand that had pummeled many a heavyweight in his youth, Hymie swung with the form—if not the force—that he had during those pugilistic days. His body could not, of course, do what it had once done, and his fist grazed the intruder's shoulder.

"Ha, ha. Look what we have here. A Jew Joe Frazier. Well Joe I'll be Muhammad Ali." The thug threw a second straight right to Hymie's face. This time he went down as blood spurted from his broken nose onto the expensive silk Persian rug.

The intruder and his partner lifted Hymie and moved him back to his chair. Hymie wasn't giving up. "You idiots, do you even know who you have chosen to attack?"

"The King of England?" The partner said.

"She is the daughter of Carmine Sabbatini. Do you know who that is?" Hymie asked.

"I don't give a shit if she's Al Capone's kid. Mafia punks don't scare me," the younger man said.

The partner ripped another piece of duct tape from its roll and sealed it across the old man's mouth. The younger thug took out a cell phone, pressed a number and placed it against his ear.

"We're in. But there's collateral damage. The old Jew's got a girlfriend." He listened for a response, nodded his head and smiled.

"Yeah. Today's not her lucky day. You coming now?" He waited. "Good."

Muhammad Ali put his cell phone back into his jacket pocket.

"This should be interesting," he said to his partner. "Maybe even spectacular."

After a few minutes the doorbell rang. A middle-aged woman with orange-red hair entered the foyer of Hymie Safier's house. She kissed the young intruder on the cheek and said, "Good job. This time let's make sure we find out if he's got what we want before they die."

CHAPTER FOUR

PSYCH 'N' ROLL

There were four of them and they filled the cramped radio studio as they prepared for today's broadcast of *Psych 'n' Roll*. The show's theme song, "Roll Over Siggie Freud Gonna Tell Dr. Ike My News," a production staff parody of the Chuck Berry classic, raved on from WNYT in midtown Manhattan and out into the FM universe. The show's intro was also a signal to the three techs— Moe, Larry, and Curly, as the staff had affectionately dubbed them–to get their butts in gear and finish their work. Ike Miller, donning his Dr. Ike persona, was the fourth person on the broadcast stage. He sat in front of his microphone impatiently waiting for the three stooges to leave as he studied his programming list and commercial script.

Stacy the weather person, a petite brunette a year out of broadcasting school, approached him from the newsroom. "Ike, I need to talk to you."

"Now? We've only got a minute before we start."

"Did I do something wrong?" Stacy asked.

"What do you mean?" Ike asked as he glanced at the clock.

"When I suggested a segue to the first weather report you jumped all over me," Stacy said.

"Really?" Ike remembered the interaction but not the insult. His response clearly must have hurt Stacy because she looked like she was working hard to hold back her tears.

"The way you talked to me wasn't you. I never heard you speak to anyone that way before," Stacy said, then turned and stormed back to the newsroom.

Ike shook his head and watched her go. But recognition trumped denial. It was an old sensation he thought he'd conquered, a squeezing tightness in his gut. Not just a "Monday, Monday" feeling on the first workday of the week. His psychology colleagues would diagnose it as a mixture of performance anxiety and claustrophobia, symptoms of which had taken the better part of the gig's first year to overcome. Today, whenever he'd looked at the station's call letters and FM address, 102.3, draped across the windowless cinderblock walls, he felt it come rushing back.

Ike eyed the time once more. The show's opening was just seconds away. Tony Keyes his producer and partner had drilled it into Ike—the way Ike's college basketball coach had repeatedly done—that the clock was his friend, and that it had to be treated with respect.

It was part of what Tony called the three Ts in radio: "teamwork, time, and timing."

"Ten seconds to Steve's intro," Tony, a heavy-set, biblically-bearded, rock 'n' roll savant, announced into Ike's headset.

The station announcer, Steve Springer, stood in a room the size of a phone booth that was to the left of the broadcast stage. Springer cleared his throat and appeared ready to speak into the ceiling-suspended microphone. Because today's show was simulcast on cable television Springer dressed as if he was still hosting his once popular TV game show. He wore a silver-gray Armani suit, perfectly pressed white shirt, and red-and-silver-striped silk tie. It irritated Ike—dressed in a blue button-down shirt opened at the collar and gray tweed jacket—that the station announcer was engaged in sartorial one-upmanship. Ike had had enough of the announcer's passive-aggressiveness and wished Springer would bring his vamp demeanor to television fulltime to host something like American Idol.

Tony counted down, "Three, two, one," and pointed. "You're on."

Springer spoke into his microphone. "Good afternoon everyone, at home or in your car. Welcome to *Psych 'n' Roll.* Our acclaimed psychologist, Dr. Ike Miller, is in his office. And he's ready to listen and help. Joining him is the legendary rock 'n' roll musicologist, Tony Keyes. Professor Keyes will play music to lift your spirits, touch your heart and soul, and stimulate your mind. If you have a question, a problem, an issue, or wish to voice an opinion on today's topic, call us here at *Psych 'n' Roll,* 800-555-5454. Now...here's Dr. Ike."

"Thank you, Steve Springer, and good evening every-one on this beautiful fall Monday here in the Big Apple. We hope you're having a wonderful day in your car, at home, or the office, or wherever it is you're listening to *Psych 'n' Roll.* I'm Dr. Ike Miller. But you can call me Dr. Ike. And you can do so on your landline, cell phone, satellite phone, Skype, or with smoke signals. We'll take your call in any form.

"Today's topic is 'loss.'" Ike spoke the word with rever-ence, and allowed for a moment of silence to highlight the idea. "Something we've all experienced: Loss as in the death of a loved one, loss of a job, breakup with a lover. But before we get to the callers, let's kick off our first musical set with Wilco's, "Hate It Here," a song about a man waiting for the woman who'd abandoned him to return home."

Tony played "Hate It Here."

Ike looked at his producer who stood at the control board on the other side of the studio's glass partition. He had his familiar "I-know-something-you-don't-know" smirk, which meant that it was musicology time. Was the class ready? Ike wasn't the only one in the industry who knew that Tony's knowledge of rock and popular music was superior to everyone else. Had "Name That Tune," the old fifties TV show, still been on the air, his partner would've been banned because his domination over other contestants would have taken the TV execs' fancy gray flannel suits to the local dry cleaners. Tony could recognize the slightest guitar strum, drum beat, piano chord, and place it to the song, the artist, and names of every individual backup musician and singer, the producer, the label, and the highest position it had achieved on the charts. His speed-of-light ability to retrieve almost any recording that would fit the ongoing psychological theme was just what Ike had wanted, actually needed, when WNYT gave him the shot to try out *Psych 'n' Roll.*

"Okay. What ya got?" Ike said.

"Wilco, right? What's the major influence?" Tony asked.

That's an easy one, thought Ike. "Hate it Here" had the soaring guitars of Abbey Road, the tricky McCartney bass in counterpoint to Lennon's rhythm guitar.

"Beatles, my bearded wonder," Ike said.

"Yeah, you'd think." Tony's eyes sparkled. That usually meant that as music-savvy as Ike had become, he was wrong.

"Not Beatles?"

Tony smiled.

"Okay, then who? Elvis? Muddy Waters?"

"Don't guess. Think a little deeper. I'll give you a couple of hints. The group became popular at about the same time the Beatles did. They started as a blues group and then morphed into a pop band with horns. The song I'm thinking of preceded *Abby Road* by about a year. That bass you hear McCartney play, the fast *doo doo doo dum* you'll also hear on this song."

Ike didn't have a clue.

"How about you do some homework," Tony said.

"Puh-lease," Ike said closing his eyes and lowering his chin.

"Didn't you tell me you wanted to be like me?" Tony asked.

"No. I said I wanted to be like Michael Jordan."

"Unfortunately, as good as you were, you know that's not going to happen, right?"

Ike smirked. He hated being reminded of his limitations.

"I know you're a Gen X guy so you may not have heard of Blood, Sweat, and Tears—"

"Hey, that David Clayton-Thomas guy, a rock-crooner type," Ike interrupted.

"Swish, Ike. But you only get credit for one free throw. When David Clayton-Thomas joined Blood, Sweat, & Tears, he made them into a pop group like Chicago. The song with the bass riff is "I Can't Quit Her" and it came before Clayton-Thomas joined them. If you get the time, listen to early BS&T and The Blues Project. You'll hear the influence."

"Hate It Here" was in its fade and Tony shifted his focus to make sure the next recording was on cue. It was time and timing in action.

"Bad Fog of Loneliness" is next, right?" Ike said.

As Neil Young's high-pitched, and warbling voice began to sing about another man's obsession with a woman who'd left him, Tony lifted his head from the sound console. Ike noticed Tony's eyelid twitching, which often meant he was feeling stressed. Ike worried. Was his producer unhappy? Could he even be thinking about leaving the show? It was a fear he'd lived with ever since he'd finally convinced the bearded and reluctant genius to head back to the states from an ashram in India to join him on *Psych 'n' Roll.*

"What's wrong?" Ike asked.

"No big deal. We've talked about your dad, how he played with Neil, how he was always on the road, and what happened to him. But you never told me this one thing."

Heat suffused Ike's head and face. "What one thing?"

"You have a middle name."

"So what?"

"Were you named after Neil Young, you know, Isaac Neil Miller?"

Ike had hoped that Tony would never discover the connection. "What are you, some kind of rock 'n' roll dick?"

Tony's look was a mixture of Hindu chillness and mock normal-guy anger. They both burst out laughing.

Tony pointed to the clock. It was time for the callers.

The show started slowly. So much of rock 'n' roll was about loss. Mostly "I lost my baby, *dom-doobie-doo-wah*" sentiments. Ike had been hoping for more. He was looking for deeper emotional, even political, content that would rivet the audience. Instead, as the show moved through the caller list, the mundane took over, like six-year-old Rebecca who was on the line crying about seeing her cat run over by the school bus. She sobbed so painfully over the airwaves that Ike asked to speak with her mother. A tiny voice called out, "Mommy," and after a moment, her mother came to the phone.

"I didn't know what to do, so I gave her the telephone to talk with you. I'm at my wits' end to help her," she said.

"How terrible for Rebecca," Ike said, moving closer to the microphone

"Horrible."

"Yes," Ike commiserated.

"What can I do?" she asked.

"First tell me your name."

"Gloria."

"Okay Gloria. What I'd like to know is: were you with her at the time?"

"Yes. I always wait with her for the bus."

"And the cat. Why was it outside?"

"We always let her out."

"I see. So when the accident happened did you remove Rebecca from the scene? Did you shield her eyes?"

The caller was silent for a moment. "Are you saying this was my fault?"

"I'm not blaming anyone. I'm trying to make this into a learning moment. Try to remember when you were your daughter's age. It helps to know how to deal with a child at any age when you can remember your own experience at that time."

"What are you saying?"

"I'm saying that if you remember what it's like to be a six-year-old you'll be more protective of your child. An example is that she's not the one who should have been on the phone when we started this call. That should have been your job."

She was silent again. Ike wondered if he'd been too harsh. Tony had a questioning look on his face. But when it came to children, Ike's first concern was their protection.

"We're getting dead air," Tony said into Ike's headset.

"Gloria, are you there?"

"Yes." Her voice was shaky. "I try to do my best. I hope you understand that."

"I'm sure you do. Just remember: she's a little girl, and giving her a grown-up's responsibility, like calling a radio show, isn't something that should happen."

"Okay. I'll keep that in mind," she said.

Ike couldn't tell if she was offended or if she'd actually taken in what he said. Maybe it was a combination of both. But the call was over, and they had to move on. Tony played Crosby, Stills, Nash & Young's, "Our House", with its reference to two cats in the yard. He tacked on Tom Jones's "What's New Pussycat" and Patti Page's "How Much Is That Doggie In The Window?" Choices that were Tony's not-very- subliminal message to get Rebecca a new cat.

It was time for news and weather.

Springer was the newsman. Ike knew the Stillman brothers, who owned the station, gave him the assignment because they were as tight with their money as the studio was tight with space.

Tony signaled to Springer that he was on.

"Couple murdered in burglary of Staten Island home," Springer read. "Eighty-eight-year-old real estate developer Hyman Safier and his companion Stephanie Russo, fifty-five, were found shot to death in Mr. Safier's home in the Huguenot section of Staten Island. What was taken from Mr. Safier's house has not been determined at this time. Police are questioning next of kin and neighbors for any information that would lead them to the perpetrators of these killings."

Ike shook his head. Here was a tragic story and Springer sounded as if he were reciting the amount of money and prizes a contestant won on his game show. The announcer's tone and cavalier attitude grated on Ike. It made his already sour mood even more unpleasant.

Stacy followed.

The old saw that radio and TV weather people never looked out the window to see the true state of local

conditions was a fact at WNYT. But it wasn't Stacy's fault.
The only way she'd be able to see the sky was to run six
stories down to the street to observe and then six stories
back up to report.

As she finished the five-day forecast, Ike was fuming;
he'd been pressuring the screeners during the break to
find him a caller with a more compelling story. He knew
he was acting crazy—what control did the staff have over
who called, anyway?

The clock ticked to zero, and Tony pointed to Ike
that he was back on the air.

"Claude from Astoria, Queens is on the line. Claude,
what's your story of loss and how can we help?"

"I have a question first."

"Sure, go ahead," Ike said.

"Does the loss of respect for another person fall under today's topic?"

Bingo! They'd finally gotten an out-of-the-box request. "Yes. Tell us, Claude, who have you lost respect
for?"

The caller cleared his throat. "It's my wife, and I
hope she's not listening. I don't think she'd listen because she hates rock 'n' roll and distrusts psychology.
We went to a marriage therapist once and she didn't
like what he said to her."

"What did he say?"

"He told her she acted cruelly toward me. That
ticked her off and she ran out of the room never to
come back to counseling."

"That must have been upsetting."

"That was nothing. I supported my wife throughout
the marriage. Held two jobs, sometimes three, to give

her and the children a good life. Her father died recently and left her an estate of...I won't say the exact amount, but let's just say neither of us would have to work again, and my kids' college educations would be paid for and—"

"So let me guess," Ike interrupted. "She wouldn't share her inheritance with you."

"How did you know that?"

"Unfortunately, that's not an uncommon problem. If you listened to the show on betrayal last week, a caller was enraged when her husband abandoned the family after inheriting a large estate. When people are left huge sums of money it sometimes drives them crazy. Literally."

"Yeah, it's something like that. But there's more. Let me ask you this Dr. Ike. For your birthday, do people give you what you want?"

"I think what you're asking is really about you."

For a moment Claude was silent. "I guess," he finally admitted.

"So did your wife give you the wrong thing for your birthday?"

"Yes. But it was a little different than that. I'd asked her to get me anything other than a tie. She always gets me ties. I have more ties than your announcer. In fact, I could donate a few to him. Mine are prettier."

Ike and Tony looked at each other and had to work hard to stifle their laughter.

"So what happened?" Ike asked.

"My birthday came, and there it was—a long rectangular box. When I opened it and saw a tie with dollar signs all over it, I almost exploded."

"You said, 'almost exploded.' Do you ever get angry or share any of your feelings with her?"

"No. How could I? You don't get angry after someone gives you a gift. Do you?"

Ike felt bad for the guy. But not so bad that he wouldn't tell him the truth about loss of respect. "Claude, I can understand your feelings about your wife and how she's treated you. You feel she's taken advantage of you, that now that she has wealth she won't share it and reciprocate for all you've done for her. But I'm sorry to tell you this, and I hope you will take it in the spirit of concern that's intended here."

"No. No. That's why I called. What is it you want to tell me?"

"What I want to tell you is that the respect you say you've lost for your wife is really more about the respect you've lost for yourself."

Claude's lack of response came over the airways like a thud. Ike could imagine the brain scrambling that was going on in his head. Finally, the caller spoke. "What do you mean?"

"I have a sense you're way too passive with your wife about your own needs. And the way she treats you is a message she's lost respect for you. When you said you didn't tell her how you felt about the tie, I concluded that you probably don't express how you feel about most things. And the fact that she got you a tie, when you asked her not to—well, it was her way of telling you she's upset that you don't share your feelings."

"Do you think it was a test?"

"If you mean she consciously planned it this way I can't know. But her unconscious mind may have set this up to get a reaction out of you, and unfortunately you didn't pass that test."

"I don't know. I just don't know," Claude said.

Ike visualized the caller shaking his head in confusion.

"Well give it some thought. We really can't control what others do. We can only be in charge of ourselves. If what I've said makes sense, then try to talk with your wife about your feelings. If you find it hard to do and you want help to learn how, you can call us back. A member of our clinical staff will give you the phone numbers of professionals in your neck of the woods."

Claude sighed. "Okay. I have to think about that."

"Absolutely. And Claude, I truly respect that answer."

Tony played The Staple Singers' "Respect Yourself." Aretha Franklin's "Respect" followed.

Ike took off his headphones and headed for a bathroom break.

When he returned, the commercial for the Child Transformation Project was in the middle of its pitch. Ike was certain that this advertisement—aired every half hour on WNYT—gave instructions about parenting that bordered on child abuse. *We will teach you ways to use punishment that is frowned upon in our politically correct world. We believe it is the lack of punishment that is the reason for so many behavioral problems. When you use our proven methods, your child will obey.*

Ike had fought the suits to remove the ad from his time slot at least, and they'd finally relented, or so it seemed. The Stillman brothers must have gotten blowback from the advertising agency that insisted it be aired during *Psych 'n' Roll* because of the show's high

ratings. Ike believed that Ross and Barry wouldn't cop
to the problems that troubled Ike about the so-called
"Child Transformation Project" because of the oodles
of cash the show made for them. It frustrated Ike so that
he shouted to Tony, "Damn it, there it is again. Just listen to the narrator, his tone, his energy—'You vill make
your child obey.' The guy sounds like a concentration
camp commandant."

"Ike, calm down. I know it's BS. But radio's a tough
business, and these guys have to make money somehow.
I'll speak to them again. I have no idea how this got into
the commercial queue."

Ike shook his head and fantasized a professional
divorce—something he'd been contemplating the
last six months into what was now his third year at the
station.

"Ike, take a breath and get ready." Tony had his right
hand in the air. "Three, two, one."

"We have Sharon on the line with a story about her
brother who was killed in a drug bust. Sharon, how can
we help?"

"Dr. Ike, Peter was my best friend. He was such a
great guy, kind, giving. In high school he was voted
'most likely to succeed.' I don't believe it. I just don't
believe this happened to him," Sharon said.

"What is it you don't believe?" Ike said, his voice
lacking the usual empathy he displayed when someone
was in such obvious pain.

"That he was involved with drugs and that he's gone."

"Why don't you believe it?" Ike asked sternly.

"What do you mean?" she answered defensively.

"Look, I'm sorry for your loss. But was your brother at the scene of a drug deal?"

"Yes, but—"

"Then your problem, Sharon, is denial. As soon as you accept what went down, the faster you'll heal from this."

The silence seemed louder than any heavy metal recording that Tony sometimes played. A dial tone followed.

Tony moved quickly. He played Dream Theater's "Take Away My Pain."

"Ike, I'm coming in there."

"Why?"

Tony burst through the door that separated the control room from the studio.

"What are you doing?" Ike asked, bewildered.

"We need to talk," Tony said.

"About what?"

"Is today the anniversary of your father's death?"

Ike's knee began to throb. A reminder of how he felt yesterday after his game.

"It's my mom's *yahrzeit*," Ike said, his eyes sad.

"What?"

"The anniversary of her death. She died from pancreatic cancer six months after my father died."

"And your dad, I know he was murdered in a drug deal gone wrong. We were shocked over at the other radio station when we heard. We were all such big fans."

"Yeah, I get it. My circumstances are similar to the caller's." And that was it, of course, the workings of the unconscious mind. His had put two and two together and created a brain freeze. It was crystallizing into awareness now and Ike didn't like what he was seeing in himself.

"Two things are important here," Tony said. "That was not professional. And the caller's brother died last week. Your father was killed twelve years ago. Don't you think it's time to get this under control?"

Ike couldn't give an answer that had any sincerity behind it. He knew what he should say and what he should do. But he needed something else to happen that would break the spell. His own therapy hadn't done it. His discussions with his Grandpa Otto hadn't helped him tie up the loose ends of this nasty business. He just didn't know where it would come from.

"I don't know what to tell you," Ike said.

Tony closed his eyes and his face softened. "Look, take a coffee break and think of a way to repair what happened with Sharon. I'll play a set of apology songs to give you some time."

As Tony played REM's "So, Central Rain" with it's repetitive mea culpa cry, a shaken Dr. Ike headed for the coffee shop on Fifty-Seventh Street to use a few moments to clear his noggin and prepare a heartfelt "my bad" of his own.

CHAPTER FIVE

AJA

The Golden Mike Pub, on Broadway between West Fifty-Seventh and Fifty-Eighth Streets, was just around the corner from the studio. The saloon catered to the media and theater industry and the infrequent locals from Hell's Kitchen just a few blocks west. Because the bar's outward appearance was an inch away from derelict, heartland visitors just off their tour buses almost always did their Dionne Warwick best to "walk on by." Mike Golden accepted their rejection with alcoholic cheer. He and his steady patrons didn't want yokel additions to what had become an overflow in-crowd happening. Burly, red-haired, red-bearded Mike, his bar, his food, his antics had become legendary in certain New York circles. He was an Irish Toots Shor, holding court behind the bar, often schmoozing with patrons at their tables. Mike's broad shoulders and thick arms were likely a nature-nurture product of blue collar Emerald Isle stock and the restaurant's headline fare: Guinness, red meat, beef fries, and fried onion rings "as big as hula hoops," Mike liked to joke.

Ike's agent had pushed him to show up at the pub, as an occasional appearance with the *Psych 'n' Roll* crew might get Ike and the show some Page Six ink. Ike had resisted the idea, but gradually came around and fell in love with the Guinness, the atmosphere, and the deliciously greasy and extraordinarily fattening menu offerings. Though Ike would have liked Tony to join him, his producer never came along for what had become a beginning of the workweek ritual. Tony was a recovering alcoholic and his presence in a joint like Mike's was dangerous to his sobriety. Whenever Ike wanted downtime with his producer, they'd dine in an Indian restaurant near Second Avenue on Fifty-Eighth Street.

Ike was seated at the bar. He held a pint glass of the dark stuff and slowly sipped as he attended to his corned beef sandwich dinner. James Taylor's "Mockingbird" played in the background. Mike Golden stood by the counter sink and dried shot glasses with his omnipresent shamrock dishtowel. "Where's the rest of your crew?" he asked.

"Hank's joining me in a couple. I think Moe, Larry, and Curly will be here soon."

Hank Grimm was WNYT's head of security. In addition to keeping out intruders, it was Hank's job to make sure that Ike and other station talent weren't the target of some psycho caller. Ike had tried to dissuade Hank from using the word "psycho," but as a former NYPD detective, Hank was going to talk the way he wanted to even if it wasn't psychologically or politically correct.

"How's the big fella doing?" Mike asked.

Ike nodded and shrugged. He sipped some more from his glass. From the corner of his eye, he caught the linebacker body of the ex-cop bull his way through the swinging pub doors and head for the bar. He inched his way in and around the growing throng of patrons near the bar, and stood alongside Ike. Hank was casually dressed, but wore a blue and red striped tie. He always wore a tie. It reminded Ike of his Grandpa Otto who also always wore neckwear whether the occasion was business or recreation. Ike wondered but never asked Hank the reason he dressed this way.

"You had a bit of a problem today, didn't you?" Hank asked. "Not your best job, eh Ikie?" Hank was the kind of guy who never missed an opportunity to tweak people, and Ike knew Hank loved to tweak a younger man who was giving advice to the world on radio, television, and the Internet.

Ike looked up from his food and stared at the ex-cop. "You do your cop thing and I'll do my shrink thing. I have no patience for your snarky shit tonight."

Hank looked taken aback. "I was just sayin'. No need to be so sensitive. Whew, what's with you lately?"

"Mike, pour me another pint of Guinness," Ike said. "It's a tough time for me, Hank. But I don't want to get into it. I'm just trying to relax and then get out of here."

"Okay. No harm, no foul, as you like to say. But just a word of warning: you need to be careful out there. You never know how someone's gonna take things, especially anonymous callers on a radio show."

"I'll remember that."

"I'm sure you will. You're a smart guy. How's the corned beef?"

Ike nodded it was fine.

Hank waved at Mike and shouted for a Guinness and a shot of rye. As he waited for the drinks he scanned the pub.

"You looking for Springer?" Ike asked.

Despite Springer's game show host manner, Hank seemed to like the guy. They got drunk together, and where they ended up was anyone's guess and often a subject of raised eyebrows and furtive gossip. But no one would ever dare say to Hank what they said to one another.

"Not here yet, is he?" He put his arm around Ike's shoulders and whispered in his ear. "Ikie, I think a long-legged beauty's got her eyes on you. Check her out."

Everyone at the radio station knew Ike was an eligible guy. What no-one knew, except for Tony, was how much hurt he'd endured in his previous relationship. This wasn't the first time Hank had tried to hook him up with some woman at the bar. They were usually not the type to bring home to mom and dad, even though that didn't matter anymore. Nonetheless, Ike gave her a stealthy peek. He'd noticed her when he entered the pub. She was sitting one stool away from the end of the counter watching Knicks pre-season pre-game interviews on the big screen TV and nursing what looked like an iced tea as she picked at a salad. Her meal was one explanation for a thin but shapely auburn-haired, blue-eyed lovely a couple of years his junior. She wore jeans, a blouse the color of ripe plums that revealed well-toned, long-muscled arms, and a beige sweater anchored around her back and shoulders.

"Why not introduce yourself? You're single, famous, and decent looking. That's enough cred, don't you think?" Hank said.

Before Ike could respond, which was always difficult when it came to explaining his reticence about making the first move, Springer had spirited his way to the bar and slapped Hank on the back. Hank jumped at first, then smiled at his nattily dressed friend. "What took you so long?"

"Something at the station. I'll tell you later," he said. "I got us a table in the back. Had to slip the hostess a twenty."

"Join us?" Hank asked. Ike knew Hank was just being polite. And Springer would have gagged if the invitation had been for real. Ike shook his head, thanked him for asking, and turned his attention back to his meal as the two angled their way toward some nook in a back corner of the joint.

Just as Ike started on his second pint of Guinness, the guy who'd been seated on the stool to his left and in-between Ike and the long-legged beauty stood, dropped a few bucks on the counter, then sliced his way out of the saloon. To Ike's way of thinking, the red sea had just parted. The salad-eating lovely smiled at Ike, grabbed the back of the vacated stool, and slid onto it. Her maneuver had the grace of a professional dancer and the assertiveness of an athlete.

"Mind if I sit here?" she asked.

Do I mind? Did I just win the lottery?

"My name's Aja," she said and extended her hand.

"I'm Ike." He shook her hand.

"Yes, Dr. Ike from *Psych 'n' Roll*," she said with an easy smile.

It was a strange and uncomfortable business, this celebrity bit. It still didn't make sense to him, as he still didn't think of himself that way. Obviously, some people did.

"Asia," Ike said. "That's a beautiful name. But you don't look Asian at all."

"It's not spelled like the continent. It's A-J-A," she said, as if she'd gone through this explanation countless times.

"Aja, huh? As in the Steely Dan recording," he sang a couple of lines from the song holding his spoon as a microphone.

"Yes. Wonderful. A regular Donald Fagen."

"May I ask how you got your name?"

"My mom was a big Steely Dan fan. She played them all the time. I think she must have played "Rikki Don't Lose That Number" non-stop while I was in the womb. I still have dreams about that song."

Ike laughed. "You know, we've got something in common already."

Her face lit up. She moved to the edge of her stool. "Really?"

"Yeah. My father was a guitarist who played with Neil Young. My middle name is Neil."

"Is that why you like Dad Rock so much?" she asked slyly.

It was an amusing but contemptuous expression he'd heard from some of his callers. It meant that classic rock from the sixties and seventies was no longer hip. "That has something to do with it. I just think that rock from back then was the pinnacle. My producer—"

"Tony Keyes, right?"

He was impressed she knew his name. "Yeah. Tony likes to say that the songs of the Beatles and Led Zeppelin are great classics. He compares them to the works of Mozart and Beethoven. He believes they'll live forever." He had to raise his voice as the alcohol-infused noise was making it impossible to hear a word. Aja moved her stool closer. Ike sensed the maneuver wasn't only to facilitate conversation. A jolt of excitement ran through his body. They made eye contact without talking for a couple of ticks on the clock. It was like staring into the sun during an eclipse, and Ike felt the need to look away. "Can I get you something to drink?" he asked.

"Iced tea, thanks."

"Nothing harder, huh?"

She shook her head. "I don't drink alcohol, but thank you anyway."

Ike caught Mike's attention and ordered what she wanted. "So if you don't drink alcohol, what are you doing in a saloon?"

"You mean what's a nice girl like me doing in a place like this?"

He laughed. "Yeah. Something like that."

"I'm waiting for a friend. She never called to say she wasn't coming and I couldn't get her when I tried to call. I know she wouldn't deliberately stand me up. So I'm still waiting." Aja checked the time on her watch then looked directly at Ike. "But that turned out to be a good thing. I got to meet you."

Electricity ran the length of his spine. He leaned closer.

"So Dad Rock's not for you, I take it," Ike said. "So what kind of music gets you to move, turns you on, makes you feel? Or maybe you don't like music. I know I shouldn't make assumptions."

"No, no. I love classic rock. I love it all. But punk and heavy metal are more my style. You know, Metallica, Korn, Slayer, Pantera, even Guns n' Roses. I went to their concerts and jumped into their mosh pits. A lot of people think it's just noise. But those hard-driving guitars, I don't know, it's something about the vibrations that thrill me."

Despite her musical preferences, Ike noticed she was free of Gen-X war paint. "Heavy metal, punk, and no tattoos?"

"You never know. Just because you can't see them doesn't mean I don't have any." She reached for his arms, turned each one over, and playfully looked for artwork on him. "Maybe it's the same with you. Who knows what you might find under a person's clothes."

Ike took a sip of his Guinness to cool himself down and decided to change the subject. "You know, the way you grabbed that stool made me think you might be a dancer."

"Close." She smiled and nodded. "I played basketball."

"You did what?"

She laughed. "I played hoops. I was a UConn Husky."

Did he get this right? "You played serious, organized ball?"

"Yup, that's me. An organized baller," she said with the sly smile she flashed earlier. She recited her hoops resume. She was the Huskies starting power forward, known for her defense and shot blocking. Her team had been to the NCAA championship game three times, winning twice. She'd tried out for the Olympics but was the last player cut. "I should have made that team. It was a terrible disappointment," she said. "It was my dream ever since I started playing at eight. I was always a jock and everyone called me a tomboy."

"There's very little boy, Tom or otherwise, in the way you look," Ike said.

She blushed and took his hand. "Thanks."

He hit the Guinness again. "What do you do now?"

"I'm a surgical resident at Langone Medical Center, you know, NYU."

Brains and brawn in addition to rock 'n' roll, and they all made it to Ike's what-we-have-in-common list in his head. It upped her attractiveness another notch.

"So we both love rock and work in professions that help people—"

"And you're a world-class baller yourself."

"How do you know that?"

"I did my research on the web while I watched you on the TV simulcast of your show. I'm a big fan. I could be one of your biggest groupies."

"I never knew I had any." *Can this really be happening?* Ike thought, feeling fortunate that he met someone of her caliber and with matching interests in a bar.

"Well, all the better if I'm your first," she said and placed her hand on his knee.

The touch was soothing. It was just what he needed to make the ache he always carried there go away.

"Do you still play?" he asked.

Her face brightened. "Why don't we go find a court and you'll see for yourself?"

Play? Go play now? Ike thought. *Wow! In the world of celebrities and groupies this had to be a first.*

He looked at his watch. It was getting close to nine. They needed three things. He had his Nikes on. She had her own sneaks. So one was easy. Two was a ball. Three was a court with lights.

"We can get a basketball over at Duane Reade and I'll leave the court to you," she said.

But where?

Ike ran through his weekend playground venues.

Harlem? Too far.

Lower East Side? Uh-uh, too scuzzy, not the best place for a first date.

Central Park? Too busy.

Then it came to him: *Swish!* Jamal's court, the playground in Hells Kitchen, just a few avenue blocks west of Mike's. He described it.

"Let's go do it," she said.

Ike grabbed some cash from his wallet and dropped the bills on the bar.

"Before we head out let me text my friend just in case she decides to show up." She made a few arcane gestures on the screen of her phone. "Okay. I'm ready." Aja took his hand and led him through the Golden Mike's swinging doors and out onto the street.

Hell's Kitchen Playground. Courts empty. Lights on.

She'd attached herself to him the whole time as if they were familiar lovers, and as they approached the courts he felt turned on by the warmth of her hand and her body nestled into his. And with a game about to commence, well, there was no doubt what he was feeling. He was smitten.

Despite the arrow to the heart, he needed to make a transition from attached to separate. He'd been holding the basketball in the crook of his arm since they purchased it, so he gave it a couple of bounces. Aja must have taken that as a signal to get ready. She let go of his hand, tied her hair in a ponytail, unknotted her sweater, and dropped it on the bench under the clock. She walked three or four feet closer to the side court line and began to stretch. The yoga moves gave Ike a chance to look at her body more clearly. Her breasts were ample, unusual for an athlete. Her butt was athlete-dancer perfect. He felt excited when he imagined her naked, a rose or butterfly tattoo in some secret place. He became a bit uncomfortable when she noticed he was staring. He lowered his eyes. But as he glanced back at her one more time, her smile told him she was happy that he was looking.

After he completed his own stretches, he said, "Let's play Horse."

She angled her head and looked him in the eye. "Think of me as an opponent," she said.

That isn't going to be easy.

She grabbed the ball out of his hands and in one motion jumped and threw up a soft, high arcing shot from twenty feet away that ripped the metal net.

"Your turn," she said.

Ike dribbled twice behind the free throw line. His shot circled the rim and fell to the ground. Aja had the honor of being on offense first.

Many times over the years, particularly now on his weekend hoops outings, guys would talk smack about this and that game, who they played for and against, and the great moves they could make. It wasn't unusual for talk to be followed by very little walk. Aja said she was a player, but there was only one way to find out. And there was this one other issue. Aja was a woman, and he was a strong, in-shape man. He didn't want to take advantage of her. Then she made her first shot and soared into the air to slap his layup out of bounds. Ike thought of Jamal and the kids he'd played against just yesterday. They'd be on him, whistling and hooting. It was clear: Aja was far from delicate, and she was out to beat him.

She stayed with him on every move. He did the same when the ball was in her hands. They created a rhythm of back and forth, stops and starts, pivots and slides, turns and twirls, a jitterbug, foxtrot, and waltz all in one. Their butts and arms and hands and legs slid and bounced against each other. Her ponytail brushed against his face and chest and back. His sweat commingled with hers. After an intense half-hour of their dance the score was Aja twelve, Ike eleven with the ball in his hands. When he drove to the hoop, followed by a pull-up move that fooled her, he let go of his shot. The only way they could tell the ball went in was by the rattle of the net, because in the split second before they heard the metallic sound, the court lights zapped off.

Knocked off balance, they stumbled and landed on their backsides. Ike reached for her. The street lamps from Eleventh Avenue provided minimal light, but it was enough to see her face and blue eyes—soft and inviting. He pulled Aja close. He kissed her lips, and she slid her tongue into his mouth. His body tingled. She moaned as he stroked her back and arms. She wrapped her long legs around him, and they pressed closer. Ike felt the curve of her hips and stroked her firm, round athlete's bottom, pulling her closer into him. She placed her hand between his legs. Growing hardness pressed against his jeans. Just as she began to unzip him, something rustled in the shadows on the adjacent side street, followed by bursts of laughter.

"Someone's here," he whispered. "Wonder if it's the Devils."

She raised an eyebrow.

"The kids who usually play here."

The moment was over. They wouldn't jumpstart it here. "How about coming to my place," he said. He stood and held out his hand to help her up.

On her feet she pulled him close, kissed him passionately and looked into his eyes. "I'd love to. Not tonight," She stroked his face. "We should get to know each other a little better. Wouldn't you agree?"

He had to admit that intense, one-on-one hoops followed by making out on a basketball court was an unforgettable way to start a relationship. Wasn't that the constructive way to frame it? The rationalization helped, but only a little.

He kissed her again. "Let's get a cab and get you home."

"That's good," she said. "But let's drop you off first."

Ike opened his mouth, but he wasn't sure what to say. He didn't know her last name, where she lived, or her phone number. She put her fingertips to his lips. But he couldn't let it go like that.

"Let me get your number," he said.

"Don't worry," she said. "I'll call you."

Ike stepped out into the street to hail a taxi. In his disappointment he thought about Big Apple bar pick-ups, one-nighters. *Was that what this is? A one-nighter with a groupie named Aja?* He held the door for Aja, then followed her inside.

CHAPTER SIX

UNSETTLED SCORE

"We should get to know each other a little better" and *"Don't worry, I'll call you"* rattled around in Ike's head. Three days after those reassuring words, Aja still hadn't called. He questioned himself: *Who is she? Is she for real? Was it a quick bar pickup with just as rapid a drop-off, after all?* Thoughts of their intimate hoops dance — the kisses, the deep embrace with their bodies urgently pressing against each other, the stroking — drove him to the point of obsession. As Dr. Ike, he had fielded phone calls by and about stalkers. He felt as if he'd turned into one when he searched for Aja on the Internet. She was who she said she was. Connolly was her last name — Aja Connolly. Facebook and Twitter postings discussed her challenges as a resident in orthopedic surgery. She was a bowler, which was a little weird. Nevertheless, he imagined her long legs loping down the bowling lane,

her body bent toward the pins, her arm forward releasing the ball.

On her Facebook page she openly discussed her political attitudes. She believed that firearms should be regulated. As a liberal democrat she'd voted for Barack Obama. She supported gay marriages and prominently displayed the same-sex-wedding snapshot of a teammate and her partner. Ike Googled the UConn women's basketball team website and saw Aja and a teammate holding up the 2002 NCAA championship trophy. Obviously, she hadn't given him jive about that. A sidebar congratulated his one-on-one opponent for being the country's leading shot blocker. True enough—he'd personally experienced her ball-swatting talent.

Tony must have noticed Ike's mood. From behind the studio glass he said, "Dude, what's going on?"

"I was at Mike's—"

"Told you not to go there," Tony said smugly.

Ike bristled at the interruption and dismissal.

"Yeah, okay. I'm all ears," Tony said.

Ike told him the story of how he met Aja Connolly and his little side trip with his self-identified groupie to the Hell's Kitchen Playground where they did their basketball dance under the lights—a game so intimate that it was nearly as good as making love. He told him about her refusal to give him her number, her promise to call, and how he'd yet to hear from her.

"Hang in there. It's only a couple of days. Try not to think too much about it. I've learned that when you plant the seeds of patience you harvest the sweet fruits of happiness and love." It was typical for Tony to transform angst into mellow with the words of his guru. But changing Ike's focus was never an easy task when a woman became important. It was why his first inclination at Mike's had been to get up and leave rather than get entangled in the kinds of feelings he was having now. Regret for not paying attention to his instincts began to form in the pit of his stomach.

"Looks like tonight's topic suits you well," Tony said. "Loose ends can be painful. But, you know, meditation helps when things aren't going the way you want. It's been a godsend for me. It teaches me to be present and gets me out of the negative stories I tell myself. I've shown you how. Maybe we can practice together, like after the show."

Ike smiled and shook his head. "You and Otto. Everyone wants me to have a spiritual life." Ike's grandfather had lobbied hard to get Ike to go to synagogue ever since he'd dropped out of religion after his bar mitzvah.

"It wouldn't hurt, you know," Tony said.

"That's exactly what he says. Only he's got a Yiddish twang."

Tony chuckled. He turned his head to look at the clock. "Time to get ready. You're doing the intro."

"Me?" Ike was puzzled. "What's wrong with Springer?"

"Nothings wrong." Tony smiled. "In fact everything's just right. When I came into the studio, suits told me he was leaving the station for a game show gig. Had no problem getting out of his contract. Bosses are searching for a new announcer as we speak."

Ike felt like yelling *yes!* Followed by a canter through the studio bumping fists and giving out high fives to the staff like a proud new papa gives out cigars. Instead, he just flashed a satisfied smile and said, "That works."

"Knew you'd like that," Tony said.

"Okay. No problem with the intro. Let's get ready for showtime."

The theme was "unsettled scores," a hip, rock 'n' roll way of discussing unfinished business, or the overused term "closure" that floated around the psychobabble universe. Ike wanted to limit his use of professional jargon on the show. One of his objectives on *Psych 'n' Roll* was to define and clarify terms like "unfinished business," something Grandpa Otto often used. Otto was an expert on living with unfinished business. You couldn't survive something as big as the Holocaust and not have thoughts and feelings of what you could have done that you didn't do and what you'd do now if you were given another chance.

Tony got Ike's attention. The producer signaled that *Psych 'n' Roll* was on the air. Ike moved his lips closer to the microphone. He began with the standard opening greeting and segued into his monologue. "Do you have something unresolved that beckons your attention? Is it emotional, like telling someone your feelings of love or anger or hurt? Does it require an action such as asserting yourself to a parent, spouse, or boss, or righting a wrong through legal means? Are you seeking redemption for a failure or horrible mistake? Or is it forgiving someone for a slight, an insult, or a trauma? And most of all, do you need to forgive yourself for your own shortcomings?

"One caveat before we get started. We want to talk about serious matters. We want you to speak about unsettled scores. Don't tell us that you missed *Dancing With the Stars* last night and forgot to set your DVR. And I know all about professional sports team disappointments. I am, as many of you know, a Knicks fan, so I feel your pain. A big *nada* to these complaints as trivialities will get you instantly cut off. So bring substance to the table. *Capiche?*"

Ike watched Tony laugh, who then spoke into Ike's headset. "I didn't know you were multi-lingual? *Nada? Capiche?* Wow."

Ike grinned and placed his attention on the caller list.

"We have Crystal on the line from Manhattan. What's your unsettled score, Crystal?"

"I want to tell you about my grandfather." Crystal's voice was shaky. "My mother and I have an unsettled score with him."

"Go ahead."

"My mother was thirteen years old nearly forty years ago when her father disappeared," she said.

"Does anyone know what happened to him?" Ike asked.

"No. She told me he went away on business and just never came back."

"How did your grandfather's disappearance affect the two of you?"

"It wasn't so much what happened after he left. But when she was a child, he abused her terribly." The caller's voice rose in anger.

"How did you find that out?"

"When I was a teenager my father got drunk one night and crashed his car into another car. He died and killed the car's driver and his wife."

"I'm so sorry you had to deal with this."

"Thank you," she said. "Right after my father's death my mother told me the terrible things my grandfather did to her."

They were walking into sensitive territory and Ike wanted to be careful about his next question. "Is it something you're willing to talk about?"

She hesitated. Then said, "Even though my dad was an alcoholic he never hurt me. Not like what my grandfather did to my mother."

"And she shared with you what that was?"

"Yes, and she was *very* graphic." Her tone made Ike imagine her eyes nearly closed, and the muscles in her face, especially around her mouth, tightening.

"This is what psychologists call vicarious traumatization—"

"What's that?" Crystal voice quivered again.

Ike realized he'd gone against his own policy to simplify professional language. He was not happy and knew he had to correct it.

"It's okay," Ike said, trying to calm her down and steer the discussion back on track. "Just a fancy psychological term, that's all. It means that even though what happened didn't happen directly to you, and because it was at an age of difficult emotions and developing relationships, your mother's trauma and the pain that came with it may have been passed to you."

"Does that mean I'm crazy?"

"No. Not crazy. Just hurt."

She was silent for a moment. "Thank you for saying that. I didn't know that was even possible." Her breath caught, then steadied. "I thought that all my problems with men, my panic attacks and anxiety, were because I was deeply flawed or mentally ill."

"No. It's not about those things." Ike said. "Like a person who catches a cold from another person, you may have caught your mother's pain."

She was silent again. Tony signaled Ike to engage her.

"Crystal will you share with us what your mother told you?"

She cleared her throat and sighed. "No," she said softly.

"That's okay. But I just want you to know you're not alone."

Psych 'n' Roll dealt with all manner of personal issues including horrific physical and sexual abuse. Its audience of millions had also spawned a core supportive community on the Internet. Ike reminded Crystal that she was anonymous and there were many people with problems like hers who could help.

"I can't talk about it." The anguish in her voice grew. She paused to catch her breath. After a moment she said, "Do you think you could play a song by a group called Dilemma? You'll understand my feelings better if you do."

In all the shows they'd broadcast no caller had made a musical request. His audience apparently hadn't thought of him in the Cousin Brucie mold. He looked to Tony for direction.

"Let's do it. It'll be interesting. It could be the start of something new and good," Tony said.

"Have you heard of them?" Ike asked.

"Affirmative. But get ready. The lead singer murdered her manager then killed herself. They had a cult following in Europe, especially in Germany."

Ike turned his attention back to the caller. "Crystal, what song do you want us to play?"

"It's called 'Love and Vengeance,'" she said.

"Tell us about it."

"Could you just play it?" She said.

Tony told him it was ready to go. "Okay. Let's listen to 'Love and Vengeance' by Dilemma," Ike said.

It was a work about revenge, a threat to settle an old score for cruelty and vicious control. The genre was heavy metal. The mood it conveyed was ominous and deadly. It started up with an eerie, synthesized sound that enveloped the studio and slid into something reminiscent of the old fifties theme song "Rawhide." Instead of snapping leather, the repetitive rhythm turned out to be exhaled breath that stayed in the background, producing an unsettling yet sensual feeling. The lead singer sang:

"I think of you always,
It's my terrible obsession.
You said you loved her
But she was your possession
You played with her like she was your tool
You owe the world for being this cruel."

Heavy metal jamming was next. As it faded, she slowly spoke these words:

"Look to your feelings
Remember this verse
Love is my gift, hatred your curse

One day to your mortal surprise
I'll look into your soulless eyes
And the world will never regret
What in eternity you won't forget.
Because you used her as your possession
Payback will be the lesson."

As the piece ended, Tony said, "I Googled the group. Their organizer and principal songwriter — Franz Danzig is his name — wore a swastika tattoo that was broken in half. Wikipedia said the tattoo was a symbol of Danzig's hatred for everything about the Third Reich. But the piece also said that some neo-Nazis revered the broken swastika. In their way of thinking, it transformed blasphemy into a positive symbol."

"Typical Nazi mentality, right?"

Tony nodded.

"Do you think this has anything to do with her call?" Ike asked.

"Check it out," Tony urged.

"Crystal, did you know the manager of Dilemma wore a broken swastika tattoo? And that he wore it because he hated the Third Reich?"

"I know," she said curtly.

"Did you also know that neo-Nazis wear it in sympathy for Hitler and his crew?"

Silence.

"Is this why you can't talk about it?" Ike asked.

By the sound of her breathing he knew he'd hit too close to home.

The caller finally spoke, "I can't handle this," and hung up.

For the moment, dead air.

"I just went to a commercial," Tony said, a concerned look on his face. "You seem upset by what just happened so I want you to take some time."

"Thanks," Ike nodded. "I'm not sure if you know this. Both of my grandfathers were Holocaust survivors."

"I knew about Otto, but not about Avram."

"It fucked him up real bad. It fucked all of us up."

CHAPTER SEVEN

OTTO

Though Grandpa Otto never burdened Ike with his troubles, there was urgency in his voice when he called and asked Ike to pay him a visit. Ike's plan for the evening was to drown his sorrows over "whatshername" with a couple of beers—maybe even a few more than a couple—at Mike's after the show. Because he never refused face time with Otto, Ike put that self-indulgent plan on hold. After he said his goodbyes to the crew, he hailed a taxi for The Hampshire Towers. Ike and Grandpa Otto lived in the same building.

Greg Finneran, one of the two doormen at the Towers, was on duty. Greg, like Jamal, was a marine and an Iraqi War veteran. Ike wondered if Greg had listened to a recent show, in which one of the callers had spoken about nightmares she'd suffered after her service in Baghdad. But Greg had never even been open to Ike's attempts at pleasant chitchat, so to bring up the door-man's war experiences would have been way too much of a stretch. *Okay, so what if the guy never wanted to have a real conversation with me?* Ike thought. *I could deal with whatever professional boundaries doormen were supposed to honor, if there was such a thing.* But Greg rarely showed civility, let alone neutrality, whenever they came into contact. Ike could take responsible detachment. More often than not, though, Greg was hostile, making snide remarks every time Ike came into the lobby carrying a basketball. Like the way he'd greeted Ike after his game with Jamal's boys: "Bet you bricked a few today."

It might be jealousy. Ike had dated Sarah Shapiro, an adorable, freckled-faced honey-blonde, for a little over a year after she'd moved into the building. When he'd raised the topic of a more serious commitment their conversation became increasingly more awkward and labored. After two weeks of this, Sarah gave him the "It's me, not you," speech, accompanied by what Donald Fagen of Steely Dan had called the *Goodbye Look*—sad-eyed, with a wish-it-could-have-been-differ-ent smile.

Sarah may have been looking for Adonis perfection. Ike's nice, but more mundane *punum*, as Grandpa Otto would say, just hadn't been for her. If that's what it was, well, okay then. He couldn't do anything about looking Jewish and nice. What Ike couldn't fathom was Sarah's more recent "let's-fuck-the-doorman" relationship.

Greg, in Ike's professional opinion, was a complete moron who lived in an overbuilt Arnold Schwarzenegger body. The fact that Sarah chose him next pissed Ike off. But to Ike, as a trained psychotherapist who knew very well the defenses of the mind it raised the question: Who, really, was jealous of whom?

Otto lived in apartment 18H. It had two entrances: one for his psychoanalysis practice, the other for his living space. For most of his life after coming to New York from Europe, Otto had lived uptown near Columbia University. A short while after Otto had his first ministroke, Ike heard that 18H had become available. At first Otto was reluctant to even think about a new place. At his age, and with his health issues, the move seemed daunting. The fact that Donald Trump owned the Towers had been a big negative that Otto jumped on as an excuse. "What a *shmegegie* he is," Otto had said. "This thing he does with women: divorce, marriage, divorce, marriage, and the women all look and act the same. The schmuck thinks they want him. They want his money, his empire. He is an insecure man. Just look at his hair." But when Otto visited the double-entranced apartment with its view of the Hudson River and Riverside Park, and its proximity to the subway, and the comforting knowledge that his grandson would live just an elevator ride away, well, it was an emphatic slam-dunk.

Ike rode the elevator to 18 and walked the hallway to Otto's place. He knocked on the steel door and waited. After a few seconds, he pressed the buzzer a couple of times, then a few extra for good luck. More time passed without a response. Otto had poor hearing, and this scenario had played out often. Ike always worried during these moments that he'd find his grandfather prostrate on his consultation room floor or in the kitchen, the two places he spent most of his waking hours.

Finally, Ike let himself in.

He passed through the foyer with its side table stacked with newspapers that Ike had to cull through weekly, and walked toward the kitchen. He noticed the faint odor of wax burning. He peered through the opening and there, on the small round table, was a candle glowing in its glass enclosure. Every fall (the specific date was dependent on the Hebrew calendar) since Ike's mother, Miriam, died, Otto burned the *yahrzeit* candle for his daughter, something he recently reminded Ike he'd do for the both of them.

Ike headed for the consultation room. In the hallway, a white sheet covered the mirror. It was Orthodox custom. When a family member passed away, survivors would veil reflective glass for the *Shiva*, the seven-day mourning period after the funeral. Ike was confused. He and Otto were the only surviving members of the Miller-Sperber clan. Ike wondered who had died.

Otto had filled his consultation room with a collection of primitive objects, Freudian artifacts that included a signed photo of the great pioneer psychoanalyst, paintings of Jewish subjects such as a rabbi blowing a ram's horn, and a sculpture of Shalom Aleichem, the fabled Jewish author. The modern world was interspersed. An HD television hung on the wall. A state-of-the-art stereo system, a present from Ike, filled the shelves of a mahogany bookcase, crowded with professional and Jewish works. On the wall opposite the analyst chair hung an Annie Leibovitz photo-portrait of Otto that the psychoanalytic society had commissioned and presented to him as a lifetime achievement award. Next to it were framed covers of the opera librettos for La Traviata and Madame Butterfly personally autographed by Pavarotti and Maria Callas. Two decorative mirrors hung on opposite ends of the room. They, too, were shrouded.

"Otto," Ike called out.

From the bathroom he heard a faint voice. "Just a minute, my boy." Shuffling followed. His grandfather arrived at the room's entrance. In the year before his ninetieth, the weariness of Otto's long, courageous, and illustrious life showed prominently on his large, round face and in his expressive brown eyes.

"Grandpa, what's wrong?"

"What do you mean?"

"You look so sad. And the apartment, and your office—what's with the sheets?"

"Isaac, please sit down," he said.

Ike sat on the patient couch, a grainy and fissured brown-leather divan.

"Can I get you something to eat, to drink?" Otto asked, still standing.

"Grandpa, please, don't change the subject."

Otto nodded and settled into his chair.

"Is there someone in our family I don't know about who's died?" Ike asked.

In his tweed suit, white shirt, and wool tie knotted in a fashion that was as Old World as he was, Otto fixed his eyes on his grandson and sighed. "I was not going to share this since you have enough to deal with—"

"Stop it!" Ike nearly shouted.

"Why are you raising your voice to me?"

"You're always trying to shield me from what's going on. I want honesty. How can you practice psychotherapy every day, a practice that requires openness, and not share the truth with me?"

"You are right. But this will be difficult, especially since it is Miriam's yahrzeit." He paused and lowered his head. "Two of my friends have died. I have attended two funerals in a week."

"I'm so sorry to hear that," Ike said. "Who?"

Otto pointed. "Please go to my desk. Bring me the picture in the top right- hand drawer."

Ike stepped over to Otto's antique roll top, and removed an unframed photo.

"Bring the chair with you and come sit by me," Otto said.

Ike handed him the picture. Sitting next to his grandfather was always a warm comfort, a feeling of caring and protection.

"This was taken just after the liberation," Otto said.

"You showed me this picture once before," Ike said, "but I don't remember the names of the men."

Otto smiled. "You know we never wanted to burden you with the stories of what we went through, so I am not surprised that you do not remember. But you have actually met each one of them."

"Really?"

"Yes. These were men who survived Barracks Seventeen in Auschwitz with me. After we settled in America we formed a survivors group. Perhaps you remember meeting them now?"

Ike nodded, then shook his head slowly as he studied the photo more closely. Their emaciated condition made it difficult to recognize any of them. They were all young—boys, really–much younger than he was now. But innocence had fled from their faces.

Otto pointed. "This man, Hymie Safier—and even here you might be able to see it in him—was a funny guy. He joked in Auschwitz, of all places. Many times we tried to keep him quiet. We were afraid the guards would think he was mocking them. But he didn't care. They, too, would laugh." Tears fell from Otto's eyes.

"Grandpa—"

"I went to his funeral yesterday. He and his companion were murdered in their home. The police said they were victims of a burglary."

At first when Ike heard Safier's name it didn't compute. Once Otto described the cause of death, Ike realized the news of the killing had been Springer's lead on Monday's program.

"Do the police know who did this?" Ike asked.

"No. They say they have nothing yet."

"Is Safier the reason you covered the mirrors?"

Otto nodded and pointed. "This is the other man who died. His name is Baruch Gittlestein." In the picture, Gittlestein's eyes reflected panic, and his body was half turned, as if he wanted to run somewhere, anywhere. "He died from a heart attack on a Manhattan street just a few days ago," Otto said.

Ike put his arm around his grandfather and gently rubbed his shoulder.

Otto sobbed. "You know this man–this man was Avram–do you recognize your other grandfather here?"

Avram's face was hard and tough, with the fuck-the-bastards attitude Ike had witnessed his whole life. Despite the physical and emotional traumas he'd suffered, he looked remarkably like Jon Miller, Ike's father.

It pained Ike to see him like this, a young man with so much rage and yet so physically compromised by the torture he must have endured.

"With Avram also gone there are now only two of us. This one here, Pierre Feldstein." He pointed to the shortest one in the quintet. "And yours truly."

"He's so tiny." Ike studied his image. "This Pierre Feldstein looks like he came through the war in pretty good shape," Ike said.

"Yes. Feldstein is a small man, but he has enormous chutzpah inside a sociopathic personality. But at least he is on our side. Perhaps you have heard about him. Pierre is a lawyer and a famous Nazi hunter. He was in better shape than the rest of us at the end of the war. There was a rumor that his father, one of the biggest diamond merchants in Belgium, paid someone at the camp so that Pierre would receive decent treatment."

Ike shook his head. "How any of you managed to get through all that is a miracle to me," he said.

"We lost so many. Besides the good fortune some of us had, what helped us survive was that we each held onto something to live for. Avram always hoped to be reunited with Rose. Hymie, too, thought constantly of his wife Estelle. With me, it was my desire to help others, especially our people in the camps. Feldstein wanted to get the bastards. The thought of vengeance or justice, I was never sure which one it was, helped him survive. As for poor Baruch…" Otto shook his head.

"He looks terrified," Ike said.

Otto nodded. "I was always concerned for Baruch. If you remember from my book, I wrote about this terrible doctor, Antonin Helm."

Twenty years before Ike was born, Otto had published what became an acclaimed account of trauma and survival in the deathcamp, "Existentialism and Spirituality in Auschwitz." Ike had read the book a number of times–first when he was thirteen and then again for a course in his graduate psychology program, and later just to go over it again.

"Yes," Ike responded. "He was the one they called 'The Cutter.' A junior Mengele, you wrote."

"Baruch was a serial victim of Helm's *verruckt* science. Because Helm used me as his assistant, I did what I could to help Baruch. It was a miracle he survived."

"Your compassion is amazing," Ike said. "I remember you talked this Helm character out of another surgery on one of the men because you knew it would kill him."

Otto nodded mournfully. "It was Baruch," he said. His eyes became distant, then focused on Ike. "My boy, I wish I could have done more to help the men and their families." Tears filled Otto's eyes. He gasped for breath.

Ike stroked his grandfather's back again. "You've done so much: the clinic for the police, your foundation to help survivors and their families, fundraisers, free therapy. Try not to expect the impossible from yourself."

Otto retrieved a handkerchief from his jacket and wiped his eyes. "I wanted to do better. Someone had to." The crying intensified, the sobs louder and deeper. Ike had never experienced his grandfather this way.

"Do you want me to get you something, a glass of water, a cup of tea?" Ike said.

"No, my boy. I just need your attention."

They sat together like this for a while, the firm ticking of the old grandfather clock the only sound.

Otto spoke. "I asked you to come today not just to tell you my troubles, but also to talk with you about your show from Monday."

"The one I screwed up?" Ike said.

Otto removed his wire-rimmed spectacles and began to alternately clean and examine the lenses. When he finished he placed the glasses back on his face. He looked gently at Ike. "Yes, but not so bad. In the end you did good by apologizing to the woman. It takes courage to know when you are wrong and to make atonement."

"I don't know," Ike said. He wondered where this was going. Otto didn't raise matters about therapy in general or Ike's show in particular without an agenda.

"Countertransference got the best of you. That is the way to think of it," Otto said. "All therapists, even the ones on the radio, must deal with this at one time or another. The woman who called spoke of the loss of a loved one, also in a violent way as happened to your father, and of course it is the anniversary of your mother's death. The *yahrzeit* of one parent will often bring back memories of the other deceased parent, and Isaac I feel you have much unfinished business about your father that you must still work out."

"That's what you wanted to tell me? Something we both know?" Ike said.

"Yes. I thought I might help you with this unpleasantness by showing you your father in a way you may have overlooked."

"What are you talking about?"

"Isaac, your tone is disrespectful. I know this time of year is upsetting. But I am someone who can help. Do you not think this is true?"

Ike sighed. Otto didn't need his abrasiveness. "I'm sorry. I didn't mean to jump all over you."

"I accept your apology."

"Okay. Tell me what I overlooked."

"I believe your father's talent as a musician came from his difficulties with Avram. You know I am ignorant about your music. I become nervous when I listen to things so chaotic and loud. But I made it my business to learn what my future son-in-law was doing for a living once Miriam and Jonny decided to marry."

"You listened to his recordings?" Ike said.

"Yes. I even attended a concert with Miriam. *Oy vey izmir!* Such a headache I had that evening."

"A Neil Young concert?"

"Yes," Otto shook his head and rolled his eyes. "The fellow with the long *shmutzig* hair and the high voice. This kind of voice is common in rock 'n' roll, no?"

Ike chuckled silently, wondering if Neil Young would have laughed as well after hearing himself described this way. "Yes, the falsetto is very common."

"I listened to your father play the guitar," Otto said. "I could hear the emotion, the anger and the sadness, the joy of freedom in his performance. These feelings were so powerful, so genuine."

"That was Jon, all right."

"Isaac, why don't you call him your father?" Otto's face turned red. "It is disrespectful to use his first name the way you do." The lines of his face seemed to deepen.

"Damn it, Grandpa. Did you forget, or is this your way of helping me get over him?"

Ike didn't mean to hurt him. Otto was grieving not only for his friends but also for his daughter.

"I'm sorry," Ike said. "I must sound like a broken record. You know he insisted I call him Jon. I don't think he was ever comfortable being a father."

"Yes. This is true."

"So why do you keep on me about it?"

"Because, in fact, he was your father, and every child needs to have one."

"I agree. Every child needs to have one. I had one. Not a good one. He abandoned my mother—your daughter— and me for the road. For sex, drugs, and rock 'n' roll. How can I have anything but contempt for him?"

"I understand your feelings. I, too, was very angry at the way he treated your mother and of course his absence from your life. But I must ask you this. If you reject him so, why have you chosen work that keeps you close to him?"

"Huh?" Ike blinked his eyes. "I'm a clinical psychologist."

Otto laughed gently.

"What's so funny?"

"My boy, yes, you are a psychologist, a wonderful and creative one. But I am laughing not at you but at the ways of your unconscious mind. Perhaps your unconscious defense is denial."

Ike tilted his head. "What do you mean?"

"You said you are a psychologist. This, by itself, keeps a good therapist close to his parents. It means you must always be working through childhood difficulties to help others."

"Of course I'm close in that way. You know how much work I've done with my conflicts around him."

"True. And it has helped sharpen your perceptions. I am certain of this. But there is one more thing."

"What?"

"You, like your father, are involved with music," he said.

"That's obvious."

Otto squinted at him. "Now, you must stop it. I know this is difficult to speak about. But we must."

"Damn it Otto, I hate talking about him. I don't even want to think about him." He got up and moved back to the divan.

"Then you are always doomed to have a blind spot in your work," Otto said his voice rising. "Other callers will have similar issues and you will handle them the same way or even worse than you did the other day."

"Thanks for predicting my future."

Otto removed his spectacles again and repeated the lens cleaning ritual. It was as if he were wiping away his grandson's anger. "Even a bad person has some good in him. Can you not give your father some credit?"

"Credit for what?"

"Whether it is nature or nurture or a combination of both, your father gave you two very big things."

"What two things are we talking about here?"

"The first is your music. You love it, use it, and have elevated it to a therapeutic art. The second is your stage presence. Like your father you go in front of people and perform. But you have taken this further. You perform to educate and heal. And I believe this comes from the pain you suffered in your relationship with him. This is why I say you are close to him."

"I don't know." Ike paused distracted by something from his past. "Do you know the story about the guitar?"

"Perhaps you told me. But I do not remember."

"For my eighth birthday, Jon–sorry—my father bought me a Fender Stratocaster signed by Neil Young. It's a special guitar, one of the best, and used by rock musicians throughout the world. But mom got me a basketball. I was always more interested in the ball than the guitar, and I think he never forgave me for that."

"Basketball is a touchy subject, is it not?" Otto said, nodding his head mournfully.

Ike knew exactly what his grandfather was referring to. "Grandpa?" Ike's tone made him sound young. "Why did it have to happen on that weekend?" In a nanosecond the memory flashed in front of him, as it had countless times ever since. Seven seconds to go. The arena electric. The Rice Owls, down by one, and the play Coach had called was for him, a simple give-and-go that was to culminate in the final shot, a sure game winner. After the timeout, the cheers of *IKIE! IKIE! IKIE!* grew like a wave throughout the stands. Ike's backcourt mate threw the ball to Ike, who took one dribble and found the team's center on the right block between the foul line and the basket. As the center dribbled to this right he was double-teamed, and Ike was free on the left, with a clear path to the hoop. The bounce pass was perfect. Ike caught it in motion, a step ahead of his man and a jump away from the game-winning layup. But as he began his elevation to the hoop, Ike's legs became entangled and instead of finishing his move he fell headlong out of bounds. His hands and the ball crashed against the hardwood and Ike watched as it rolled toward the crowd. Game over. Game lost. And to add injury to insult, Ike tore the ligaments in his right knee.

He looked to his grandfather for an answer.

"I know," Otto said as he stroked the bald dome of his head. "This is difficult to explain. One could say that unconsciously your father tried to hurt you by being in the wrong place at the wrong time, in the apartment of a drug dealer on the weekend before you were to play the most important game of your life. Another explanation was that his addiction was so great he gave no thought to what you were doing."

Ike banged his fists against the couch. "It's all bullshit."

"I agree with you. These two explanations are false."

"Then what's yours?"

"I believe—no I am sure, because your mother and I discussed this before she died—that your father was nervous for you. He was thrilled but anxious that you were playing in this big game on such a big stage. He was both proud and frightened."

"Yeah, right."

"Isaac, you do not have to believe me for my sake. But I want you to think about this. Your father had difficulty with emotions, so he used opiates to calm them. Feeling too much outside of his music caused him great pain. This is why he stayed away from his family and his own parents. His parents were the cause of his greatest sorrow. It is the case for many children of Holocaust survivors. In a way his trouble is the trouble of the Jewish people and so it is yours by extension. Hitler, his henchmen, and their evil philosophy still live in the psyches of the survivors and their families. Even in you, two generations past the war."

Though he tried not to think about it, Ike knew it was true. A family therapist colleague once told him that a trauma as big as the Holocaust would take surviving families many generations to resolve.

"When we came to America," Otto said. "All the men, including myself and your grandfather Avram, carried emotional satchels. Unlike the satchels that transported our material possessions, the emotional ones were never emptied. They stayed full with all manner of distress. And when various life pressures came into our lives, as they did with Avram, terrible things happened. Do you know what they were?"

Ike nodded. "Rage, abuse, and emotional explosions."

"Yes. When these forces are set free, they become a monster like you have seen in horror movies. And this is what happened too many times. Your grandfather released the horrors in his soul onto poor Jonny, your father. This is why I wished I could have helped more. And if I could have done more, maybe your father would not have resorted to killing his pain with drugs. And maybe your mind would have been free when you played in the championship game."

If only, Ike thought. "Do you really think my fall on the last play had something to do with all of this?"

"Tell me my boy. How could it not? It was as if you wore a satchel on your own back filled with the weight of your father's death, three days before your big game. As much as you tried to compartmentalize what happened, I believe an emotional monster crashed through your

psyche and caused you to fall. I have always believed that."

"I don't know," Ike said as he tried to let Otto's explanation sink in. "Coach used to say. 'There are no tears in hoops.'"

"I am sure he is an expert in basketball. But in my opinion, in psychoanalysis, he is only a *pisher*."

They laughed together.

"Have you spoken with Feldstein now that it is only you and him?" Ike asked.

"He was at both funerals. He made a joke. He said, 'which of us will be the third?' It is the superstition that bad things happen in threes."

A chill rushed up and down Ike's spine. "Don't think that way. We don't need that as prediction too, you know."

"Don't worry my boy. I have deluded myself into believing I will live forever," Otto said. He chuckled and his face brightened.

Ike smiled wistfully.

"Are you sure I can't get you something to eat?" Otto said.

"Yes, Grandpa. I'm sure. I'm going to head over to Mike's to get a bite. You want to come?"

Otto shook his head wearily. "If I eat in that place and am exposed to the noise I will certainly not live forever. But thank you for asking."

"I'd love to get you out of your apartment." He nodded at the draped mirrors.

Otto waved his hands. "No, my boy. You go and enjoy."

"Okay then, I'm out of here," Ike said.

He stood to leave.

"Ah, ah, ah. Before you go you must give your grandfather a hug."

Otto had always said to treat goodbyes as if it were the last time you might see the person. Ike turned and came back to his grandfather. They embraced. But something about the hug was different from the way Ike had experienced it in the past. The deep affection, as always, was there. Now, Ike felt a sensation of tightness in Otto's upper body. It was as if his grandfather was holding on for fear this intimacy would soon end. Ike considered, of course, that Otto would feel this way at his age, more so after two of his friends had just died. But what Ike was sensing was greater than looming end of life. The feeling was spooky, stronger than an intuition, more like a premonition. Like Otto's friends who kept their emotional satchels closed and close, Ike decided to do the same about what he was sensing, at least for the time being.

Ike kissed his grandfather and headed for the elevator.

CHAPTER EIGHT

THE BROKEN HEART

"Surprised to see you in here tonight," Mike Golden said.

Ike, leaning against the bar, turned and scanned the saloon. "Place looks a bit empty."

"Midweek at nine-thirty, past dinnertime and who knows what else." Mike seemed relieved. "What can I get you?"

"Let's start with a pint of Guinness and a cheddar cheeseburger."

"Cheeseburger, huh? A bit risqué for you, wouldn't you say? I thought Monday's were your only junk-food-junkie day." Mike gently laughed and then called the order into the kitchen.

"Yeah. Don't give a shit right now," Ike said.

The saloon proprietor eyed him closely. "Is this about the woman you left with the other night?"

Ike hesitated, averted eye contact. "Yeah," he finally said.

"What happened? She looked like she was really into you."

"I don't know. She wouldn't give me her number and told me she'd call me. She hasn't yet."

Mike slid closer on his side of the bar. He looked toward the ceiling, raised his hand and showed Ike three fingers. "Let me be the shrink now. It's only three days, Ike, just three days. Relax. Maybe she had important business out of town or something. If you don't hear from her by, I don't know, the middle of next week, then it was a one-night stand and you'll just have to lick your wounds."

The burger and stout came. Mike signaled Ike that he had to take care of the customer to his left who was sitting on the barstool Aja had first occupied the night they met. In the background the Stones were playing, and Mick Jagger was belting the lyrics to "Blinded By Love." Ike, in a burst of laughter, almost spit out the bite of burger he'd been working on. *I must be channeling Tony wherever I go,* he thought.

"Hey. Ain't you the shrink guy on TV and the radio?" a voice queried from Ike's left.

Ike zeroed in on a rough looking dude about his own age. He was solidly built with hard brown eyes and a scraggly stubble that barely covered a scar that ran the width of his chin. He wasn't anyone Ike had seen in Mike's before.

"Yeah. Hi. Ike Miller. What's your name?"

"Frankie. My name's Frankie." The guy had a smoker's voice.

"Nice to meet you," Ike said.

Frankie's shot glass of vodka arrived and he swallowed its contents at the speed of light and then asked for another.

"That's your third in just a few minutes. Don't you think you should slow down?" Mike said.

Ike half stood and gave the place a one-eighty perusal for a table in a dark corner. He didn't need a sloppy drunk intruding on his wound licking. He wanted to be left alone to eat in peace.

"Hey, it's cool, man," the guy said. "I won't bother you." He stood, put his hand in his back pocket and retrieved his wallet. As he took out some cash, Ike saw a tattoo on the top of his right hand — a broken swastika.

"Excuse me," Ike said. "Your tattoo. You ever hear of the German rock group Dilemma?"

Frankie stared at Ike.

Ike continued. "The organizer of that group wore a tattoo just like that. We played one of their songs on the show today," Ike said.

"Fuck that, man. No one else has this," Frankie snarled.

Ike didn't want to mess with this guy, who, though smaller than Ike, looked packed to explode, and with a few vodkas in him besides.

"I hear you. But before you go could you tell me what it means?"

"It's like a fucking broken heart. That's what it means."

As Frankie pushed away from his barstool and walked out of Mike's, Ike came to the conclusion that he'd been sharing counter space with a neo-Nazi, definitely a turnaround from Monday night.

Mike looked over at Ike. "Hey, you okay?"

Ike shook his head. "Did you see the guy's tattoo?"

"Can't say I did."

"It was a broken swastika, like the guy from Dilemma."

"What's a Dilemma? And so what? People get tattoos." He showed Ike his, a shamrock inside a heart inked onto his forearm.

Ike didn't want to get into it. He downed the rest of his Guinness and pushed his dinner plate toward the back of the counter. "I'm going home," he said.

"You want me to wrap the rest of the burger?" Mike asked.

"No, that's okay."

"Call you a cab?"

"I'm going to walk. I need some fresh air."

"You sure?"

Ike nodded.

"Okay. But remember. Do as I said. Be patient."

"Yeah." Ike put money down on the counter.

"Have a good one and be careful out there."

Thursday night in midtown was relatively quiet, that is relative to other nights. Ike's walk took him onto West Fifty-Eighth Street on his way to Columbus Circle, and then Broadway. As he turned west onto a street that was both quiet and dark at this hour, he fixated on the broken swastika, which in a sense was better than thinking about Aja. He remembered Otto quoting Feldstein about events coming in threes. Well, if that were the case,

Ike now had his third. Three Nazi incidents to make him wonder if this particular troika–Dilemma's song, "Love and Vengeance," Otto's stories about his friends, survivors of Auschwitz who'd recently died, and now the guy with the broken swastika on his hand–meant anything at all. One of the takeaways from his meeting with Otto was how Ike's father's suffering and, by extension, his own was due to the insanity of Hitler and his underlings, like the bizarro Dr. Helm in Auschwitz. Ike had inherited his father's, and grandfathers', unfinished business and it pissed him off. But he didn't know what to do with his anger. He didn't know how and with whom he could settle that score.

As he turned the corner, it happened fast and out of nowhere. It was like a distracted pedestrian walking into a telephone pole, except instead of an unyielding street fixture, the bone and meat of a fist struck him under his left eye. He staggered. Blood streamed down his face. His consciousness faded as he sunk down to the sidewalk. Through his cloudy vision he was sure the attacker was the guy from Mike's and not just your ordinary garden-variety New York City mugger. As he tried to catch his breath, the vodka drinker who'd identified himself as Frankie kicked Ike hard in the stomach, rolled him over, and felt for his butt. Punch-drunk, Ike wondered if if he was about to be a victim of a sex crime. Frankie pulled Ike's wallet from his back pocket, drove his knee into Ike's back, bounced up, and ran away into the darkness of Fifty-Eighth Street.

Ike pushed himself up, staggered, and sat up against a parked car. He scanned his body for injuries, but all he could feel was throbbing in his face and blood streaming into his mouth and down his chin.

A police car pulled up and two cops approached. One of the officers bent down to look at Ike. "That's some nasty blow to your mug. You're going to need a shitload of stitches."

"Did you see who did this to you?" the second cop asked.

"Yeah. I'm pretty sure," Ike said, still working his way through his mental haze.

"Okay, who was it?" the first cop asked.

Ike squinted and shook his head to get some clarity. It hurt to do so. "I think it was a Nazi I met in a bar."

The officers looked at each other.

"I'm sure you know what that means," the first one said. "Why don't we take you to an emergency room, and you can tell us all about it there."

CHAPTER NINE

HOOPS DREAM

The emergency room doctor stitched him up and sent him home. Ike was lucky — no internal bleeding, no broken bones, just some bruises and bumps and a shiner he'd have to sport for a while. A nurse told him to ice the eye. She gave him some painkillers that he'd probably throw away. The cops took down the description of the attacker, and told Ike they'd follow up with a visit to Mike's to get the saloon owner's account.

The idea of some kind of awful threat grew in Ike's mind. Either his grandfather wasn't putting two and two together about these events, or he was aware of their meaning and purposely kept Ike in the dark, as was the family custom. He needed to talk with Otto. He'd schedule a post show meeting with him for tomorrow.

The next day when Ike walked into the radio station, the whole crew--Stacy the weather person, Moe, Larry, and Curly, and even the Stillman brothers--voiced concern about his facial wounds. Tony was the only one Ike was willing to talk to about it.

"If I told you I walked into a pole, would you believe me?" Ike said.

"Not with the setup you just gave me. Were you in a fight?" Tony said.

"Sort of. I had a visit with Otto, then went to Mike's."

"That's one of the reasons I never go." Tony smirked.

"You going to be Tony the snark, or are you going to listen?"

"Sorry."

"Thanks," Ike said letting out a soft sigh. "Okay. So some guy is sitting next to me. He recognizes me from the show, and he's drinking vodka shots one after another. As he gets up to leave, I notice he's got a broken swastika tattoo on his wrist. I ask him about it, and he gets defensive. I don't follow up because he looks pretty rough, and his blood alcohol level is probably off the charts. I leave shortly after. I'm on Fifty-Eighth Street. It's dark. No one around, and someone out of nowhere belts me."

"You think it was the guy with the tattoo?"

"I'm sure of it. Weird. Right? What are the odds? We play a song by an artist who wore the tattoo, and I'm in Mike's and the guy next to me has the same branding. Then no more than fifteen minutes later—boom."

Tony shook his head. "That worries me. You speak to Hank?"

"Not yet. Funny thing, last Monday in Mike's he told me to be careful," Ike said and winced in pain.

Tony stroked his beard. "Who could know if this is or isn't a coincidence? And if it's not, what the hell is going on? Tell you what, you go take care of your face, and I'll speak with Hank. This is something he should know about."

"Thanks."

"Okay. Just a reminder, we've got 'Dreams' as the topic. You still good to go?"

"Yeah, easy enough. You know I'm always interested in dreams. Had a strange one last night. I was in the NCAA championship game again, taking the final shot. What else, right? So instead of a ball, I'm dribbling a gun, and the damn thing goes off my knee, the bad one, and bounces out of bounds."

"Wow. I'm not a shrink, but for this I don't have to be. I mean, your dream tells me you're one worried puppy."

"I don't know about the puppy part, but yeah, I'm worried about a lot of things. But now's not the time to get into it."

"Okay. You go take care of that thing. Try to relax. Try the meditation I taught you, and get ready for the show. Make sure you've got plenty of content on that golden tongue of yours." Tony paused to look at Ike's face again. "Boy, that is ugly. Good thing it's radio only today," Tony said as he headed for the phone to speak with Hank.

Dreams: Freudian, Jungian, New Age, old age. It didn't matter. Ike was available to talk with callers about their REM experiences, with golden tongue and golden ears alike. The callers were savvy. Some wanted to know about the unconscious meaning of symbols. Others wondered if their dreams offered a glimpse into the future.

Roberta from Manhattan was a seventy-year-old widow who'd been on the air with Ike a number of times and whom he'd once met at a WNYT community outing. Roberta believed her dreams offered premonitions.

"You say you had a vision last night," Ike said.

"Yes. A woman will come back into your life," Roberta said.

"I hope you're right." Ike flushed when he realized he'd revealed too much about himself.

"So there *is* someone. I knew it," Roberta said, obviously excited by her power to know. "She must be beautiful because in the dream she was quite so. Not only that—the two of you are very well matched. You're on the same wavelength. Just the way my husband Bob and I were."

"Could it be the dream was about him? I mean, perhaps you miss Bob." Her husband had passed away more than five years ago. Ike was only too glad that he had this information to divert the conversation away from him.

"That could be, but I don't think so. It didn't feel that way. This one was about you," she said resolutely.

"So is that all it was?" Ike eyed Tony, who shook his head and smiled smugly. They weren't going to play the Peggy Lee classic.

"No. Though the two of you loved each other. Other loyalties — no, more like responsibilities — got in the way."

"What do you mean?" Ike asked.

"The dream got murky at that point."

"So that was it. No more."

"Yeah. That's all."

"Well, Roberta, thank you for sharing your dream. And one more thing: thanks for being such a dedicated fan."

Tony played "Dream" by the Everly Brothers.

In his headset, Ike heard his partner laughing.

"What?"

"Roberta's predicted you're going to hear from her. You know, the nameless one you met at Mike's. You can stop worrying now."

"Yeah, right. And what's going to follow the Everly Brothers? By the way, that's a no-brainer of a choice," Ike said.

"Yeah, hotshot. The next one is by Van. What do you think it's called?"

Ike's face said "no idea."

"It's called, 'Caravan,' with lyrics about the radio and about a gypsy fortune teller. Next time Roberta calls, you might ask her if she's got some Romani blood in her," Tony said, breaking into the lyrics of the Van Morrison song. Unfortunately, his voice fell many notches below his production talent.

The show was coming to an end. Ike broadcast his goodbyes to the audience with a voice-over to the Van Morrison recording. As Ike shed his Dr. Ike persona and became the ordinary Ike Miller, the great feeling of being in the flow with callers and the music came to an end. Thoughts of the mugging returned. This was bigger than some random attack on a dark New York City street. He realized that his catastrophic thinking was exhausting him. He wanted to get home and lose himself in a long sleep. Maybe he'd have his own fortune-telling dream that would show him what was "really wrong," as Van sang. But before he'd have the chance to lay his body down, he had to get through his appointment with Otto.

As Ike made his way out of the studio, Tony stopped him and gave him a hug.

"Great job."

"I thought it sucked."

"You usually do. Believe me, it was good and, I have to say, interesting. Some of what you talked about has an overlap to stuff my guru says."

"Yeah. Maybe you can tell me about it another time. My face hurts like hell."

Ike got his gear and headed for the elevator. Once inside, he became absorbed in his turmoil and lost track of the elevator's position. When the door slid open on the ground floor and began to slide shut, he realized a round trip was in the offing. He thrust his hand into the doorstop just in time. He stepped into the lobby and stopped cold.

"My God. What happened to you?" Aja said. She moved close to him and brought her hand up as if she wanted to touch the wound under his eye.

Ike took a step back. They stood and looked at one another.

"You must think I'm a real bitch for not calling you."

"Bitch is not exactly the word I was thinking of."

She laughed. "That bad, huh?"

"That bad," Ike said, but he tried not to show how hurt he was.

Her mouth turned up in a smile. "I couldn't stop thinking about the other night."

"I was working real hard not to think about you," he said.

She took his arm. "I can understand that."

He felt the electricity of their hoops dance on the Hell's Kitchen Playground court. All the pain–the hurt and confusion and the throbbing under his eye–seemed to dissipate.

"Do you want to go somewhere? Starbucks? Any place, to eat and talk. It'll be on me. I want to hear what happened," Aja said.

"I need to spend some time with my grandfather," Ike said, disappointed that he was bound by his appointment.

"Okay, maybe another time." She let go of Ike's arm. They stood silently.

"Why don't you come with me?" Ike asked. "My grandfather, Otto, lives in the building. You can wait in my place. After I'm done, maybe we can think of something."

She smiled. "That sounds perfect."

Greg was on duty when they arrived at the Towers. He tipped his hat to Aja and gave Ike a strange look, as if he couldn't believe that someone like her was going up to Ike's place.

They took the elevator to the thirtieth floor, and walked to his apartment. He inserted his key, pushed open the door, and turned on the light.

"Wow. Great place, Ike," Aja said, turning to take it all in.

"Thanks," he said smiling. "Look, there's food, stuff to drink in the fridge, coffee in the cabinet. On the table over there are remotes for the TV and stereo. Make your-self at home. This shouldn't take too long. If you need me I'll be in Eighteen H. Phone number's on the fridge."

"Thanks. Take your time. I'm not going anywhere," Aja said.

As he began to leave, she put a hand on his shoulder, turned him around and kissed him on the lips and then gently under his eye. He walked to the elevator and as he waited for it to come, touched the spot where she'd kissed him.

"Otto. Otto. It's Ike," he called out.

In the kitchen, the memorial candle still burned. But Ike's grandfather wasn't at his table sipping a glass of tea and reading the New York *Times* or one of the many news magazines he subscribed to. Nor was he in his consultation room. Opened and overturned professional journals lay across the seat cushion as if they were his proxy. Ike glanced behind the desk and the patient's divan to make sure Otto hadn't fallen or worse.

He called out louder this time. "Otto. It's Ike."

His anxiety about his grandfather's wellbeing made his stomach tight and bubbles of sweat covered his brow. He headed for the bedroom. On the way he heard rustling.

"Isaac, I'm sorry I didn't hear you," Otto said, fumbling with his trouser zipper and suspenders as he stood at the bedroom entrance. "How are you, my boy? Please, come and let's sit in my office. Can I get you something?"

Ike waited for Otto to notice his shiner.

"*Oy yoy yoy!* What happened to you?" Otto asked.

"Mugged on the way home last night. It's nothing. I'm fine.

"I thought the city had cleaned up this type of trouble. You know I have connections with Bloomberg and will speak—"

"Grandpa, please. I don't need Bloomberg or the police commissioner or the FBI to help me, thank you, and besides the mugging is not why I came to speak with you. At least it's not the main reason."

"Okay. But tell me this. Did you go to the police?"

"A witness in the building across the street called them. But it was dark. The cops didn't get much of a description. Right now someone is running around with my wallet and ID."

"Credit cards, money… What did he take?"

"I had about fifty dollars on me. I called my bank about the credit cards. I'll get replacements tomorrow."

"You will be okay then?"

Ike nodded.

They entered the consultation room and sat in their traditional places. Otto focused on Ike's shiner. "You are doing the right things for that, yes?"

"Yes. But that's not why I'm here." He was getting impatient with Otto's questions.

"Is there something more important than this?" Otto asked. His hooded brown eyes looked worried.

Ike pulled out a computer printout from his jacket pocket. "After our talk last night, I became suspicious. Two deaths from your little group in such a short time is a little too coincidental, don't you think? So I did some digging."

Ike handed it to him. Otto read without changing his expression.

"Helm may still be breathing and this isn't troubling you?" Ike asked.

Otto waved his thick, liver-spotted hands. "I see no reason to waste my time worrying about rumors and innuendo. Do you realize if Helm were alive today he would be older than me? And with the international war crimes community always on the lookout for fugitives, where could he possibly go, and what could he do?"

"What about the third paragraph down—about his daughter and grandson?" Ike asked.

Otto gave it a quick inspection. He removed his spectacles, and began busying himself with his lens-wiping routine. "My boy, this is an old story. Besides, what would that have to do with any of us, with the deaths of Baruch or Hymie? That mother and her son, their fight is with German institutions. They believe they are entitled to inheritance or life insurance money because Helm is dead. Since there has been no corroboration of his death, they cannot get a penny."

Did his grandfather have the correct take on the backstory? But how could Ike question him? Otto was connected to the world of war crime investigations, not only of Nazi fugitives, but also for the newer breed of genocidal killers through his association with Pierre Feldstein and with the Wiesenthal Center. If Otto was confident that his friends' deaths were random events, then maybe he should let it go… *but not just yet.*

"Grandpa, you remember I went to Mike's last night?"

"You gave me an invitation." Otto smiled.

"Yes. Anyway, some guy is sitting at the bar two chairs over from me. He recognized me from the show. We exchanged names. But the guy is drinking heavily and I think he's going to be obnoxious. So I'm looking around to move to the back of the place, when he tells me he won't bother me and he gets up to leave. He drops money on the bar and I see a broken swastika tattoo on the back of his hand. When I ask him what it means, he tells me it's like a broken heart."

Otto raised his shoulders, lifted his hands and expanded them. "A neo-Nazi with a sentimental feeling for Hitler? What else is new?"

"This is what's new. I think—no, I'm sure—he was my attacker."

Otto remained unmoved. "I believe there must be many of these screwed-up young men living in New York. Young men with unfinished business in their families who need a scapegoat to feel important."

Ike tried a different tactic. "You're all about intuition in your work. My intuition says this is more than some Aryan Brotherhood thug."

Otto stroked the top of his head. "What you are saying is that the circumstances of my friends' deaths, followed by the attack on you, are related and connected to Helm. Is that correct?"

Ike shrugged. "Yes."

"My boy, Baruch was the paranoid one, not you my own grandson," Otto said with a caring look.

"I hope you're right. I hope it's nothing more than my own trauma response to the mugging."

"Try to remember that after such an event your thinking can go to the darkest corners of your psyche."

Ike nodded. But as he watched his grandfather closely, he thought he detected a change in his eyes. A tiny flicker that Ike had come to know signaled apprehension. The explanation was likely a simple one. Otto was worried for him. But what was he worried about?

"Are you okay?" Ike asked.

"Yes. Please, no more talk about things finished decades ago."

"All right," Ike said. But he felt dissatisfied by the way their talk was ending.

Otto nodded. "Good. Now can I share with you some food?" Otto asked.

"No Grandpa, I have a date." This was news that Ike's grandfather would celebrate. Otto wanted nothing more for him than to find a partner and get married.

"Wonderful. You have not told me about her," Otto said, his face brightening.

"Just met her," Ike said.

"I hope she is nice. Go. Enjoy. And before you leave, give me a hug. And Isaac, try not to worry about these Nazi stories."

Aja was asleep, curled up in a question mark on his living room sofa. The innocence of her quiet breathing and her hand tucked under her cheek made him think of how she might have looked as a little girl. He retrieved a blanket from his hall closet, placed it over her, and gently tucked her in. She stirred, opened her eyes and smiled, then closed her eyes again. She wrapped herself around the woolen cover and pulled a corner of it against her face, then turned toward the back of the couch. Ike kissed her forehead and headed for the kitchen. He opened the freezer door, removed a bag of ice he'd prepared earlier and tiptoed to his bedroom.

Ike turned on his bedside radio. Nightfly Thomas, WNYT's overnight DJ, offered a delicious mix of jazz, blues, and rock. Ike undressed and sat on the edge of his bed, ice bag to his face, and stretched out over the quilt cover. He began to settle in for the night—a surprisingly soft dozing off considering all that was going on around him—as he listened to Nightfly's soothing mix of sounds. Somewhere in the middle of Ella Fitzgerald's, "I Only Have Eyes for You," he fell into a deep sleep.

He woke up at the end of another crazy basketball dream, one in which his college coach looked like Sigmund Freud and directed Ike to settle the score with the Hell's Kitchen Nazis. He felt an urgency to take a leak, rolled out of bed and almost tripped over his ice bag before stumbling into his bathroom.

On his way back to bed he sensed a presence near him in the darkness of the room—a motion in the corner of his eye. Before he could turn, Aja jumped onto his back, her legs straddling his hips. Giggling she kissed him on the neck, then slid off his rump to stand on the floor. She turned him around and their lips met, the kiss like the ones they shared on the Hell's Kitchen playground. She took his hand and led him to the wall. With both hands she stretched their arms over their heads. Ike moved his body against hers. Their equivalent size, elongated now, skin to skin, was the most sensual feeling he'd ever experienced.

"I want you to fuck me like this now," she said.

Ike placed his hands firmly underneath her buttocks and lifted her. She wrapped her legs around him and guided him inside. He was surprised by how turned-on she was, and a wave of excitement flowed through him. With her heels, she pulled him in more deeply, her hands holding firmly onto the back of his neck.

The wall was now their bed.

First slowly, and then as their passion intensified, their rhythmic motion increased. Their breathing became louder. Cries of pleasure filled the bedroom. They climaxed together, laughing and kissing and holding each other. After a while, they separated and Ike gently supported her as she placed her feet onto the floor.

She touched his face.

"Does it hurt?" She asked.

He shook his head. She touched the spot again and kissed him deeply,

He took her hand and led her to his bed. They lay side-by-side holding hands. After a few moments, she stretched herself out on top of him and nestled her head into the crook of his arm. Ike held her, kissed the top of her head, her neck, and face. He stroked her back and arms. She mirrored his motions, gliding over his skin from his shoulders to the tips of his fingers. Somewhere along the way their hands met again. For a good while, they lay still, palms and fingers entwined. Like this, they entered into a confluent cadence of breath. Ike felt her shiver and he trembled in return. He heard her heartbeat, smelled the sweetness of her skin, and thought that this was it, the perfect lover he'd always wanted but never believed he'd have.

Aja gently removed herself from their embrace. She turned her head and torso toward his feet with her lips and tongue sliding over his chest, belly, and legs and then to his inner thighs. She began to stroke and kiss his cock and then placed her lips around it. He released a gasp of pleasure and moved his hand between her legs and felt her wetness. He put gentle pressure on her, intensifying his touch as her moaning led him on. He placed his tongue inside her, licking and kissing her. Time disappeared. Ike was locked and lost in the bliss of their touch, taste, and scent. Aja turned her body around, rose above him, and guided him inside. As before, they entered into a rhythmic ebb and flow. Her orgasm came with an explosion of screams. His release followed quickly after. Aja lowered herself onto Ike's chest. His arms surrounded her. He kissed her, little kisses, over her face, shoulders, arms, fingers, and palms.

Later they made love again—a decidedly more mellow version, but one so tender, so generous, so sensual and loving that tears were the only answer. After, they fell asleep in each other's arms.

It was eight a.m. when he awoke—much later than he'd wanted his day to start. He turned to reach for her. She was gone. He jumped from the bed.

"Aja!"

After a few seconds of silence, Ike grabbed a t-shirt, put on his jeans, and walked into the living room. He found her sitting on one of his swivel chairs. She was wearing the long-sleeved Rice University nightshirt he'd given her after their lovemaking. She was turned to the view of the Hudson River and the GW Bridge. He took the chair next to hers.

"Are you okay? I called to you…" He stopped speaking when he saw her face, pale and sad. Otto had once told him that he was attracted to women whose broken wings he seemed compelled to fix. "Be careful about this tendency, my boy," he'd said. Was that it? Did he see Aja as a broken bird?

"Are you okay?" he asked again.

Her eyes were distant and tears streamed down her cheeks. "I don't want to be hurt."

No one wants to be hurt. Yet everyone is. He wanted to reassure her, tell her "Don't worry, I'll never hurt you." But would she do the same for him? Besides, who could make this promise and not feel totally full of shit? Instead, Ike pulled his chair close and put his arms around her. He kissed her ear, her cheek, and her neck.

"Let's go back to bed," she murmured into his neck.

"You don't know how tempting that is. Too much to do."

"Can I use your shower?"

"Of course. And before you leave, I want your phone number." He retrieved his cell phone and put in the number she gave him. She slid over to him and kissed him once more, her mouth open and her tongue caressing his. "Something to remember me by," she said.

"Don't worry. There's no way I'll ever forget you."

She giggled and ran off to the bathroom.

CHAPTER TEN

EGG SANDWICH

To anyone who may have noticed them strolling along the brick path, they appeared an ordinary twosome, as typical as any middle-aged mother and her young adult son. He wore a black leather bomber jacket and baggy jeans drooped below his waist. Black running shoes.

Mother's name was Maria. The gold and orange autumn leaves on her dress matched her red hair and the ruddiness of her skin. A white cashmere sweater covered her doughy arms. Black woolen socks inside Birkenstocks. A backpack slung over her left shoulder. They strolled the narrow strip of parkland on Riverside Drive adjacent to the Hudson River to the west and the Hampshire Towers to the east. The leaves on the trees had begun their color turn from green to orange, to red or gold. Some, the smaller and weaker ones, tumbled onto the ground when a brisk breeze swept through their oak and maple homes.

The woman gestured to an empty park bench, and they sat. Around them, pigeons were busy feeding on pieces of bread and soft pretzel remnants. At eight A.M., residents of the neighborhood were in full commuter mode, schlepping one thing or another, busy as the squirrels that overpopulated the park, walking in different directions to board buses, subways, cabs, or to move their cars for alternate side of the street parking. Runners with determined faces ran past, while occasional bike riders did their Lance Armstrong impressions.

Maria was just past fifty. FP, as she called him, was nearly thirty—an unemployed high school dropout who'd seen the inside of state and federal prisons at least a half dozen times. But Maria always said, "Who's counting?" when anyone brought up his less-than-illustrious resume.

She removed a sandwich from her bag and handed it to him.

He grimaced—an automatic response whenever she fed him, probably modeled by watching his father despise everything about her.

"Don't worry. It's a fried egg sandwich, just the way you like it."

He examined it more closely, then devoured it as if he hadn't eaten in days. FP, short for Franz Paul, aka Frankie, never missed a meal. He wasn't fat but he had the hardness of a running back, having inherited the mesomorph body of his father, who'd abandoned the family when FP was twelve and was later found dead on the short end of a biker gang shootout. That had been her first husband. The second hadn't been much better.

Maria admired her son's physical prowess, but wished he had inherited the brains of her own father, to become a professional man like him: a doctor, maybe even a surgeon.

FP wiped grease from the sandwich onto his tattooed hand and got up from the park bench. "How many times do I have to tell you to put ketchup on the eggs. Why don't you ever listen to me?" He nodded toward the Towers. "He should be leaving soon."

"Yes. Meantime, go say hello to Mr. Feldstein. I'm sure he's got some interesting stories to tell you. While you do, I'll keep an eye on Miller's grandfather."

CHAPTER ELEVEN

THE NAZI HUNTER

Pierre Feldstein was one of the tiniest men that most people would ever meet. If the Nazi hunter was close to four-foot-eight, it was because he wore shoes with thick heels and soles. He couldn't care less about the rest of his attire, a plain pair of brown slacks held up with suspenders on a coffee-and-soup-stained white shirt that parted at the neck like the Red Sea to reveal white chest hairs. At his age, the correctness of his wardrobe was no longer a priority. But his office mattered. It was grand. Portraits of war criminals and framed press clippings of his role in their capture filled the walls behind him and made him feel tall. The office décor included rich brown leather chairs, cabinets of the finest wood, floors covered in colorful and obviously expensive oriental rugs and tall arched windows that remained uncovered to provide a breathtaking panoramic view of Manhattan from high above it here on the seventy-ninth floor of the Empire State Building. The tiny man in one of the tallest building was likely the smallest man ever to work in any form of war crimes investigation and apprehension.

Feldstein punched the intercom. "Yossi, I need you to go to the cafeteria and get me a tuna fish sandwich, a coffee with a prune Danish, please. Repeat, Yossi," Feldstein listened to his order played back to him. "Good. Make it quickly."

The Nazi hunter leaned back in his plush leather chair and eyed the Chagall painting to his right. Feldstein couldn't care less about art, especially for the work of Chagall. He'd known Chagall in France before the war and thought the artist was one miserable bastard. But, then again, Feldstein thought that about most people. Had he been educated in psychology–which, if he'd considered it, would have been a useful tool in his line of work–he'd understand how projection of his own miserable self could make everyone he disliked into bastards. Nevertheless, as much as he despised Chagall and was disinterested in art, he proudly hung the Jewish painter's work that the Boca Raton Warsaw Ghetto's Survivors Group had presented him for a lifetime achievement battling bigotry and hatred.

Despite his simmering rage, controlling personality, Napoleonic complex, and permanent joylessness, Feldstein had, in fact, achieved greatness in his field. He'd been part of the Eichmann find. He helped determine Mengele's whereabouts. His people gathered information that uncovered where Demjanjuk and other lower-level murderers had found safety. Yet, despite it all, he had never accepted how small he was. That,

coupled with his role as an Auschwitz kapo, caused him
to feel rotten in the deepest part of his soul. He ventured
on despite these feelings. A week shy of ninety-one, he
still hoped to have one more discovery: the true fate
of Antonin Helm. Now, with the seemingly coincidental
deaths of two men from his landsman group, he wondered if the violence that caused their passing was the
smoke that could lead him to the fire that was the Nazi
surgeon.

Feldstein heard the outer office door open. He hit
the intercom button. "Yossi, dammit, what took you so
long?"

Yossi didn't answer.

"Yossi. Did you hear me? I am starved. Get in here
now."

No answer again.

Feldstein was an intuitive man. It was one of the
reasons he'd survived in the viper's den that was the
death camp and in the world of Nazi hunting, where
there were many others who wanted to make a name
by catching a ten-most-wanted war criminal. He had
trained Yossi too well for him not to answer when called.
But he was prepared for moments like this. He reached
into the top drawer of his desk and retrieved the Beretta
he'd taken off the body of an SS Captain after the liberation. As he pulled it from its hiding place he heard
an unfamiliar voice.

"I wouldn't do that if I were you."

Feldstein surmised the situation quickly and pointed the gun at the intruder, a solidly built young man
who held a pistol. The young man was, of course, much
quicker than Feldstein and blew the Berretta out of the

Nazi hunter's grasp before he could pull the trigger. Blood and bone sprayed across the room and onto the Chagall.

His hand and wrist smashed, and with blood flowing like water from Moses' rock, Feldstein had every right to whimper in pain. Instead, hardness learned in Auschwitz took over, and he betrayed no emotion to the young intruder who sat on the desk, leaned forward, and burrowed his gun's muzzle into Feldstein's head.

"You have something I want. Tell me quickly and I'll kill you without pain. If you give me a hard time, I'll make you suffer like you never have before."

Pierre Feldstein was diminutive in size. But, like the cinema legend King Kong—who stood at the top of this very building in the film named for him—he was huge of heart and extremely difficult to move.

"There is nothing you can do. I will give you nothing," Feldstein said defiantly.

"Where are my grandfather's jewels?" The intruder asked.

"Who is your grandfather?"

"The Cutter, you Jew scum."

At first he wasn't sure whether he'd heard this correctly, or if he was in the beginning stages of terminal delirium. "You are Helm's grandson?"

"What's so funny?" The thug raised his gun arm, as though he might pistol-whip the old man.

"I don't know what you are talking about." He had trouble getting the words out, his tongue felt thick, his mouth dry. Beads of sweat covered his brow.

The office door opened. "Mr. Feldstein, I have your—"

"Yossi, go…run."

Yossi's, underweight body shook like a Chihuahua, and he dropped Feldstein's lunch. The coffee splattered in a starburst on the fine wood floor.

Helm's grandson pounced. He pulled Yossi by his sidelocks onto the pool of blood that was forming next to his mentor's chair. He drew a knife, and held it against Yossi's throat.

"Feldstein, if you want me to have mercy on him you'd better tell me what I want to know."

But Feldstein knew nothing, and could do nothing anyway because the spirit in his body was leaving on a jet of blood from the severed artery. The old Nazi hunter's only emotion was fear for his young assistant, because he knew Helm's grandson was determined to get information from Yossi that he, Feldstein, didn't have. Before Feldstein died, he witnessed this third generation Nazi carving up Yossi's body like his evil, psychotic grandfather had done with other young men in Auschwitz. Was this his punishment for what he'd done in the death camp? Feldstein didn't live to see the young Nazi—in a rage—tearing apart the expensive Empire State Building office, looking for a safe-deposit key, bank statements, a will, anything, something.

He found nothing.

That, at least, would have been Feldstein's only consolation.

CHAPTER TWELVE

ALL YOU NEED IS LOVE

Ike stretched his legs across the steel desk that must have been in this office during an earlier incarnation of the radio station, perhaps during Father Coughlin's reign of radio terror. He could just hear Grandpa Avram say, *"These people are cheapskates. Must be Holocaust or Depression mentality. What? They couldn't afford a nice desk for you?"* And of course Otto would follow, eyes twinkling, with his own opinion. *"Being tight in their business is a sign of unfinished emotional issues, my boy. It is unfinished business for sure."*

Ike thought about Otto. The death of his two friends—both fellow survivors from Auschwitz, no less—in such a short time had to be devastating. Given Otto's age, Ike and his grandfather weren't guaranteed many more days together. Maybe they could hang out more. Take a weekend in the Catskills. Even though it wasn't the same vacation spot that it had been back in the day, Otto would enjoy it there. They'd walk mountain trails and continue their discussions about the Holocaust and its impact on their family—in particular, Ike's relation-ship with his father. Their talk would be about unfin-ished business.

That's right. Unfinished business. Unsettled scores. Same thing. Didn't everyone have them? Could anything really be finished, fixed, repaired, settled? The Hatfields and McCoys never finished a damn thing. The Israelis and Palestinians? Forget about them settling anything. Liberals and Conservatives in Congress? Real collabora-tion and compromise? Never happen! As often as Ike had read or watched, Romeo and Juliet, the Montagues and Capulets were at each other's throats, and it was still going on, last he looked, between the Sharks and the Jets. And of course, that final shot, the move to the basket that looked like a game winner but was a knee breaker instead. How could he ever settle *that* score?

Tony appeared at the office entrance. "Ready to go over the show?"

"Yeah. I've got a terrific idea."

"You seem excited. What's your thinking?" Tony asked.

"We've done programs on love, on falling in love, on losing one's love, on the differences between sex and making love, on unrequited love, and even crazy love. We've even done a show with the J. Geils Band's, "Love Stinks", as the kick off to a discussion on rotten love—"

"Ikie, whoa. You saw her again, didn't you?"

A Cheshire cat smile stretched across Ike's face. It was met by a Tony laugh that was close to a Santa "ho, ho, ho," followed by a more serious demeanor. "Dude. You've fallen in love with this chick already?"

Ike nodded.

Tony shook his head.

"Aren't you happy for me?"

"Listen, I'm not your mom, here. Yeah I'm glad if you are. But you know I've seen this with you before, and you fall fast and fall hard."

"I know but—"

"You said 'I know but' the last two. How many times have you been with her?"

Ike raised two fingers.

"Twice. One time making out on a basketball court and the second time all the way?"

Ike nodded, but he avoided Tony's eyes.

"Dude. When you meet a woman in a bar and she knows all kinds of shit about you and she tells you she's your groupie it adds up to caution lights and not fireworks and sirens blaring. But I'm just sayin'."

Nobody likes to have his face splashed with cold water, but maybe Tony was right. There was no point in arguing Tony's logical view versus his emotional one.

"So you want to go with a "Love Stinks" reprise, seeing that you don't believe this is good for me."

Tony did his Santa laugh again. "We can go that way. But since you're in a good place, why burst your bubble? Your energy's positive, and the audience will love it. Let's start with "All You Need is Love," and believe me, I got a list of love songs, silly and otherwise, longer than our arms combined."

"Two Lennon and McCartney references in one communication," Ike said.

"Nice going, Ike. Let's see if the audience gets it. Now get into the studio to give everyone some love."

The radio stage was dead still when they entered. Support staff was nowhere to be seen. Ike looked at Tony. The question mark on Tony's face matched Ike's bewilderment. Tony lifted the house phone receiver on the broadcast desk.

"Stacy, where's everyone?"

The speakerphone was on. "We're all in the news room looking at a report about a murder in the Empire State Building. The cops think it's a neo-Nazi terrorist attack or something."

Normally, Ike paid little attention to these reports. He lived and worked in Manhattan. As the famous bumper sticker so eloquently stated, "Shit happens," and all kinds of excrement occurred on a daily basis in the Big Apple. But, the recent events that included a neo-Nazi he'd met in a bar doing a number on him, and the death of Otto's friends, had him terrified by what might be coming out of the tube. Ike ran into the newsroom, a space smaller than most walk-in closets. Tony followed. Seven people were now crowded together watching three television screens attached to the wall.

"World Famous Nazi Hunter and Assistant Murdered in Empire State Building Office." Each of the three networks flashed a nearly identical caption. Ike zeroed in on the CNN reporter who was interviewing a NYPD detective: "*The man murdered was Pierre Feldstein, a world famous Nazi hunter and "Never Again" advocate. Detective*

Romano, do you have any clues as to who perpetrated this horrible crime?"

Ike never heard a word of the detective's answer. He'd gone into shock. Much like what happened to him when he'd learned his father had been shot to death right after his team won the semifinal game on the Saturday before the NCAA final.

"What's wrong? You're as white as the computer paper over there," Tony said.

"Feldstein's the third."

"What?"

"Look. It's too much to get into now. I have to go home and check on Otto. Start the show without me. If everything's okay, I'll be back in an hour, and he'll be with me."

"But Ike, why don't you just call and—"

"I don't have time to explain. I'll be in touch. Do the show. You have before."

And with that, he bolted out of the studio. Ike heard, "All You Need is Love," piped through the stairway speakers as he ran for Otto's life.

CHAPTER THIRTEEN

DOOR AJAR

No one stood at the building entrance. Finneran or Wagner always manned the door or supervised the reception and security desks, which were also unattended. Ike approached the reception area. Security monitors flickered. He studied each one. Pasted to the desktop were instructions on how to enter the floor number on the keyboard. With a shaky hand, he clicked in the data. An image of the hallways popped onto two of the three screens. His floor and Otto's were clear. He bypassed the elevator and pushed his way up the building's stairway with frantic speed.

He arrived sweaty and winded. Ike turned the corner of the hallway and saw pools of darkness along the passageway. Bulbs smashed in their sconces. Glass scattered on the carpet.

For a moment he stood frozen. How many times had he seen it in a movie? The foreshadowing of something horrible, yet the hero continued on. "Don't!" he'd called out to the screen, his warning unheeded. The same voice now in his head repeated the cry. But Ike pushed on anyway.

He turned another corner and heard the sounds of a sitcom through an apartment wall. Its laugh track seemed surreal. Rap music, "Empire State of Mind," Jay-Z's duet with Alicia Keyes, hip-hopped its way from somewhere down the hallway. A couple fought in an apartment behind him. Life as usual, but nothing felt usual. The apartment door letters were in reverse order: M, L, K. He turned the corner, J, I, Otto's office entrance, then, H–18H.

The door to his grandfather's apartment was partly open. Ike's heart pounded. He pushed on the door. Something moved, barely. He threw his shoulder against it. It moved enough to show him the impediment. Two bodies, soaked in blood, a jumbled mess of tissue and thick, oozing red on the parquet foyer floor. The gashes in their necks were long and deep, their heads nearly severed from their torsos. Finneran, the doorman, and Sarah Shapiro in a bloody heap. The doorman, a security guard, could be explained. But Sarah—what the hell was she doing here?

Nausea overcame him, and he threw up near the bodies. He stepped outside and leaned against the wall, breathing deeply to push back a second wave, but he couldn't control it. The little that had been left in his gut was now on the hallway carpet. His tears blinded him. He worked to catch his breath, hoping to recapture some semblance of calm and regain the ability to think.

He'd come for a reason.

"Otto!" Ike cried out.

Nothing. Silence.

Ike pushed himself to move. He jumped over the bodies and ran through the apartment. On the kitchen table was a glass of tea, three-quarters full, a half-eaten cheese Danish straddling the plate and table, and a professional journal bent open and laying upside down. Otto's chair leaned on its back legs against the windowsill. As Ike continued through the rest of the apartment, he noticed the place looked like a gale force wind had invaded its confines. Papers and books and clothes and artwork were strewn all over. Drawers, if not on the floor, hung from the desk and cabinets. He looked for Otto, hope against hope that he was still alive. But there was no one in any of the rooms, the only sound, a dripping faucet in the bathroom.

"Otto!"

Maybe the murderers went to my place? What if they have Otto and they're still there? He called 9-11 and gave the dispatcher his apartment number—30B. But he couldn't just wait for them to arrive. Each tick of the clock was precious.

"Time and timing," Tony had said. "Time and timing."

He ran to the stairway.

His apartment door was also slightly ajar. He felt dizzy and was afraid he'd pass out. He entered to a demolition much worse than the destruction of Otto's place.

"Otto… Grandpa… Otto… Grandpa." The lack of response was like a magnet that pulled him through the rest of his apartment as he moved cautiously through each room of his apartment. He entered the master bedroom. His bedside lamp was on the floor smashed, its shade beheaded from its base. The bed's quilt looked tousled as if someone had rolled on top of it, the four pillows lay in random positions on the area rug. Ike felt a surge of panic move from his gut to his throat. He could hardly breathe. He looked over at the bathroom. The door was shut. He never kept the bathroom door closed when he wasn't in it. He stepped slowly toward it and inched it open. What he saw–blood everywhere and Otto, his throat slashed, laying in the bathtub—sent a shockwave through his body. Ike shouted, "Why did they do this to you?"

He passed out.

A cop was kneeling over him when he regained consciousness. "Okay now, easy does it. Let me help you up."

He didn't know where he was and couldn't remember what had happened. Then it hit him. Otto was murdered, the image of his blood-covered body too surreal for him to comprehend.

The cop assisted Ike to his sofa.

Then another thought crashed through to his consciousness. He was now the sole survivor of his family, much the way both grandfathers had been at the end of the war, sole survivors with no siblings, parents, or grandparents. Not just a solitary survivor, but a traumatized one like they'd been.

Technicians gathered evidence. Two of New York's finest removed Otto's body in a long black bag.

The cops wanted to know what he knew.

He told them about the death of Baruch Gittlestein, the murders of Hymie Safier and his girlfriend, Stephanie, and Pierre Feldstein and his assistant. He mentioned the coincidence of a caller to the show whose music was produced by a guy with a broken swastika tattoo, only to meet some guy in Mike's with the same branding. He rambled about the mugging that had followed and his suspicion that the neo-Nazi in the bar was the mugger. He heard himself speaking and thought it all sounded like gibberish.

"That can't be all," they repeated, and each time he told them the same story.

Detective Romano, interviewed on TV after Feldstein's murder, was the homicide investigator in charge. He persistently asked two questions: "Why were the apartments turned upside-down? What were they looking for?"

Ike, numb as gums after Novocain, could only shake his head. His body shook. Romano directed one of the officers to get Ike a blanket and a cup of coffee. Romano took a seat opposite Ike on the sofa. "I was well acquainted with Dr. Sperber."

Ike nodded.

"I don't know if you know this, but your grandfather organized one of the first PTSD clinics in the city through the Patrolmen's Benevolent Association. It was a godsend after 9/11."

Ike nodded. "My grandfather was a great man. Who would do something like this to him?"

Romano leaned forward. "We need your help with this. Whatever you can tell us. The perpetrators were looking for something. That's the MO in all of the murders — places trashed, drawers pulled out, and closets ransacked. It looks like the killers were after something specific. Do you have any ideas?"

Ike stared ahead without expression. He pulled the blanket more tightly around him as he coiled his body into the back corner of the couch.

"All right. Try to think about it. Maybe something will jar your memory, like a discussion you had with your grandfather. Maybe you'll think of something else that's relevant," Romano said.

Ike's apartment door opened. A tall, bald guy, oozing authority, entered and began talking to one of the uniform officers. He removed something out of his coat pocket and showed it to him.

"Detective Romano, he's here," the cop said.

Romano stood and beckoned the man over.

"I'll take over now," the tall guy said.

"Hi, Ike."

Romano backed away.

"Who are you?" Ike said from someplace that felt like the ceiling. Penetrating his dissociation was the thought, *how do you know my name and why so informal, so casual at a time like this?*

"I'm Special Agent Simon Cone of the FBI."

Ike stared at him. He wanted to say something, but his dry mouth felt disconnected from his brain.

"I know this is a bad time. But we need your help," Cone said.

"In the condition I'm in, I don't think I can be of help to anyone."

"I understand. Perhaps after the funeral. Being Jewish myself, I know it has to take place tomorrow. No wait. Tomorrow is *Shabbat.* The funeral will likely take place on Sunday."

Funeral? What funeral? Who died? Ike wanted to say. Then it hit him again. How was he going to arrange for a funeral? Someone like Otto didn't have an ordinary memorial service and burial. He was too big for that, and Ike felt too small to make something like that happen.

"Yeah, after the funeral, maybe," Ike said, from a tunnel far away again.

"Okay. But could you answer one question?"

Ike shrugged. It was all the energy he could muster.

"Did Otto, I'm sorry, Dr. Sperber, your grandfather, ever mention anything about a Nazi fugitive named Antonin Helm?"

"Of course. It was in his book."

"Anything else?"

"Look, I told the cops fifty times already. Ask them. If you haven't got anything different to ask, then could you just leave me alone?" The anger brought him back to himself. Despite Ike's emotional state, he saw that Cone was trying to stay calm but frustration was creeping in. Despite the horrific events and his horrible emotions Ike sized up the agent from some weird competitive place. He was power forward big. On the court he'd be a plodder. He'd be good at grabbing boards, but as soon as he brought the ball down, Ike would steal it away.

"Did your grandfather ever say anything to you about jewels, a stash of riches, gold, diamonds perhaps?"

"No. Otto didn't give a damn about money. He was lucky he had me, otherwise he'd never pay his bills."

"So he never said anything about any of the other men, the ones who were murdered, having a hoard of diamonds and gold?"

"Uh-uh."

"What about your other grandfather?"

"Avram Miller? How do you know about him?"

"We know all about your family and the families of the men who died. It's all part of our investigation into these murders."

Ike just shook his head. He had nothing more to say and he hoped that Cone got the message.

Cone handed Ike a business card. "If you think of something, remember a conversation with either grandfather, about hidden gold or jewels or recall unusual spending habits, let me know. Call me."

Ike nodded again.

"One more thing. The police will watch this place tonight. Don't leave your apartment. If you have to, for whatever reason, get in touch with me first. After the funeral we'll talk."

Cone stood. He said something to Romano and left. After a final round of whispering, gathering, and moving things out of the apartment, so did Romano and the remainder of his cadre of the Finest. Ike was only too glad to be left alone. At least that was his first thought.

CHAPTER FOURTEEN

NO TEARS IN HOOPS

He was listening to his courtside mentor, urging him to hold back the tears. There would be time for grief in its deepest and fullest expression, but it wasn't now. His interrupted sadness became leg-twitching restlessness and it told him to get a move on. He found himself in the lobby ignoring Agent Cone's advice (had it been advice or an order?) to stay put. His body pulled him forward to Otto's apartment. Cone's and Romano's questions about diamonds and gold seemed absurd. But who knew? His family had kept so much from him that anything was possible. Maybe there was something in this destruction that would bring him clarity.

He jogged down the stairs to Otto's floor. Once on the landing, he cautiously opened the fire door and walked to 18H. The cops had strung yellow crime scene tape across Otto's front entrance, but they'd neglected to do the same for the consultation room door. He entered it and turned on the light. He saw for the second time the destruction the murderers had left. That priceless autographed photo of Freud and the Annie Leibovitz photo portrait torn apart, the librettos in shreds, the speaker covers ripped from their wood frames, the television and stereo smashed and pulled apart, shards of glass and wire and insulation scattered across the carpet.

He went straight for Otto's desk. The killers had emptied the drawers, six of them, and tossed them every which way around the oak rolltop. He knelt and examined each paper, object, and artifact—checkbooks, pens, pencils, pads, notebooks and handbooks, American Psychiatric Association files, and a couple of article manuscripts in total disarray. But he found nothing that mattered. He felt like a stone. He rose wearily and headed back to his place.

Once inside he plopped himself on the couch and closed his eyes. He just hoped he'd be able get through the night, to sleep a dreamless and stone-like sleep. But as he lay on the sofa he could no longer heed Coach. "No tears in hoops" only worked for normal losses like meaningless basketball games, and ordinary pain like banged-up knees. The stone that he was turned to water as he began to weep. Alone, completely without any distractions, Ike Miller fell into mourning followed by a nightmare-filled sleep.

CHAPTER FIFTEEN

IF YOU SEE SOMETHING...

When the heard phone rang he was in that gray, dusky area between sleep and wakefulness that psychologists called the hypnagogic state. It was a condition in which objects were distorted in size, and music seemed channeled directly into his brain. Groggy and disoriented, he found the damn cell phone under a throw pillow and picked it up.

"Ike, can I come up?"

He couldn't identify the voice.

"Can I come up, darling?" Someone said.

Come up where?

"Do you hear me? Can I come up?"

"Aja? Is it you?"

"Oh, Ike, I can't believe what's happened. I want to be with you."

"Of course. I'll buzz you in."

"No. Cops won't let me come up unless they have your okay. They want you to come to the lobby and identify that I'm not a threat to you."

The stone-like feeling returned. It had now overtaken his entire body and he felt like a six-foot-one granite statue secured by huge bolts to the floor. "Can't they come to the phone? I'll verify you are who you say you are."

"No. They want to see you. Please come down."

He did what she asked, and when he arrived on the ground floor, she was standing next to a uniformed officer. Ike nodded that she was okay. The cop allowed her to go with him.

She looked around from room to room at the devastation as he walked behind her. But when they got to the master bath, the door was closed and police had rolled crime scene tape across it. "You don't want to see what's there anyway," Ike said.

Aja embraced him. Tears streamed down her cheeks and onto Ike's neck. "How horrible," she said and held him more tightly.

He stood in her arms but felt nothing. She pulled back.

"After what he'd endured and survived, he had to go through this?" She shook her head repeatedly.

"I have to make a funeral, and I don't know where to start," Ike said.

"Otto belonged to a synagogue, right?" She asked.
Ike nodded.

"Let's call them and see how they can help."

"It's *Shabbat*. There won't be anyone to take the call."

Aja put the palm of one hand on her forehead, her index finger of her other hand in the air. "Go rest. I'm going to make some calls."

Ike didn't know what she was talking about. But getting back on the couch sounded like it was the only thing that made sense. She pulled a blanket over him. Somewhere in his psyche he recognized that she was doing for him what he'd done for her only the night before. Before he fell into a sleep fit for a granite man, his mind flashed the thought, *has it only been one day?*

Seven A.M. light woke him.

He rolled off the couch and stumbled his way into the guest bathroom. When he first saw Aja standing near the door he thought for a moment that he was still dreaming. After he shook himself into reality, he said, "Where did you sleep?"

"On your bed."

He made an anguished face. "Too close to the bathroom for me."

"I figured."

"Thanks for coming over. I have to find out what to do about Otto."

"I worked it out."

"You what?"

"I called the police and they connected me to the morgue. The clerk gave me contact information. Turns out the rabbi was waiting for your call. He wants you to meet him after services this afternoon, around one-thirty. He said not to worry."

Her kindness warmed him, but for some reason that made little sense, because in his current mental condition nothing was making any sense, it also disturbed him. Was he right to doubt Aja? He was a grandchild of Holocaust survivors and now a survivor in his own right. How could he trust anyone, considering all that had gone down?

The "1" train pulled in almost simultaneously with their arrival on the platform. They found two seats together in the middle of the car and sat quietly holding hands. In front of him, an ad pitched the famous New York City warning: *If you see something, say something.* He looked at the faces of the other riders, but they were absorbed in their own thoughts, newspapers, conversations and grooving to music on their headsets. Aja must have noticed. "What's wrong?"

He pointed to the poster. "There were signs. I tried to warn him. Maybe Otto would still be alive had if I'd managed to convince him." Tears softened the granite feeling again.

She said and put her arm around his shoulders.

They sat like this until the train came to the Eighty-Sixth Street and Broadway station. The warning ad was still on his mind as he and Aja headed onto the street. Each person they passed felt like a threat and Ike, shaking his head, remembered how Otto had said, "Baruch's the paranoid one. Not you, my grandson."

The West Side Jewish Center's circular stained glass window rose for three stories above the heavy oak doors. Ike held the door open for Aja.

"No," Aja said. "I think it's better if you do this without me. I'll get some coffee, make some calls to the hospital, and wait for you here. How long do you think you'll be?"

"No idea."

"Okay. No worries. I'll be here when you're done." She brought him close and kissed him.

He went inside.

The rabbi wore dark slacks, a white shirt with its sleeves rolled up, a tie loosened at the neck, and a hand-woven, navy yarmulke bobby-pinned to his graying hair. He met Ike in the middle of the synagogue hallway. He extended his hand. "Dr. Miller. I'm Rabbi Joseph. I'm so sorry for your loss. We are all shocked by what has happened." He shook his head mournfully. "Please follow me."

They walked into the rabbi's study. Ike sat next to his desk.

"First. Do the police know who committed this terrible crime?" the rabbi asked.

Ike squirmed in his seat. "Rabbi, I've never done this before. I don't have a clue about making arrangements—"

"Please, don't worry. The synagogue is organizing the funeral at the behest of your grandfather who left instructions with his attorney. The attorney contacted us after he received the news. So there is nothing for you to do except to arrive at the cemetery tomorrow."

"What about all the people who'll want to attend?" Ike asked.

"Dr. Sperber's instructions were clear. He wanted a small gathering and a gravesite ceremony only. If you want, I'll give you the list of those who have been contacted."

Ike shook his head. It didn't matter to him. In a way he was glad it would be small. Perhaps at some point after the mourning period he'd muster up enough strength to have a memorial gathering.

"Where will it be?" Ike asked.

"Beth Abraham Cemetery, in Middlesex County, New Jersey. My secretary will give you instructions."

It was the family plot. Grandma Lainie, Ike's mother and father, Grandpa Avram and Grandma Rose were buried there. All Ike had to do was sign a couple of documents and arrive in the morning. But there it was again. Even though relieved, Ike felt resentment, diminished in stature, like he was still a kid. Even beyond the grave, his family treated him like a child and hadn't trusted him to handle such an important life event.

"Rabbi, can I see my grandfather?"

"Yes. I'm glad you asked. You know most people are too upset to look at the body."

"Where is he now?"

"The Central Park West Mortuary on Seventy-Fifth Street, just a few blocks from here. I'll call ahead and arrange it."

"Thank you." Ike stood and shook the rabbi's hand again and left the building.

Aja was waiting when he walked onto the street. She took his arm. "That must have been rough."

"Numbness works wonders."

"Where should we go now?"

"I want to see Otto." His voice cracked, the words almost inaudible.

"The funeral home?"

"Yeah. Not far from here."

"Do you want me to come?" she asked softly.

"Yes. But if you wouldn't mind, I want to be alone with him."

She nodded. "No problem. I'll wait outside."

They headed toward Central Park West and walked four and a half blocks to a brick building with a green awning and the name of the funeral home printed along its side. The receptionist was waiting for him. She introduced Ike to Barry Weintraub, a bald, forty-something man wearing a fine tailored gray suit. For such a depressing vocation, Barry was a friendly and cheery sort, which in Ike's state of mind was irritating. They shook hands. Barry led the way to a room in the rear of the building.

"I'll open the casket," Barry said.

What Ike saw inside was someone who looked something like Otto. But it wasn't the great man he knew. The body looked more like a wax figure than the once-lively being whose energy and spirit were three standard deviations above the mean. Ike began to weep the racking and hiccupping cries of a child. Barry put his hand on Ike's shoulder. Ike shook his head. The funeral director nodded and backed out of the room, closing the doors behind him.

"Otto," Ike cried. "I'm so sorry. I should have done something."

From somewhere, a memory of his forgiving and accepting kindness perhaps —or maybe in a room like this Otto could actually speak to him — Ike heard, "*Please, no shoulds. Just do the best you can, my sweet boy. Just do the best you can.*"

He took a breath, bent into the coffin, and kissed Otto on the forehead. Then he closed the casket and wept.

When he came out, Aja was waiting, leaning against a car. As he approached she smiled warmly and in a subdued tone said, "How was that?"

"The person inside the casket wasn't my grandfather. It didn't even look like his body and face. It was just a...I don't know. I feel so devastated. I just can't believe this has happened. I don't have enough words to describe what I feel."

She put her arm around him, kissed him and put her face against his cheek. Ike felt her tears on his face.

"I hurt so much for you," she said. "The thought of someone as close to me as Otto was to you being murdered is just too much to bear."

Her words were just a jumble of syllables and sounds. He was far away, lost in a memory of Otto attending one of his high school basketball games. How, after the game—in which Ike scored thirty to help Madison High School win the South Brooklyn title—his grandfather, who knew little about the sport, was beaming with pride. Ike remembered how he'd wished his father–who was on the road (*Wasn't he always on the road?*) touring with Neil Young—would have come to see his big moment and how grateful he was that Otto had filled the void the way he always had.

"Tell me what you're thinking?" she said as she brought him closer to her.

He shook his head. "Maybe another time. Now I'm just bushed and need some rest."

"Let's head back to your place," she said. She took hold of his arm.

"I don't want to go to my apartment."

"Then come to mine. I'll make you dinner and you can rest."

"I don't have clothes for tomorrow," he said. The awareness that he didn't have the proper outfit put him into a panic. He became restless and pushed her arm away.

She seemed to read his mind. "Let's find a store."

He was agitated and light-headed. He thought he was going to faint.

She brought him close to her again, stroked his head, arms and back. "Breathe, slow and deep," she said softly.

He did what she instructed. The breathing and her gentle touch helped him calm down. He felt so young inside. The simple act of going to a men's shop and buying a suit completely overwhelmed him.

So on the day before his beloved grandfather's funeral, Aja accompanied Ike to buy a black suit, shirt, tie, and shoes in a clothing store on Amsterdam Avenue. They left the place looking like a normal young couple who had enjoyed a shopping spree on a typical autumn day in New York. They hailed an ordinary cab, which took them to her place, an apartment in a limestone on Riverside Drive near Columbia University. But their lives were no longer ordinary, nor typical, nor normal. He worried it was about to get a whole lot worse. There were killers on the loose—sadistic murderers who'd caused Otto horrible pain and suffering, something that never should have happened to this wonderful man, his grandpa.

CHAPTER FIFTEEN

THE FUNERAL

They entered a sparsely furnished two-bedroom apartment. It was as if Aja had recently moved in and was still waiting for more deliveries. Minimalism was another possibility—she seemed to get by with the basics: queen bed and dresser and a well-worn living room sofa. The only other places to take a load off were four chairs around an oak dining room table and another one next to a desk. Ike was surprised to see bare walls, except for a small oak-framed mirror in the entryway. "No book cases, no books? Don't you have a lot of reading for your work?"

She smiled. "Of course, silly boy. I'm sure you've heard of libraries and computers. My iPad holds all the reading material I need."

"I guess after a tough day you just want to kick back. This place is perfect for an ascetic, someone who practices meditation with very few distractions." Kidding her, for the moment, helped pull his attention away from the awful feeling in his gut.

"Not quite me. I sublet the apartment from a friend who's in Europe for two years. This is how she had it, and I didn't want to add anything because I'll have to leave in eight months anyway."

"I didn't know that." An old feeling of abandonment mixed with his grief.

"Yeah. Not sure where I'll be going next."

Ike had the impulse to invite her to move in with him. Then, the quick reminder in the form of Tony's voice: *You hardly know her.*

"Why don't you put your stuff in the bedroom and then take the garbage to the incinerator? It's on the first floor under the stairwell," she said.

Ike deposited his suit and shopping bag on her bed and grabbed the bulging trash bag she'd left at her door. They exchanged loving smiles as he exited the apartment. The hallway was dark and its air smelled of fried fish. For the first time today he was hungry. The feelings and thoughts of the past two days seemed to melt away as he thought of the possibilities with Aja. He felt energized and took off down the stairs as if he were on a downhill fast break. He found the incinerator and dumped the bag of garbage into the chute.

Something rustled nearby. Probably nothing. As he turned at the corridor wall, someone ran up the stairs. Someone who reminded him of Frankie. Fear jolted through him and he moved cautiously to the building entrance, a glass and wood-frame door that needed a key or buzz to secure entry. It was locked. He inched the sheer curtain away from the door and peeked out onto the street. A Land Rover idled in front of the building — a red-haired, middle-age woman behind the steering wheel. A figure he couldn't see clearly occupied the front passenger seat. The woman turned, appeared to notice him, then faced forward and pulled away.

Intuition or paranoia? Ike asked himself.

Maybe it was both working together like a point guard and a center on a pick- and-roll. It got him to move. He climbed the stairs two at a time to Aja's floor. Once on her landing, he looked down a short hallway. The corridor was empty and the stairway was quiet. He heard Jay-Z and Alicia Keyes in his head and realized he was having a trauma flashback. He shook out the noise and sprinted to Aja's apartment door. It was locked. Had he unlocked it when he left with the trash? He knocked. A few seconds of silence answered him. He knocked again. Silence still. He pounded on the door.

"Coming," Aja called out.

She let him in.

His shaky voice barely spit the words out to tell her what had happened.

She put her arm around him and pointed to the hallway. "The person you saw was probably a guy named Levy. He's a Columbia student who lives one flight up—a marathon runner on the track team. I take care of his cat when he goes out of town for meets. I have to call him anyway, so I'll check if it was him." She took out her cell phone and pushed a button. "Tom, was that you that just ran up the stairs?" Aja nodded and put her hand over the receiver. She mouthed, "It was."

"Thanks," Aja said into the receiver. "I'm glad I got hold of you. I can't watch Mickey tomorrow. I have a funeral and who knows what else. Can you get some-one?" She nodded her head. "Good! And good luck in Boston."

She hung up the phone.

"You look exhausted." Aja opened her arms to him and they embraced. "Why don't you rest? I'll put some-thing together for us to eat."

He nodded. She led him to her bed, kissed him on the forehead and on the lips. She closed the door be-hind him. *What kind of wimp must she think I am? I can't seem to control my emotions anymore.* Before he could spend time worrying about it, Ike fell asleep. He didn't wake up until the next morning—Sunday morning—the morning of Grandpa Otto's funeral.

The sky was overcast and the air carried the damp chill of mid-November. Ike noticed four or five small scrums of people near the grave site. Some he recognized from professional meetings he'd attended with Otto, others from the synagogue. They turned toward him as he and Aja made their way to the mourners' seating area. One by one they came over to offer condolences. Ike introduced Aja, who wore a simple black dress under a gray raincoat. People whispered to each other as they nodded their heads in her direction. Ike didn't care what they thought. He was here to say goodbye to his grandfather.

He was about to head for his seat when he felt a tap on his shoulder. Tony, dressed in white Indian garb, hugged him. His eyes filled with tears. "I'm so sorry. I don't know what else to say." When they let go of each other, Ike introduced him to Aja. Tony took her hand, kissed it, and looked into her eyes. "My guru says, 'The greatest religion is to be true to those you love. If you do, your soul will live forever.'" He bowed. Aja clasped her hands and raised them to her heart and bowed in return.

The rabbi asked everyone to take seats. Ike and Aja were directed to chairs in the center front. Ike pulled Tony along to sit with them, and looked past the burial site to see the tombstones of his Grandma Lainie, his mother, father, Grandpa Avram, and Grandma Rose— painful reminders that he was the last of his family.

As the rabbi stepped in front of Otto's casket, a figure some fifty yards behind him caught Ike's attention. A tall man in a dark suit leaned against a sedan parked on the cemetery road. Simon Cone. *Not here,* Ike thought, but remembered Cone's promise to speak with him after the funeral. Ike shook his head. *Why can't it wait?*

The rabbi, after reciting the traditional prayers, invited Ike to speak. Standing in front of the mourners the numbness Ike had felt the last two days dissipated. Anger welled up. He turned to the casket. "Who could have done this to you? Why? For what reason in the world, after all you've been through and after all the good you've done?" He stopped and scanned the attendees, conscious that he'd misspoken at this solemn time. But his words had resonated: his bewilderment, sadness, and anger were reflected on so many faces. He was about to let go of more outrage when he noticed Tony's compassionate look. Ike stopped and breathed deeply. *There'll be time for anger later,* he thought. He

cleared his throat, made eye contact with a few mourners, and turned back to the casket.

"Grandpa." The tears came. "You will always be
remembered by the people who crossed your path as
being a man, the way a man should be. Your strength,
intellect, and kindness are a model for the world.
You were my mentor and friend. But most of all you
were always, and I mean always, there for me. You
guided me like a father when I really needed a dad,
and you were also my grandpa with all the wisdom of
your many years and your incredible life experience.
Thank God I had you. I love you and will never forget
you."

Sobbing, Ike sat. Aja kissed him on the cheek and
took his hand.

The rabbi spoke. He lauded Otto, a Holocaust survivor who had gone on to do great things for the world
as an untiring speaker for social justice, for New York
City as the lead psychiatrist in the police PTSD project,
and for the synagogue and the Jewish people, as Otto
had been a passionate and even-handed advocate for
peace in the Middle East. The rabbi followed with the
Twenty-Third Psalm. For Ike, the line, "though I walk
through the valley of the shadow of death, I will fear no
evil" stood out in all of its boldness. He prayed Otto had
been without fear at the end.

The service ended with the *Kaddish*. When the rabbi
finished, he signalled gravediggers to lower the casket.
"Once the casket is in its resting place, I ask you to come
forward and to help fill the grave with earth," the rabbi
said. Ike wasn't staying for it. He hated the sound of dirt
and rocks hitting the box, the finality of it all. He took

Aja's hand and quickly led her away from the gravesite and to their rental car.

"Ike, slow. What's the rush?" Tony said as he hustled to catch up.

"I can't handle the sight of Otto's coffin going into the ground. Besides, Cone's here and I don't want to talk with him now."

"Who's Cone?" Tony asked.

"I see him over there. He's headed for our car," Aja said pointing.

"Shit. Whatever. I'll just have to deal with it," Ike said. Her comment about Cone sparked something in him, jarred him really, but he couldn't put his finger on what it was.

"Do you need anything? Can I help in some way?" Tony asked.

Ike shook his head, a head that was spinning from too many disruptive things going in.

"I've got to get back. But if you need me, call," Tony said.

Ike nodded and smiled weakly.

"Almost forgot. Everyone at the station sends their love—"

Ike raised his hand. "Tell them thanks. I'll see them tomorrow."

"The Stillman brothers said to take your time. We've got it covered until you're ready," Tony said.

"I'll be there," Ike insisted.

"Okay," Tony said. He hugged his friend, bowed to Aja and headed for his car.

Cone was already standing on the driver's side of the rental vehicle when Ike arrived with Aja.

"Hi, Ike. My condolences. I'm really sorry. I read up on Otto's life and checked out his book again. Your grandfather was truly a great man."

"I appreciate that. Sounds like you're working hard to connect the dots," Ike said, aware that on some level he sounded like a moron.

"Yeah. We're committed to tracking these bastards down. For me it's become a personal thing. I've got relatives that were killed in Europe."

"I can't do this," Ike said, looking at Aja.

"Your life is in danger, and we want to protect you," Cone said. "We need you to tell us everything you know. You never know, you might tell me something you think is unimportant and it could turn out to be a lead."

The thought of dirt covering Otto's coffin intruded. Ike floated above the scene. Aja must have noticed his disconnection and took his hand and squeezed it.

"My head's too jumbled," Ike said.

"Maybe some food or coffee will help," Cone said. "Please, Ike. We can't waste any more time. Think about it. Don't you want justice for the murders?"

"I'll go with you," Aja said.

"I'm sorry, Miss...?" Cone shook his head.

"Connolly."

"Miss Connolly. I can't have that. Our conversation has to be just between the two of us," Cone said.

"I'll follow you to wherever you're going and wait in the car," Aja said.

Ike looked up the road. Tony was still standing by his car, talking on his cell phone. "No. Go with Tony. I'll take the rental car back when I'm finished. I'll want to be alone anyway."

"Thanks Ike. This won't take long. I promise," Cone said.

They sat at a table in the back corner of the Mount Olympus Diner, a short drive from the cemetery.

"Get whatever you want," Cone said.

"Big expense account, huh?" Ike didn't want to be angry. There was no need to take it out on the guy who was just trying to do his job. *Yeah? So what?* Ike thought. *My grandfather was just put into the ground because some cretins decided to slice him up. How could I not be angry?*

Cone didn't respond.

"Sorry. I'll just have coffee, thanks," Ike said.

The waitress came and they each asked for a cup. Cone added a toasted corn muffin to the order. "You sure you don't want to eat something?" Cone asked.

Ike shook his head.

"Okay," Cone said. "First, let me tell you what we know."

"Sure," Ike said. The fact that he was even having this conversation, in this place, after what had happened felt completely surreal.

"We believe all the deaths are related, including the heart attack that caused Baruch Gittlestein's demise," Cone said.

"That's what I told Otto. But he didn't believe me," Ike said.

"Gittlestein's Brooklyn apartment was trashed in the same way Safier's and Feldstein's office and Otto's and your place were. Witnesses at the post office said he was under duress and was shouting something about someone coming for him. We believe he was followed. We know he had a history of mental illness with paranoia as a feature, but paranoia sometimes speaks the truth, at least the partial truth. In this case Gittlestein knew he was in trouble, and he was right."

The waitress brought their order. Cone took a sip of his coffee. Ike held his hand over the mug. The warmth was soothing.

"You sure you don't want to eat anything? It'll do you good."

"Look, I can't eat. Please don't ask again."

"Okay," Cone said and took another sip of his coffee. "We don't have witnesses but we have this." He reached inside his coat, pulled out a black-and-white mug shot, and slid it across the table.

"That's the guy," Ike said, remembering the meeting at Mike's and the blow to his face.

"His name is Franz Paul Schmidt, aka FP, or Frankie Schmidt. He's got a rap sheet as big as this table."

"Not surprised," Ike said.

"Have you seen this person?" Cone handed Ike a color photo of a woman.

Ike's first reaction was to shake his head. But as he looked at the picture more closely, it came to him. "I think I saw her yesterday. She was the one double-parked outside Aja's apartment house. She was looking toward the door. When she saw me, she drove away." It chilled him to make this connection.

"Good, Ike," Cone said, nodding his head. "That helps. And it helps confirm our theory that these killings were committed by Helm's daughter and her son."

"I read an article about them on the Internet," Ike said. "They were denied insurance money because there's no corroboration of Helm's death."

"That's right," Cone said.

"Are they US citizens?"

"Yeah. It's a long story. But I'll give you the short version. Helm must have come to the US like a lot of Nazi scientists, doctors, and technical people. He started a family and tried to sink into the background. But once the various Nazi hunting organizations and authorities got on his tail, he left without a word to anyone. He's been all over, but we think his last stop was Egypt. The redhead is Maria Jordan— name is from a second marriage, but her birth name is Maria Strauss. Anthony Strauss was Helm's first alias, and Maria was Helm's only offspring as far as we know. She grew up a typical sixties-seventies kid. For a while she lived on the streets of Haight-Ashbury."

Ike had this strange thought that typical American hippie Maria could have been a Neal Young fan and by extension, a fan of Jon Miller's. He decided not to share this with the agent.

"Okay," Ike said. "They can't get survivor benefits, so what are they looking for?"

"That's what we want to know. What could they possibly want that would make them commit multiple murders?" Cone's eyes made Ike think the agent believed he knew the answer.

"In your apartment I asked if you knew about unusual spending habits that either of your grandfathers or grandmothers had. Did Avram or Otto come up with money they couldn't possibly have had that helped pay for college or graduate school or anything else? We want you to brainstorm this because we think there's a big wealth secret out there, and it has to be what the murderers are looking for."

"Like I said, Otto didn't care about money. As for Avram, the only thing I can tell you is that he was a man who kept everything, including his feelings, close to the vest. If he had a secret about money, it went to the grave with him."

"You sure? Who paid for college and graduate school?"

"I got a full athletic scholarship to Rice and a half scholarship to NYU. I'm still paying off the other half."

Cone lifted his cup to sip his coffee. "Let me try something else. Have you ever seen any of the women in the family wearing fancy diamonds?"

Ike shook his head. "My mom was just like Otto, modest to a fault. Lainie, Otto's wife, was a beautiful woman who dressed well. But she did most of her shopping from catalogs. She wore some trinkets here and there, but nothing like what you're talking about. Avram's wife, Rose, was such a quiet, unassuming person. I never noticed any jewelry on her except for her wedding ring and a gold watch that I think her synagogue sisterhood gave her."

The waitress came again. "Is everything all right?" she asked.

Both men nodded.

"Can I get you something else?"

"Not for me," Cone said. "You sure you don't want to eat?"

Ike nodded.

"I'll bring you the check." She turned and left.

Just as she walked away, a busboy dropped a load of dishes. Ike nearly jumped out of his seat.

"Easy, boy," Cone said. "I know what's happened the last few days would fray anyone's nerves." Cone looked compassionately at Ike. "Come to think of it, you've been holding up pretty well, considering."

"Thanks," Ike said and took a breath to calm down.

They sat silently for a time. Cone finished his muffin. Ike just stared into his coffee.

"What's going to happen next?" Ike asked. He was certain he sounded like a six-year-old.

Empathy mingled with a hard look that Ike had seen before on Cone's face. "They're going to come after you."

"What?" It was as if he couldn't hear what he didn't want to hear.

"They're going to come after you."

Ike sat frozen.

"But that's both a good and bad thing," Cone said.

"What do you mean?" Ike's voice quivered.

"If you do what we tell you then we'll get the opportunity to catch them. That's the good. But the bad is… look, we can't offer any guarantees…" his voice trailed off as he shook his head and stirred his coffee.

"No guarantees for what?" Ike's voice bordered on shrill.

"Listen, Ike, go back to your place. Do what you'd normally do. When you're up to it, get back to work. We'll have our people watching. They'll be undercover so you won't know they're around. I'll come by from time to time, as well."

"You said, 'no guarantees.' What can't you guarantee?"

"Perfection," Cone said. "We can't promise that we can protect you perfectly. We're going to need you to help us by keeping your eyes open, and you have to have my phone number programmed and at the ready."

Fear blasted through Ike's guts. Whenever he felt this way his best remedy was to move his body. It was one of the reasons why hoops had been so good for him. He wanted to, needed to move now—to get up and run.

Cone must have noticed. "Just one thing before I take you back."

Ike sighed. "What else?"

"This woman, Aja Connolly," Cone said and paused. "Are the two of you engaged or going steady or something?"

"I don't see how this is relevant to anything we've been discussing." Ike was angry.

"It may or may not be," Cone said. "Just want you to be careful, that's all. We have our concerns. You two met at a saloon near your radio station around the time Gittlestein died and Safier and his girlfriend were murdered. You spent a total of one evening and two nights together including last night, and this morning she's your companion at the funeral. Have you given any thought that how you met her, out of the blue, during the time these murders were taking place is more than just good luck on your part?"

Ike was exhausted and didn't want to give into his anger and defensiveness. Instead, he managed a smile. "In a way, you're right. I'm one lucky guy."

Cone nodded. "I guess you are. Okay. Let's get out of here."

CHAPTER SIXTEEN

THE KITCHEN TABLE

After dropping off the rental car, Ike felt agitated and lost, walking aimlessly through the city streets. In his head he replayed his conversation with Cone and replayed it again. He talked to the agent as if he were walking alongside, then wrestled with his own impressions and conclusions. It was good the Feds had suspects. But the questions about secret wealth troubled him. Ike knew that Otto would never keep information like this from him. If, by any chance, he'd come into the kind of treasure Cone alluded to, his grandfather would have given it away to worthy charities. If anyone could have kept clandestine wealth it would have been Avram. But if that were the case, he'd have taken the secret to his grave. Avram had left little in his will for Ike: twenty-five thousand dollars and a few *tchotchkes*, nothing of the magnitude the killers were likely searching for.

So lost was he in his mental jumble that he hadn't realized he was headed midtown west. He found himself at Hell's Kitchen Playground. A game was in progress: The Devils versus The Harlem Blues. Ike strolled over to the spectator-filled bleachers. He tried to watch, but he couldn't concentrate on the action. Whatever he looked at seemed gray and far away.

Jamal must have noticed him and trotted over to Ike from the opposite side of the court.

"Heard about what happened. I'm really sorry, my man," Jamal said.

"Thanks," Ike said. The sight of his schoolyard teammate made Ike wish he could roll back the clock and be out on the court, running a fast break, playing tough "D," and shooting his long-range jump shot like Jamal's boys were doing right now.

"Wasn't the funeral today?" Jamal said. "And what happened to your eye?" Jamal stared at Ike's shiner.

"Just got back from the funeral. Don't want to talk about my face right now." Ike said. His tone was as flat as the surface the kids were playing on.

"So why are you here? I mean, you're welcome and all, but it seems like this would be the last place to go."

It was at that moment that Ike got it. "Courts are my spiritual home. That's why I came."

Jamal's face said he understood. Ike sobbed. Jamal's eyes teared up, and he put his hand on Ike's shoulder.

"I know what it's like to lose someone like your granddaddy, believe me. But Ike, I'm sorry, I've got to get back to the game. Call me if you need someone to talk to. My invite still stands. When you're ready, come by the Garden."

Ike nodded and looked out at the scoreboard. "Looks like the boys are having their way."

"Yeah. They're playing one hell of a game. You take care now."

Ike decided to catch the subway at Forty-Ninth Street going uptown. He was going home, ignoring his internal warning that it was unsafe, though Cone told him it was okay to go back. Okay or not, he wanted familiar surroundings.

He avoided the building's main entrance and used the garage in the rear. He took the stairs to Otto's floor. At the door, he noticed the yellow tape was gone. He didn't know if their having vacated the premises was a good or bad thing. He thought about what Cone had said: *They're going to come after you.* But it didn't matter right now. He just wanted to be in Otto's place again.

He sat at the kitchen table. The *yahrzeit* glass was still there, the remnants of a wick at the bottom. The sight and feel of the round wood *tish* flooded Ike with memories: the taste and smell of Friday night chicken soup and noodles that Grandma Lainie made with Otto's matzo balls that he joked were as light as a fender. The joy Ike and his grandfather shared playing board games like Scrabble that Otto always won because he got away with phony words that started with Z and Q, their laughter that brought them both to tears when they acted out Abbott and Costello's Niagara Falls skit. Ike would say the name of the landmark waterfall, and Otto, with mock-crazy eyes, hunched-over body, and an exaggerated Austrian accent, would recite, "Zlowly I turned, step by step, unt inch by inch…" and Ike, giggling hysterically, would run and hide in the bath-tub, the shower curtain his cover.

The table had also been the launching pad for out-ings: ball games, theater, and the music Ike learned to love after an initial and understandable childish revul-sion—the opera. Otto, Lainie, and his mom had taken him to *La Traviata, Aida,* and *Rigoletto.* Even though Ike had always been a rocker, it was because of his family that he'd learned to love all kinds of music.

He began to weep.

In the midst of his tears, he thought of something. He left his seat and walked to the consultation room. Rummaging through the destruction, he found the photo Otto had shown him. He studied it and put him-self among the men in the picture. This faded snapshot was a record of five survivors at the end of their war. His war was still unfolding.

His cell phone vibrated.

"Ike, where are you?" Aja sounded frantic.

"I'm in Otto's apartment."

"Why didn't you call?"

He sighed. "I don't know. I've been out of it since I got back. I walked around the city. Before I knew it, I was at the Hells Kitchen basketball court watching the Devils play. Then I came here." This time he thought he sounded like someone immediately after a head injury.

"Ike, it's dangerous. You know that, don't you?"

"Yeah. I don't care right now. Besides, Cone said to go back to my place."

For a moment there was silence. "Can I come over and be with you?"

"Come if you want. I'll be in my apartment. I've got things to talk with you about anyway." What had sparked in him at the cemetery was turning into a raging fire.

"I'll be there in a flash," she said and hung up the phone.

By the time she arrived, Ike had filled half-a-dozen large trash bags of his things the killers had strewn throughout the apartment. It didn't matter what was in the mess. He just picked up whatever he saw and stuffed it. He'd made it possible now to sit in the living room and sleep in his bedroom—on second thought, that wasn't going to happen—without crap being in his way. But he also knew that instead of tidying up–a completely mindless emotional act–something inside warned him to get out despite Cone's orders to stay. But like heroes in so many movies and books, he wanted to go home. Here, the danger he was sensing could be ignored. It was denial, of course. But it helped him pretend that everything was normal.

Aja kissed his cheek. "Come sit with me."

"I don't feel like sitting."

"Okay. Do you mind if I sit?"

He shook his head slowly. He felt like his brain was in the last row of the Garden.

"What's wrong?" she cocked her head.

"My grandfather was murdered, and he was buried today."

"I know that. That's not what I'm talking about. You're acting strangely toward me. Cold." She took the swivel chair that she'd sat on the morning after they'd made love. She patted the one next to her and smiled at him. "Sit with me. Let me warm you up."

He shook his head and began to pace the room.

"I know you're in pain. Talk to me. Tell me what you and Cone discussed."

He stopped pacing and stared at her. "Who the fuck are you?"

"What do you mean?"

"How the hell do you know Cone?" he asked.

"Why are you asking me that?"

"That was a bullshit answer," Ike said.

"I don't know what you're talking about. I think we should be getting out of here. I feel we're vulnerable. Don't you?" She said, gesturing to the door.

"I'm not doing anything with you until I get the truth."

She turned the swivel chair away from him and faced the window. She sat like that for a moment then turned back. She gave him what looked like a forced smile and patted the chair again. "Ike, please, come sit by me."

"I don't want your phony sweet talk. I want answers. Something happened that didn't register until I did my zoned-out walk around town. We were in the cemetery and I was pulling you to the car. Tony asked me what was the rush and I said I needed to get away from Cone or something like that. And do you know what you said?"

Aja's eyes were open wide. She seemed to be searching for a point of reference.

"Yeah, right. It was a slip, a big slip. You said, 'I see him and he's coming this way.' But how could you possibly know him? You were never with me when Cone was around."

It was all hitting him now. All of the suspicion and uncertainty, other people's lack of confidence in her: Cone's questions, Tony's disbelief, Greg the doorman's reaction. The reality bludgeoned him like an elbow to the head from a seven-foot, three-hundred-pound center. He'd met this woman a week ago in a bar. He knew nothing more than her teary declaration about being hurt, some tweets and posts about hoops, bowling, and politics, and that she lived in a nearly empty apartment and was leaving it in a few months—to go where? He had learned how she wanted him to fuck her, and that she knew how to turn him on. But what else did he really know? Did she have a family? What relationship did she have with her parents? Did she have brothers, sisters? What were their names? What challenges did she face at work? Come to think of it, he didn't believe she was a surgical resident. So what work did she really do? Who had broken her heart? What nightmares woke her in the middle of the night? He didn't even know, other than the salad she'd eaten at Mike's, what foods she liked. There was nothing, nada, not a morsel of data about any of these things. The dearth of information combined with the biggest crack in the Sperber-Miller family tree that had been left for him as his legacy: a large and very profound mistrust.

Aja was slow to answer. Finally, she stammered, "By his looks, you know, a detective or cop, or some kind of—"

"Bullshit. You didn't ask, 'Is that him?' or 'Is that the guy?' No. You were emphatic. You knew him. So *Who The Fuck Are You?*"

Aja took a breath. "Okay." She rose from the swivel chair and retrieved the handbag she'd placed on the dinning room table. She removed a wallet and unfolded it. "I'm Special Agent Aja Connolly, FBI." Her serious face stared back at him from a plain blue and white ID.

"This is too screwed up," Ike said. He blinked and shook his head. "Is that ID even real?"

"Let's get out of here. Then we can talk about it." She reached for his arm.

Ike stepped aside. "I'm not going anywhere, and definitely not with you."

"Will this convince you?" She pulled a gun from her purse.

"You've got to be kidding. So what are you going to do, shoot me if I don't go? First you have sex with me then you shoot me?"

She put her revolver back into her purse. "You're right. That was dumb."

"Is that some police technique you learned in the Bureau? Is that how you say it, 'the Bureau?'" He stopped for a moment as a realization came to him. "Wait a second. So you work with Cone? I don't get it."

"I don't. I'm undercover. I know about him. I don't know if he does or doesn't know who I am. I don't think so. But he's very well-connected in the agency, so it's possible."

"Pretty weird, isn't it? At the end of our meeting, Cone suggested that the way we met, you know, in the midst of all the murders, was more than just good luck on my part."

She came over to him and took his hand and tried to pull him close to her. He pushed her away. He just wanted answers. That's all. Then he'd insist she leave. "So was that it? Something more than my good luck?"

Aja looked away. "It's really not material. You and I—we—are in danger. I can tell you that everything I did and said when we were together was real. But what difference does it make now? We have to focus on something more important than our relationship."

"I want you to tell me the truth," he said. "What was your reason for coming into my life?"

She walked around his living room, stopped and appeared to look out at the Hudson River, and then pivoted around toward him. "I was a marine MP in Iraq. After I came back from the war I was recruited by the Bureau."

"Nice resume. But you didn't answer my question."

"My job was to get close to you. I never thought it could even be possible that I'd fall..." she avoided eye-contact, shook her head, and breathed deeply.

Fall? Like in fall in love with me? No, he needed to hear her answers before he could allow himself, if ever, to trust any kind of emotion from her.

"My job was to keep an eye on you and Otto," she said. "We believe that Antonin Helm is alive and that either he's entered the country or is about to. We believe Otto had something Helm wants."

"Cone said nothing about Helm. He gave the impression that Helm wasn't even in the picture. Their investigation concerns Helm's daughter and grandson."

"We're interested in them too. We don't know if they're working with him."

He stared at her. "You did a hell of a shitty job keeping an eye on my grandfather. Maybe you were too interested in fucking me to keep him safe."

She bristled and walked away from him.

"It was my fault," she said from the window. "I didn't act quickly enough after the Safier killings. When that happened, my superiors called me in. That was when I was out of touch with you. They wanted to know if I needed help. I told them I could handle it. I could always handle this kind of pressure. I did in the war and in hoops. So maybe I had an overinflated view of myself, because I messed this up miserably. My job was to learn everything I could about the case and also to protect the two of you. I failed with Otto. Now I don't want to make it worse by having something happen to you. That's why we need to leave, and soon. Like now."

He knew she was right. They couldn't stay much longer. But he didn't want to go with her. He knew that made no sense–it was only his wounded pride that was rejecting her warning. After all, she was the pro with a gun, and he had no way to protect himself. He walked toward the back of the apartment.

"Where are you going?" she asked.

"I need a shower. I feel dirty." Ike could see his words had hurt her. He didn't care. He needed time to think and the shower was always a good place.

"Let me come in. I'll sit and talk with you."

"You've got to be kidding," he said.

"I'm not."

Something about her look of disappointment made him want to give in. He stepped into the bathroom and locked the door.

She knocked. "Ike, please. We didn't finish."

"Later."

He started the shower and took off his jeans and t-shirt. He caught a glimpse of his face in the medicine chest mirror. The discoloration around his eye was the same, but the swelling had gone down a bit. He looked stressed and tired and his whole body felt tight and sore.

He heard a knock on the door. "Please, Ike, we've got to get out of here."

"Go away!" he shouted.

He stepped over the wall of the tub and extended the shower curtain. A waterproof MP3 player was attached with suction cups to the wall tiles. Sarah Shapiro, of all people, had given it to him as a birthday gift. He shook his head mournfully at the thought of what had happened to her. He needed to play something loud. Loud enough to drown out his thoughts—loud enough so that he wouldn't hear Aja talking to him through the door.

He turned the player on. Tina Turner's version of "Proud Mary" was the first song in the queue. The opening fast doo-wops of the backup singers flowed through the tiny speaker and filled the shower space. Then Tina came on. Ike envisioned her performing with her long, toned, sexy legs strutting Jagger-like across the stage, making love to the microphone. He entered into a fantasy of Aja as Tina Turner holding and stroking the real thing. Ike and Aja, Ike and Tina, he chuckled at the rock connection. He became hard and wondered if he should change his mind and invite Aja in. But how could he feel this now? In the opening pages of, *The Stranger*, by Albert Camus, a man and a woman are making love shortly after the funeral of the man's mother.

Ike remembered talking with Otto about it. His grandfather had smiled and said, "Life goes on my boy. Life
goes on. Always remember that." Despite the memory
of Otto's compassionate message, Ike felt ashamed that
he was thinking with his dick at such a dangerous time.

And then he heard something.

At first, he thought it was a flaw in the "Proud Mary"
recording, a scratch or a nick. He decided to turn the
damn thing off and the shower as well. He stood chilled
and wet in the tub and waited to hear the sound again.

It was quiet. Ike exhaled. He turned the shower back
on and let the hot water roll over his body. He switched
the music player back on to Tina and the Ikettes.

They were wailing about rollin' on the river. Their
doo wops rose to a crescendo and then...*CRASH*.

He turned everything off again. He heard a ruckus,
shouting, but he couldn't make out the words. Ike
jumped from the tub and put his clothes on. He checked
the door. It was locked. That would give him some time,
but what about Aja?

A shot rang out. A muffled voice said, "Drop it.
You've got no chance. It's three guns against your one."

"Where is he?" Ike heard a man's voice demand.

No response.

"Go look for him," the same voice ordered.

They were going to test the bathroom door any second now, and Ike had to think fast. He had no gun or
knife, just his hands and some inspiration. He'd probably read it or seen it in a movie. There were two items
he knew he could use: his hair dryer and an iron. He
turned on the tub's spigots, placed the stopper in the
drain, and poured water from the tap into the iron,

plugged in both appliances in a socket close to the bath-
tub, and turned the iron all the way up. He waited. His
clothes were drenched. His heart pounded.

"Ike, get away from the door. They're going to shoot
the knob!" Aja cried out.

"Shut the fuck up," another voice ordered.

Ike jumped away from the bathtub just before a
bullet blew the doorjamb apart. They were coming in.
But the door was only big enough for one at a time.
Shaking, he got ready.

The first man entered. He looked around at head
level, but Ike wasn't there. When he looked down, Ike
rose from under his sink and turned on the hair dryer.
He upended the intruder into the tub as he tossed the
appliance into the water. The lights went out. But Ike
had no time to congratulate himself. The second man
followed the first inside, coming up short behind his
partner, who was still convulsing in the electrified water.

Ike pushed the iron into his mouth, nose, and eyes.
The guy screamed, put a hand over his face and ran out
of the room. Ike knew there was at least one more he'd
have to deal with, but he couldn't see in the darkness.

"Miller, don't try anything else. I've got a gun on
your girlfriend, and I'll have no problem shooting her."

The lights flickered back. Ike tried slamming the
bathroom door shut. But the guy who called himself
Frankie threw Aja onto the floor and aimed his gun at
her. Behind him stood the man with a suppurating burn
on his face in the shape of an iron. Frankie pointed his
gun. "Make this easy on all of us," he said.

Ike decided instead to commit a charging foul by
bull-rushing the prick. Frankie pistol-whipped Ike on

the side of his head and he went down. Aja reached out toward him. Something sharp pierced his butt cheek and he let out a scream. All of his senses–sound, sight, and feeling–deserted his body. And just before everything faded to black, a vaguely familiar voice barked out an order: "Get them the hell out of here."

PART II

CHAPTER SEVENTEEN

MOST WANTED

Only his cook, Anat, and Tarek, his attendant and body-guard, knew who he was. In this gated suburban community outside of Cairo his neighbors were aware of him as a rich, elderly woman, who entertained few visitors but attended the morning call in the local mosque always dressed in a blue or green chiffon hijab. The lightness of the fabric enabled him to tolerate the year-round desert heat. Although beginning now, in October, the temperatures moderated and the morning breezes made this the best time to be outside. This was not the season he would have chosen. He wished this could have come together during the sandstorm months. But that was not something he could control. Even at ninety-three he hoped for more delightful autumns, times when he could feel whole again after what had been taken from him in what seemed like another life and time.

This morning he sat in the Chrysler limousine instead of heeding the call of the muezzin. They were going to Cairo International Airport where Tarek Hussein would play the dutiful son of Habibi Hussein as he pushed her wheelchair onto the EgyptAir flight for JFK airport in New York City.

The sun had been the best cosmetic. It had made his face dark, wrinkled, and leathery. Being a small and slender person anyway, it was a perfect disguise. But even with everything in order, he was anxious whenever he left the villa. In the disorder of the world, some kind of mishap could always occur, and Tarek was the one who had to field his apprehensions.

"You spoke with Anat?" the old man asked.

"Yes," Tarek said as he started the automobile's engine.

"She is to go about her duties as if I am still there, and she must not leave the house for any reason, not even for a family emergency."

"She has been told."

"If all goes well, she will be rewarded, as will you."

"Thank you."

The old man's face turned grave. "If we fail, the authorities will deal with you cruelly."

"Yes. I am aware. We will not fail," Tarek said. His jihadi training had made him obedient and reliable to the point of infallibility. The old man, who was an expert in non-verbal facial cues, could see that his bodyguard was confidently resolute when he gave his response.

"Good." There was no more that needed to be said. The old man gave Tarek a forward wave of his hand, the signal that he was ready to leave.

Tarek drove the car onto the main road. Once, the old man would have enjoyed the ride through the desert and the small villages on the way to the airport, as had always been the case when Tarek drove him to meetings of the Brotherhood.

Not today.

Until he was in the clear at his destination, there could be no feeling of comfort, no moments to enjoy the stark vastness of the Egyptian landscape.

Nevertheless, Tarek performed according to his training. The car traveled exactly at the speed limit, traffic lights and stop signs were observed to perfection, and all of the necessary papers were in order and ready at each of the checkpoints, and the most important one, the entrance to the airport. The two of them did nothing to arouse scrutiny. It had worked well for the twenty years he'd lived in Egypt. So well that the search for him had stopped.

They boarded the plane without any questions concerning the passport and visa of one elderly woman named Habibi Hussein or her dutiful son. It was New York that worried him, but Tarek, had managed it. He had even managed to secure a vital connection in law enforcement without whom they would have had little chance of success. The old man was convinced. He had to be. There was no going back now.

Most of the way he slept in the comfort of first class under the influence of a strong sedative. Tarek stayed awake, exercising his duty to watch over him.

At JFK they rolled through customs without a hitch. Everything was going according to plan. He was here in the city of the Jews, the financial capital of the world—a man who'd been one of the most wanted, but a man who had never been found.

CHAPTER EIGHTEEN

METRO STATE

For a time after New York State evacuated the Metro State Psychiatric Center in the 1980s, the abandoned three hundred acres remained a beautiful campus of red brick buildings encircled by oak, maple, and mountain laurel trees, azalea and rhododendron bushes. The park-like surroundings made the institution look more like Harvard than the reputed snake pit it had once been. As the years passed, the buildings fell into disrepair. The trees and bushes and grass grew unruly. And on a blustery day like today, the vast grounds gave the appearance of a windblown ghost town in a B western—without the tumbleweed, of course.

Despite the eyesore it had become, it was the perfect safe house for Frankie, his mother, and a couple of their business associates, as Frankie liked to call his friends from the federal penitentiary system. The State had handed the grounds over to a caretaker, Peter Bremer, who'd been a member of Frankie's prison network. The Division of Mental Hygiene and the State Interior Department, in partnership with a prisoner release rehab program, had put Bremer in charge of minimal security. His job was to shoo away pot-smoking teenagers as well as the wildlife that made its way onto the property from the woods along the Long Island Sound behind it.

What was most appealing to Frankie and his mother about this vast medical complex were the underground corridors, the meeting rooms, and the padded holding cells that at one time had been home to the criminally insane. The place even had a surgical theater, where neurosurgeons had once performed lobotomies and psychiatrists had practiced electro-shock therapy. Frankie thought that if his grandfather were alive, he'd love this place just for the chance to do the experimental surgery he was famous for.

Frankie and his mother followed Bremer to one of the padded rooms. Back in the day, these rooms had held the real nutcases–psychos who had to be put in stright-jackets and kept from hurting themselves. Bremer told them this would be the best place to put Miller. Bremer was a cheap vodka-soaked alkie, but like most of his associates there were few things Frankie could count on him for. The trick was knowing what those things were, and always holding out the promise of that share of the big score. Bremer slid open the spy window to Miller's cell, and there he was, tied to a metal folding chair.

"It should be easy," Frankie said.

"It's not going to be as easy as you think," Maria said.

"Leave me alone with him for five minutes and I'll beat it out of him."

"No. We have to keep our eyes on the prize, okay?" Maria said. "Let's try the easy way first. If that doesn't work, well, then you can do whatever it takes."

Frankie would have voted for the Bush crew if he'd been allowed to vote and if they were still running for anything. He loved it that they'd use torture to get information, and he admired them for never shying away from their hard beliefs. Dick Cheney was his hero just for that reason and the fact that he'd never apologized for anything, including shooting a friend.

"Have it your way. But trust me, we'll have to hurt him."

Maria unlocked the door and they headed down a short staircase to visit with their prisoner.

The first thing Ike saw was a thick fog. His rapidly beating heart sent a thousand pounding drumbeats to his temples. He began to shiver, probably the aftereffects of whatever drug they'd pumped into him. His face still hurt from Frankie's pummeling– worse than before, if possible. Ike coughed hard—an allergic reaction that told him he must be in a damp place, maybe a cellar. But the coughing helped clear his head and allowed his other senses to come online, like the sensation that told him his hands were tied behind a metal chair, his feet were bound together, and a blindfold covered his eyes. His surgically repaired knee was throbbing in a way it hadn't in years.

A door opened and footsteps came toward him. The scent of rose perfume revealed it was a woman. She removed his blindfold. His eyes ached and burned from the sudden shift into light. Everything was a blur.

"What about the rest?" Ike said.

"No. I think it's safer to leave you this way."

"Funny how everyone wants to protect me," Ike said. His eyes cleared and he focused on the red-haired figure of an overweight middle-aged woman.

"What's that suppose to mean?" the woman asked.

"Never mind."

An uncomfortable silence followed, like dead air on the radio. Finally, he blurted out, "What is it you want?"

"I think you know," she said.

"Whatever you think I know, I don't know."

The fact that she thought he did scared the hell of him. "I don't have anything to give you, so why don't you just let me go now."

"Please, Dr. Miller, we haven't gone to these lengths just to let you go. First we get what we want, and then you go free."

Ike tried to focus in on her. *This has to be Maria Jordan, the woman in Cone's photo, the one who was driving the Land Rover just...what day was it?* He had no idea. *Yeah, right. You get what you want, and I go free. You killed Otto and the others, and that's what you expect me to believe. Bullshit!*

"Where's Aja?" He coughed.

"Who?"

"The woman who was in my apartment when your boys broke in."

"Ah, yes, the FBI agent. Don't worry. She's in good hands. What happens to her will depend on what you do for us, of course."

Aja's wellbeing depended on something he had to do for these criminals, and he didn't know what in the world it was.

"So where is it?" she said, the phony sweetness gone.

"I don't know what you're talking about." Ike's voice cracked under the stress and fear.

"You're the only one left from your family and the survivor's group. They had nothing, and they're dead. You're the only one left who could know. Tell us where it is, and your reality and your girlfriend's will be different from theirs."

His reality was that he wanted to get loose to kill this bitch and the others. He wondered where the rest of them were.

Ike heard a door open and saw the fuzzy outline of someone headed toward him with something long and thick in his hands. He'd better stay alert to what was coming his way.

A man's voice: "Did he tell you anything?"

"No," the woman said.

"Let me have a shot at him."

As the figure emerged into Ike's field of vision, he recognized the guy with the telephone pole fist, his abductor, the man with the I-Heart-Hitler tattoo who went by name of Frankie. The nature of reality, Ike's reality, as his eyesight grew more focused, was that the guy responsible for the mayhem to his body, Otto's and his friends' deaths–the man who knew where Aja was–carried a baseball bat on his shoulder and was coming his way. He imagined the bat smashing his head in and nearly passed out. He couldn't talk even if he had something to tell them.

"My grandfather's stash — tell me where it is or I'll bust up your knee," Frankie said.

Ike remained frozen.

Frankie lifted the bat, and just as he was about to swing it at Ike's leg, his mother pushed him aside.

"Don't."

Their reign of terror over the last week had been a brutal guessing game that had led them to Ike. He was now all they had. They believed he had something that belonged to Helm. Ike didn't know what that was, but not knowing was likely going to cause him excruciating pain before they found out he was telling the truth.

Then, Ike thought, *they'll have no choice but to kill me.*

Ike couldn't tell how long he'd been sitting. Just the forced posture itself, on a steel chair with his hands tied behind him and his feet bound, was torture enough. From time to time he dozed off and had dreams or hallucinations—he couldn't tell the difference—about Otto and Avram and about Tony and Coach. The message was clear. Fight the bastards. Avram told him to be tough. Otto wanted him to finish unfinished business, to settle old scores. Coach wanted him to be a warrior, and Tony talked about time and timing. Another dream had Otto in Auschwitz. He was speaking to another inmate who looked like a composite of the faces from Otto's photo. He said, *"When you make it out of this evil place, you must find your love. You must not stop searching for her until she is in your arms."*

Was his unconscious mind reminding him of Aja? That he shouldn't forget her and that his first responsibility was to help her? He felt the pileup of his mortal losses and the fear that she had become another one of them. He heard Avram. *"Be tough. I looked for Rose and found her."* And Coach: *"Always remember to be there for your teammates. Never let them down."*

He dozed off again and awoke with a start when he heard the door open. A bandaged-faced thug entered, followed by Frankie.

Frankie spoke first. "You know Miller, you proved that even a skinny Jew like you can be dangerous with an iron and a hair dryer. One of our men is dead, and Fisher here is going to need a lot of surgeries to fix the hole you put in his face."

"After what you've done to my loved ones, I'll do it again if I get the chance."

"Fuck you," Fisher said. "I think you better say you're sorry."

This goon, this murderer, was so sensitive that he needed Ike to apologize. Was that a joke? "I'm not sorry about what I did to you. Just like you're not sorry about the death of my grandfather."

He knew he'd pissed them off, but what difference did it make? Apologies or not, they were going to do what they wanted. And just as the face-pressed thug moved in position to throw a big-fisted punch, the door opened and Ike heard the voice of Maria Jordan say: "Stop it, now! Franz Paul, I want you meet your grandfather."

CHAPTER NINETEEN

THE LAUNDRY

On the northern border of the Metro State Psychiatric Center campus stood an unusual building. Its vast, beige canvas roof bubbled over glass and steel made it more reminiscent of an indoor sports facility than the cleaning and maintenance center it had been from the time it was built in the 1960s. Workers had dubbed the structure "The Laundry" because it had been the repository for every sanitation issue the hospital faced—piss, shit, blood, surgical waste, institutional detritus, and the possessions of the deceased, who were either buried in the cemetery out back or cremated in the hospital's cremation facility. Bizarrely one side of the building looked out onto an eighteen-hole golf course with the Long Island Sound inlets and coves as its water hazards.

In its cinder block depths lay a platoon of rusted Dumpsters and corroded Hazmat containers standing perfectly in line, as if waiting for marching orders that would never again come. Adjacent to this vast indoor parade ground and bordering the exit ramp to a campus road was a series of office cubicles with windows that once offered an oversight of the goings and comings of dump trucks, hazardous material vans, and body transport vehicles.

The window of the room in which Frankie had deposited Aja had no such view because for some reason workers had painted the glass panes black. So when Aja woke up she had only a cotton-headed awareness of the darkness and airlessness of her surroundings. Her captors had bound her to a metal chair, and she'd lost track of how long she'd been on it. Her faced burned and throbbed from the pummeling she'd endured when they brought her to this space completely absent of any sounds. She felt the impulse to break the silence, but recognized it as anxiety. The marines had trained her to notice but not act on her emotions–that silence could save her life. In a condition of ambiguous threat, like this one, it was better to preserve her strength and prepare her mind to withstand possible interrogation and torture. They'd trained her to sit alone, on dirt or concrete, bound and blindfolded without human interaction, to keep her mind active, to avoid negativity, to think about what was good in her life and what she could look forward to. But as hard as she tried to remain focused on the good, she knew she had failed to protect Ike Miller and his grandfather.

Whispering, followed by footsteps. A doorknob turned and a door creaked open. Lights blinded her. A figure emerged into clarity—a red-haired woman wearing a flowery dress and Birkenstock sandals. She pointed a pistol at Aja.

"Hello, Ms. Connolly," she said.

Aja held steady and said nothing.

"My father welcomes you into his house."

Her father? Was Helm here? But Aja wouldn't engage her about him. She didn't want to give anything away.

"Okay. You won't open your mouth to talk. But I bet you will for food."

She remained silent.

"All right, then," Maria said. "When my father arrived—I've been scratching my head about who must have told him, I mean after all these years, and of all places, he found us here–we were shocked and overjoyed that he was alive. But the great surprise was that he came with this handsome Arab. His name is Tarek. He'll bring you dinner. But don't let him touch you. He has a habit of putting his hands on women," she said with a strange smile that Aja interpreted as firsthand knowledge.

"I can take care of myself," Aja blurted. But she knew she'd made a mistake.

"Really?" Maria said as she touched the shiner under Aja's eye. "Don't be so cocky. You may be a cop, but you're still a cop without a gun. So be careful. Do what he says and you'll be all right. I'm going to untie you. Don't try anything stupid. Remember, I'm the one with the weapon."

She'd fallen into a light sleep sitting up against a corner wall. Footsteps and voices outside the door roused her, and she strained to hear what they were saying. "Do what he says and you'll be all right," the woman had said. *That depends on what it is, doesn't it?*

The lights burst on. The man Maria said was named Tarek entered, but without any sign of food. He was young and wiry, with large hands. He gave off an energy she'd seen countless times from young Arab men in Iraq. When her male colleagues had spoken with them, they showed restraint and respect. With her they became hostile, insulted by her implied power over them. Tarek had a worse attitude–he had all the power here, and he wasn't hesitant about showing it.

"I was told to bring you food. But I ate it." He grinned.

"McDonalds hamburgers are not *halal*."

He laughed. "Yes, they told me your were a Marine stationed in Iraq. You know a lot about my religion." He shrugged. "I do not have your food, but I can give you something else."

She got his drift and it mobilized her instantly. "There's nothing else you can give me. Nothing."

He began to circle his way closer.

"What do you think you're doing?"

"I am admiring how beautiful you are," he said.

He closed in, even as she backed away. The distance between them narrowed. She was ready, or so she thought. But Tarek was quick as a wolf and took her down to the floor before she could make her move. He pressed himself fully against her. She smelled his stale breath and felt his bulge between her legs. He began to maul her breasts. She flailed at him, using elbows and knees, tearing at him with her nails, and head-butting him. But he was strong, much stronger than his wiry frame indicated, much stronger than anyone she'd ever grappled with. Everything she threw at him, he caught and pushed away. Her resistance changed nothing. He turned her over and pulled down her jeans, keeping her arms pinned with one hand while he ripped off her clothing with the other.

She still had a chance. He couldn't go any further without separating himself, even for a moment and for a few inches. When it happened, she rolled over, pulled her knees to her chest, and kicked him, like jumping up to swat away an opponent's layup. His pants were halfway down his legs, and he stumbled backward, but recovered quickly, gathered himself into the predator that he was, and pinned her again.

There was one thing left. "I'm unclean. I'm getting my period!" she shouted.

For the smallest moment he hesitated. Then he smiled and said, "All the better for the both of us."

This time he got to do what he wanted. Not before she whacked him with a karate chop that she was certain broke his nose. He punched her under her other eye, knocking her unconscious, which turned out to be a good thing, as she remembered nothing. Finished, he left Aja on the hard cold floor that was now streaked with their comingled blood, her clothing strewn throughout the room.

CHAPTER TWENTY

THE SURGICAL THEATER

Rubber straps held Ike in place. A huge rectangular lamp hung over the center of his body. It jarred him into the realization that he was on an operating table. Terror rolled through him. The walls loomed over him, closing him in. He gasped for breath and struggled to get past the illusion. The room they'd put him in was cavernous. It was like being tethered at the bottom of a great, wide-opened chasm with nothing around him but rows of empty chairs ascending to the top of a surgical amphitheater.

Ike felt a presence emerge from the emptiness. As it came close, he smelled dentures, decay, and camphor–an old person, a very old person.

A German accent: "Yes, yes, look who we have here."

"Yeah. Sperber's grandson." It was Frankie.

"The grandson of my esteemed colleague Dr. Otto Sperber." The old man sounded relaxed, quite sure of himself.

"Whatever. The son of a bitch won't tell us anything," Frankie said.

"We will see about that. Please bring me the towels and my surgical bag. In the meantime, I will introduce myself to Dr. Miller."

The presence stepped over to the back of Ike's head and gently stroked his hair. Ike looked up and saw a small man—not as small as Pierre Feldstein, but a diminutive figure nonetheless with a sun-darkened, weathered face. It was a face that projected great intelligence, maybe even as great as Otto's. The evidence was in his cunning, quick, and incisive blue eyes.

"I am so sorry for your loss," he said. "I was devastated, truly upset, to hear about the violent death of my old colleague."

Anger burst through Ike's body. He clamped down on it and kept his mouth shut.

"Dr. Miller, do you know I am able to get your show in Cairo? Streaming audio on the Internet, a marvel of technology."

It was surreal–like watching a Hollywood Nazi sadist, frightening and comical at the same time.

"Yes, yes. I am not surprised the grandson of Otto Sperber offers advice and provides a deep understanding of his listeners' problems."

Ike remained quiet.

"So, if you will indulge me, I would like us to engage in a role play, or psychodrama, as some of your analytical colleagues might call it. I will pretend to call into your radio show with a particular problem. Let us say the show is like the one you aired just a few days ago. I am sure you remember. It was called, 'Settling Scores,' I believe, or some such title. Yes, yes, so I call in, and you ask me what is my score to settle and I tell you and then you give me advice. Do you understand?"

The old man slid along the side of the table, stopping midway down Ike's right leg. He began to touch the surgically repaired knee, gently, softly, the way he'd stroked Ike's hair. "So what say you, Dr. Miller? Will you play?"

Ike looked away.

"Come, my young man. It will be fun. Much more fun than this." He placed his hands on Ike's knee and twisted it. The echo of Ike's scream filled the emptiness of the auditorium. He gasped for breath. Tears filled his eyes.

"So," the old man asked again. "Will you play?"

Ike, trying desperately to calm his breathing, nodded.

"Good," the old man said, almost giddy at Ike's acquiescence.

Silence followed.

The old man looked at Ike and Ike at him. Then he nodded in recognition. "So sorry. You must get a cue from someone that you are on the air. Let us pretend that has already happened. Begin, please."

Ike exhaled. "On the line with us is…"

"Yes, yes, I am so sorry, again. I did not introduce myself to you, very rude, very rude, indeed. I am Dr. Antonin Helm. For the sake of our enactment you can call me Tony from Cairo…Egypt, that is."

He'd known it was Helm, but the sound of the name coming from the war criminal's lips touched a deep and primal terror. Ike's breathing came in gasps. His throat was closing and he wondered if he could speak. He took a breath and pushed himself into the role-play like the professional that Tony his producer, not Tony from Cairo, wanted him to be.

Yeah, Professor Keyes, what choice do I really have?

"On the line with us is Tony from Cairo, Egypt. Tony, tell us your unsettled score."

"It is a terrible thing. Dr. Miller, have you ever had valuables ripped away from you? Through robbery, larceny, or burglary? Has someone gone into your home, into your place of work, and stolen precious diamonds, gold, and envelopes filled with currency?"

Ike shook his head. "No."

"This has happened to me. It is my unsettled score," Helm said.

Ike wanted to say, "What about the Jews you killed and looted it from?" Instead, he continued with the charade.

"Do you know who stole these valuables from you?"

"Yes, yes, you are a smart lad. It took me many years to figure it out. Actually it was not until I read the magnificent work of your grandfather Otto Sperber that it came to me."

"'Existentialism and Spirituality in Auschwitz?'" *Helm had read it?*

"His world-famous account of survival in a place I knew very well. It is interesting to me, and perhaps to you, that Auschwitz-Birkenau was not so different from the campus where we currently find ourselves.

I read in an article on the Internet that this Metro State Psychiatric facility of yours extends three hundred acres, with dormitories and medical facilities. I am truly at home here. But I have strayed from the topic. We were talking about Otto Sperber's book. Beautifully written—a psychological masterpiece. In the dedication, Dr. Sperber tells the reader of his surviving Jew brothers: Gittlestein, Feldstein, Safier, and of course your other grandfather, Avram Miller." The old Nazi moved back to his original position behind Ike's head and began stroking his hair again. "You see, it made me aware that I was betrayed by one of my own men."

"Your unsettled score is with a subordinate?"

"No," Helm said forcefully. "I shot the fool."

"With who then?"

"As Auschwitz was being evacuated, one of the barracks guards told me he had killed the man who was to become your paternal grandfather. I believed him. To my surprise, some fifty years later, I read in Otto Sperber's fabled document that Avram Miller still lived. How could this be? I agonized over this news for many days. I had sleepless nights with terrible dreams, dreams about Jews shouting from the ovens that they had my treasure. But here is what may be of interest to you as one who studies the mind. I never before had these dreams."

He shuffled around to Ike's knee again. "You must be curious what happened next, no?"

Ike nodded. He felt the fear one feels in the presence of a world-class psychopath. Dead air filled the fake radio.

"We are broadcasting your show, remember?" Helm said, his voice rising.

"Yeah, okay. So Tony from Cairo, what happened next?"

"I realized my dream was a message. Perhaps from Hitler in the nether world." He laughed. "You do not believe that do you?"

Ike shook his head.

"Good, neither do I. But I do believe it was a communication. Do you not?"

"Yes. The unconscious mind has a way of showing through dreams important material our conscious mind may not notice," Ike droned. Even this much effort seemed almost more than he could manage.

"Yes, yes. Impressive. That is exactly what happened. I put one and one together and I came up with two hundred million, which is what I believe my treasure is worth. And your Avram stole my treasure. It is the only possibility."

"How did you conclude that from—"

"Please do not act as an innocent. It is right there in Otto Sperber's book. His dedication was to the men of his survivor's group. Avram was, of course, one of them. I had hid the satchel of diamonds and other valuables behind a wall there so that my thieving comrades, who would never step foot near the ovens, would not find it. I left the building to conclude final preparations for my escape. Your Avram removed the satchel and ran from the camp. I believe it is still in your family's possession, and since you are the only family member left, it must be in yours. Because if it is not..." His voice trailed off, and Ike felt Helm's cold hands on his leg once again, twisting the kneecap. Ike lost consciousness. He came back to the stench of ammonia, and Helm holding a vial under his nose.

"You must understand," he said. "I know this about you. You are a fine athlete. Like Achilles you have a weakness. I know what it is, and I am quite ready to exploit it. If you cooperate and get me what I want, I will be generous. A one percent finder's fee! I am sure you can use two million dollars."

Ike's knee throbbed, and he was afraid Helm had displaced the kneecap. But he knew nothing, and not knowing was going to cause him a great deal of pain and his life. Somewhere inside another part of him, the part of him that had learned how to perform during crunch time on the hardwood, took charge.

"Are we still playing *Psych 'n' Roll?*" Ike asked.

"Yes." Helm nodded emphatically.

"Tony from Cairo your unsettled score is with Avram Miller. To settle it you want your treasure back?"

"Yes, yes. That is what I want, and all will be forgiven, plus commission, of course."

"I see." Ike tried to adjust his body. "But I have some questions."

"Yes?"

"First: if you knew it was my grandfather who took your treasure why did you kill the rest of them?"

"It is what happens unfortunately when you have incompetent people making crucial decisions on limited information. My family believed I was dead. They have made a mess for me. When I learned about the deaths of Safier and Gittlestein, I knew it was time to involve myself. That is why I am here. To rectify what has happened.

I am sure you will help me in that regard," he said as he stroked Ike's hair once more. "Your next question?"

"Why now? Sixty-five years have passed."

"That is an intelligent query, I must say. Let me put it this way: I read Dr. Sperber's book only ten years ago. If I had read it when it was first published, I could have come here as a younger man. But even with knowledge of your grandfather's revelations, I did not have the insider connection that would allow me to make my travels until very recently."

"Last question, Tony from Cairo," Ike said.

"Yes, yes, what is it?" Helm sounded impatient.

"Why are you so sure that I have the treasure in question?"

"It is well known that Jewish families try desperately always to help their offspring. I know that your grandfather Avram was the culprit. He passed away six months ago, if my information is correct. He had to leave it to you in a will or in a private communication. It matters not to me how. What matters is that you retrieve it and return it to its rightful owner."

"But I'm telling you I know nothing about it."

"What you tell me now matters not, because in the end you will give it to me because of this." He made his way back to Ike's knee. At first he placed light pressure on the joint and then increased the stress in small increments. The pain knifed through Ike's leg and radiated through his body.

"What will it be?" Helm said.

Gasping, Ike shouted, "It's the truth!"

Helm's face twisted in anger. He placed his other hand on the joint and with each hand turned the ends of the kneecap in opposite directions. Ike screamed. The amphitheater began to spin, and he felt himself slipping into darkness.

"Still no truth from you? Well if that will not convince you to cooperate, then maybe this will. Franz Paul, come now!" he ordered.

Frankie rushed toward Helm from someplace in front of the operating table.

"Get ready to help me," Helm said. "My grandson has received a crash program in medical assistance. He is now familiar with the tools I use." He stroked Ike's knee gently. "One more thing, Franz Paul, bring me the bone saw. Just in case we must use it."

Frankie approached with an apparatus that to Ike's horror was a rectangular blade attached to a gun-shaped object. Ike squirmed, flailed about, and pushed at the restraints. In his panic he screamed, "No!" The echo of his terror bounced off the amphitheater walls. Frankie pressed a button. The saw made a high-pitched keening sound. Frankie zeroed in on Ike's leg.

"Turn off that stupid thing. There is a time and place for everything," Helm shouted. He addressed Ike. "Now when I am called on to do surgery in my new country I always do it humanely. Not like that terrible rumor that has followed me since the end of the war. But in your case, I want you to know I will use all extremes to get what is mine. Franz Paul, scissors."

Ike struggled and cried out, "I don't know what you're talking about!"

Like an operating room nurse, Frankie firmly handed a pair of scissors to his grandfather.

"Thank you. Now gag him. All this noise ruins my concentration."

Frankie stuffed a rag into Ike's mouth.

Helm removed Ike's shoes and socks, then cut the right leg of Ike's slacks above his knee and pulled it from him. His cold hand rested on Ike's leg.

"You will feel excruciating pain. Your body will try to compensate for the injury by putting you into shock. By then you will have gone unconscious."

Ike's mind had already traveled to the night he met Aja. Hell's Kitchen Playground. Courts empty. Lights still on. Their ballet took him far away from this atrocity. So absorbed was he inside his dissociation that for a moment it didn't register what was emerging from the shadows behind Frankie.

"I will now make the incision," Helm said. "Scalpel."

Frankie slapped a surgical knife into his grandfather's hand.

Seeing the gleam of light reflected from the knife jarred Ike back to reality. He thrashed and struggled to tear loose. A tall, bald man emerged into the light. *Hallucination?* Cone put an index finger to his lips. *No, that's him. That's really him.*

Helm bent forward. Ike felt the point of the scalpel against his skin.

"FBI. Drop everything!" Cone's order echoed throughout the surgical theater.

Helm straightened and dropped the scalpel.

"You're under arrest." His gun drawn, Cone approached the operating table. "Are you Antonin Helm?"

Helm puffed out his chest and stood at attention.

"Are you Antonin Helm?"

The old Nazi maintained his position.

"Ike. Is it Helm?"

Ike nodded.

"Antonin Helm, you are under arrest for murder and for crimes against humanity." Cone recited Helm's Miranda rights and handcuffed him to the surgical table. Frankie–possibly aiming for a place in Nazi folklore—rushed the agent. Cone fired. Frankie fell to the floor, his shirt pooling with blood.

Cone pulled out a cell phone. "I've got the Nazi. Unfortunately, I had to shoot his grandson. If he's not dead, he's damn close. Send an ambulance and get in here ASAP." He clicked the phone off and placed it inside his coat pocket.

Cone untied Ike and helped him to his feet. "Doesn't look like he cut you." He pointed to Ike's leg.

Ike nodded.

"You okay?"

"I guess. But I think I fucking aged ten years."

"I don't see any gray," Cone told him, grinning.

"Yeah. Anyway, thank God you came."

"I told you we'd keep an eye out for you."

CHAPTER TWENTY-ONE

BIG MEN

Cone led a limping Ike Miller out of the surgical theater. Something seemed off. "You just going to leave him like that?" Ike asked.

"Not a problem. Other agents are in the building. Meantime, I want you out of here so you get home sooner than later. I have to debrief you first."

"Wait." Ike stopped in his tracks. "Where's Aja?"

Cone hesitated like a physician about to give a patient bad news.

"What is it?" Ike asked.

"I didn't want to tell you this now. I thought once we were more settled I'd—"

"What? What!?"

Cone grabbed Ike's shoulders, held him in place, and looked at him with compassion. "They killed her. I'm sorry, Ike."

"What?"

"I'm sorry. She's dead."

"What happened?"

Cone sighed. "I don't know if I should tell you now. Maybe after we talk and you tell me what they did to you and what they wanted," he said.

"No. I want to hear it now," Ike said.

Cone looked anguished. "Are you sure?"

"Yeah."

"I don't know if I—"

"What did they do to her?"

"Someone—" he shook his head. "Someone raped her, then slit her throat. My men found her in the basement of the Laundry building."

"I see," Ike said. His mind fled to the now familiar place up above and outside his body. He'd become the stone man again. Cone gently, but firmly, tried to move him. "Come on Ike. We've got to go."

"Where is she?"

"On her way to a morgue in Riverhead." His head pointed in the general direction.

"Can I see her?"

"Maybe later. More likely tomorrow."

Ike separated himself from Cone and punched his fists into the air as if he was boxing the sky. "If only I'd listened to her," he said, remembering their conversation in his apartment. She'd begged him to leave. He'd responded with stubborn petulance. He had cost them both. She didn't have to die, and all because of what? His ego? Hurt feelings?

"It's my fault she's dead."

"What are you saying?" Cone asked.

"I should have stayed away from my apartment."

"This isn't your fault. I was the one who told you to go back. Put it on me if you have to blame anyone," Cone said. He continued to push Ike to the car. "Blaming yourself is useless. It's over now. Time to work all of this out."

"For what? Why all these killings after all these years?"

"I know. It's terrible. The why is what we have to learn, and it starts with what you witnessed, your testimony."

Cone led him outside through what was once the emergency receiving area. His black sedan was parked where ambulances and police cars had once brought drugged-out young people, the criminally insane, and violent patients wrapped up in straight jackets. Aja's brutal death in some abandoned basement room was now part of the hospital's snake pit history.

Ike shook his head. "Are you sure?" He asked.

"Am I sure of what?"

"That she's dead."

Cone blew out a breath, either from frustration or empathy. Ike couldn't tell.

"Sorry Ike. I'm so sorry to be the one to give you this news. But it is what it is." He helped Ike Miller into the passenger seat and drove out of the hospital grounds and onto the bordering local street. He turned to Ike. "You need anything? Water? Food? We can stop at a diner on the way," Cone said. "Maybe something to eat will help you deal with this better."

Ike's spirit was floating at the top of the sedan, and nothing that Cone was saying made much sense. "I don't need anything," he said.

Cone glanced at Ike again. "Reach in the back seat for my windbreaker. It's getting cold, and I think you'll need it."

Ike was a statue again.

Cone half turned and retrieved the jacket from the back seat. "Go ahead, put it on."

He clumsily pushed his arms into it. "Thanks," Ike said weakly.

"No problem."

They headed onto a main road. But to Ike it made no difference where they were or where they were going. Aja was dead. Ike the stone was on the verge of becoming Ike the explosion. He felt like screaming, breaking the windows, and kicking the dashboard. But coach's voice intervened: *Don't get angry. Keep your head. Let the game come to you.*

Ike looked over at Cone. "I have to ask you something."

"Go ahead."

"Did you know that Aja was an undercover FBI agent?"

Cone's eyebrows shot up. "Really?"

"Yeah. Before we were abducted she told me," Ike said.

"She's really good. I didn't know and would never have suspected it."

"She recognized you at the funeral. But you don't know her?"

"She was the one undercover. I never met her before the funeral."

After a moment Cone said, "What you just told me makes an issue out of how this was handled."

"What do you mean?"

"My people need to know. Her body was sent to a local morgue. But it should have been processed through proper channels. I have to make a call." Cone held onto the wheel with his left hand, pulled a headset from the center console and placed it on his head. He pressed a key on the phone and waited. "Gundersen. I'm glad I got you. There's an issue with the woman they found in that laundry building." Cone nodded. "So you know that already. Okay, can we go see the body, and if so, where?" Cone continued to nod. "Okay. Thanks."

He hung up, removed his headset, and looked over at Ike. "They know. They moved her to the morgue in lower Manhattan. Not only can you see the body, but they want to ask you some questions."

Ike thought of Aja on some stainless steel slab, looking at her body the way he'd looked at Otto's at the funeral home. He couldn't believe he was going to see the lifeless form of this incredible woman he'd made love to just a few days ago.

"When?" Ike asked.

"In the morning. Ten a.m."

"So you can take me to my place now, right?" He needed to escape to the familiar. Even his apartment, tainted with murder and mayhem, was still the best alternative to being anywhere near Metro State. He just wanted a quiet place, a place with a bed and sheets and a cover to crawl under so that he could fall asleep and awake in the morning to find out that everything that had happened was just one horrific dream, and only that.

"After I debrief you at the Hempstead office," Cone said.

"Damn it. Why can't this wait?"

"I know you're upset. But it can't. Protocol is that we do our questioning as soon as possible after an operation."

"Fuck that," Ike wanted to say. But he just didn't have the energy to plead with Cone anymore.

Traffic moved at a steady pace as Cone took one of the state parkways onto the Long Island Expressway. The "World's Largest Parking Lot," as commuters not-so-affectionately called Interstate 495, was living up to its reputation. The stream of cars slowed to stop and go. Ike became agitated and felt trapped. He looked over at Cone, who banged the heel of his hand against the steering wheel.

The sun was low in the sky, and Ike was bothered by the glare. He closed his eyes and was startled when he felt Cone move his arm close to him. "Just making you comfortable," Cone said as he pulled down Ike's visor and then did the same for himself. "It's not going to move for a while, I'm afraid. Why don't we listen to the radio? Your show is on."

Ike was too numb to care. He flashed to the image of Aja's body in the morgue, the look of gray-white death on her face.

"Do you want me to turn it on?" Cone asked again, nodding toward the radio.

Maybe the distraction would help. "Okay, go ahead," Ike said.

Cone pressed the radio button. WNYT was already programmed to go. Bob Dylan's "A Hard Rain's Gonna Fall" was playing. Dylan's blue-eyed son line got Ike's attention. He thought about Aja's blue eyes. How soft they were when they'd made love, how fierce when they'd played ball against each other, how sad when she talked about Otto's murder.

Finally, traffic began to move. After about ten minutes, Cone turned off the highway and onto a main road in a heavily populated area. On the radio, Springsteen's "Missing" segued onto the Dylan song. Tony was sending Ike a shout-out, or that was how he was interpreting the set. He looked over at the agent who seemed lost in a driver's trance. After a few traffic lights and stop signs, the car slowed down and Cone pulled it over to the front of a concrete and glass building. A sign announced, "Federal Building."

"We're here. Let's get this over with," Cone said.

Except for a cleaning service and a handful of overtime workers, the building seemed empty. On a directory, Ike read, FBI 4th FLOOR.

"You okay?" Cone asked as he leaned against the back of the elevator.

Ike's knee throbbed. Despite what Helm had done to him, he knew it would be okay. He just needed some time and a little soothing treatment.

"Maybe some ice?"

"Yeah. I'll rustle it up from the galley kitchen."

"Thanks."

The elevator headed up. Dad Rock tunes, as Aja would have described them, were on the elevator music bill. The great sounds of the past were the canned sounds of the present. The ending strains of Phoebe Snow's "All Over," seemed to disappear through the top of the rising lift. The Allman Brothers Band's "Ramblin' Man" followed.

They arrived on the fourth floor and walked a long corridor to a large glass door with the agency's letters on it. "This is one of our back offices, so we don't have as much activity here as in lower Manhattan." Cone removed a set of keys from his jacket pocket and opened the entrance. "Follow me," he said.

They entered an interrogation room, not much different from what Ike had seen in the movies. There were two chairs and a table. On it was a phone, and a two-headed microphone, its cord running into a small opening in the wall underneath a two-way mirror. The observation set-up was similar to the type they had in his graduate psychotherapy training. Ike felt the coldness of the space and wondered why Cone had to question him this way. He wasn't the suspect, after all, just a victim a few too many times over.

"Let me get you the ice," Cone said and jogged out of the room. He came back with a small cellophane sandwich bag with a half-dozen cubes inside. He handed the package to Ike, who placed it on his knee, his leg now resting on a chair.

"Sorry, it was the best I could do," Cone, said, pointing to the baggie.

"It's good enough. I'm getting better already," Ike smiled bitterly. "Look let's do whatever it is you want me to do. I want to get home."

"Got ya." Cone picked up the phone. He pressed a key and waited. "Cone here. Maury, it's you. Great. I need you to witness an interview." Cone nodded. "Tape is set up, yeah." He nodded again. "Okay, we'll start in a couple." Cone placed the receiver down on the phone's cradle.

"Am I going to meet this Maury guy?" Ike asked.

"No. He stays behind the glass. It's to prevent interview bias. He's already in the room." Cone pointed to the mirror.

What the fuck? Interview bias? But then again, how could he or anyone make sense out of any of it? Otto dead. Gittlestein frightened to death. Feldstein and his assistant murdered. Safier and his girlfriend shot to death. And Aja, raped and whatever else they did to her. Ike took a breath.

Cone turned the microphone on. "I'm ready. What about you?"

Ike nodded.

"I know enough about Otto and Helm. What we want to know is what Helm's relationship with Avram was."

"Relationship? That wasn't a relationship. How could you call it a relationship? He was in a death camp, for God's sake."

"Wow. Take it easy, Ike. I didn't mean anything by it."

"Sorry," Ike said, but he wasn't. Didn't Cone have family members perish in the Holocaust? He should know better than to ask that kind of question.

"Okay. Let me put it differently. What did Helm do to your grandfather?"

"I know very little. Only what Otto told me just before he was killed."

"What did he tell you?" Cone asked.

Ike told him about Otto's picture of the five surviving men. "That photo was the first time I heard anything about Avram's life in the camp. He was very secretive about most things but especially about what happened to him in Auschwitz."

"You mean to tell me he never spoke about being a *Sonderkommando?*"

"A what?"

"Really? You don't know what that is?"

"No. I don't think I ever heard that word."

"It's a German term. The *Sonderkommandos* were the cleanup detail. They were mostly Jews, some Christian Poles, and gypsies. They transported the bodies from the gas chambers to the crematorium. It was their job to remove gold teeth, watches, rings and other personal belongings from the dead and then burn the bodies, remove the ashes, and cart them to a dumping ground or a stream."

Ike visualized the photo. No wonder Avram lived with rage, and that he never talked about it. Who would want to talk about that? And who would tell a child— even a child who's grown into an adult—about that specific horror?

"Thanks for identifying a part of my legacy," Ike said, shaking his head.

Cone squinted at Ike. "You being sarcastic?"

"No. I mean it. It helps me understand why Avram was the way he was to my father. Another piece to the family puzzle—that's all I mean."

"I see," Cone said. "The reason I'm bringing this up, Ike, is that the Bureau wants to know where Avram was the day before the Russians liberated the camp. As part of the cleanup detail, was he in or near the crematorium? So we're asking you if he told you what happened."

"No. Like I said, he didn't tell me anything."

"Really?" Cone drummed his fingers on the table.

Ike shook his head slowly. "You know more than I do. How did you get this information?"

"We have files with testimony from surviving Jews and surviving Nazis, their family members and from Nazi hunters, like Feldstein. A lot of it is in the public record. There are books about the Nazi doctors who not only spoke about their own atrocities but often mentioned Helm as one of the worst perpetrators."

"The whole thing was so fucking sick, right?"

Cone paused and shook his head ever so slightly. It looked to Ike like he was debating whether to say something. "I want you to know I overheard the whole conversation Helm had with you on the operating table," Cone said.

"Yeah?"

"So are you saying your grandfather never told you he hid in the crematorium?"

Ike shook his head in astonishment. "What? You think Helm's dream really happened?"

"Just asking, my friend. Just asking. Again, your grandfather never said anything to you about that, about a satchel of gems hidden behind a wall and that he took it from the camp?"

"No." Ike was getting sick of having to answer questions he'd already answered.

"I watched you do a great job denying under duress what Helm asked you. But the answers are vital to our investigation. So if you can tell me what your grandfather told you about jewels he took from the camp I'd be much obliged. For your grandparents' sake—at least do it for them. It will be the last piece of evidence we need to complete the case."

"I need to ask you something first," Ike said.

"Go ahead."

"You said you heard my whole conversation with Helm, right?"

Cone nodded.

"So why the fuck did you wait so long to get me out of there?" Ike asked.

"I had to let it play out," Cone said. "Sorry Ike. I was just following procedure. That's all I can say about it."

A knot formed in the pit of Ike's stomach. These "procedures" and "protocols," and the incessant questions about things Ike had denied over and over again. *It's not right.* "If I had the answers, don't you think I'd give them to you? I want this over with. Can't you see that?"

"I know. I get it. Sorry. But one more thing: did Avram ever tell you about a safety deposit box or a special hiding place?"

"Damn it, no!" Ike shouted.

"Or at the reading of his will was a key to a safety deposit box, or the combination to a safe passed to you, or does your family attorney have any of these things in his possession?"

"How many times do I have to say no? I'm exhausted—fucked-up. I want to go home. If I remember something like that or come across what you just told me I'll call you as soon as it comes to me."

Cone stood and paced the small room. "I'm going out for some coffee. I'll get you a cup, too."

"I don't want anything," Ike said.

"I'll be back in a flash." Cone walked out.

It's not right. The timing of the rescue. Where were the other agents? Cone had been working alone as far as Ike could tell—come to think of it he'd always been alone. Didn't these guys work with partners, or was that just in the movies? Was there anyone behind the two-way mirror? It all seemed so fake, even Cone's exaggerated concern for him.

Then there was Aja. Ike had a hard time believing she was dead. Was he just in denial or was it something else? Did Cone spin a story about how she was killed to create fear and sorrow and become the comforting confidant? Confidant. A person who by showing sympathy creates confidence, *as in confidence scheme.* Clearly, a huge treasure was out there, and both Helm and Cone had relentlessly pressured Ike about it. But wasn't Cone supposed to be on Ike's side. Yes? No? Circle the correct answer.

Ike stood and placed the now water-filled cellophane bag on the interrogation table. He looked at his haggard expression reflected in the two-way mirror. He remembered what Aja had said: "I don't know if he knows me. But he's well-connected, so anything is possible."

Coach would say: *"You play the game from the inside."* Otto, *"Trust your instincts."* Avram had something different to tell him. *"Trust no one."*

Cone returned holding two Styrofoam cups of coffee and handed one to Ike. "I know you said you didn't want it, but, hey, I hate getting something just for myself."

Ike nodded and put the cup on the table. "Thanks. Can we get done with this?"

"Yeah. You're right. How's the knee?"

Ike shrugged.

"Just one more thing, and I'll take you to the city," Cone said.

"Good."

"Okay. So no one in your family, not Avram, his wife Rose, Otto, your other grandmother Elaine, or your parents ever told you anything about diamonds, gold, cash, you know, like Helm said, 'worth two hundred million dollars'?"

Ike slumped. "No. Pretend I'm George Bush the father. Read my lips. N. O."

Cone shook his head and stood. "Either you're a total innocent or you're just full of shit. In either case, it's not okay."

"What do you mean it's not okay?"

Cone reached under the armpit of his jacket and pulled out a revolver.

"You're going to shoot me because I don't know what you're talking about? Or is it even worse then that? A Jewish federal agent in partnership with a Nazi war criminal?"

"Fuck you, Ike. Get up. I think the only way to get this out of you is on the operating table."

In every big game, there's a moment when being in the flow needs to overcome the fear of losing. Ike found himself completely focused. "Do you know what they say about big men in basketball?"

"No, what?" Cone seemed caught off balance by the question.

"They say they their biggest vulnerability is when they grab a rebound and bring the ball down to their waist." Ike moved an imaginary basketball downward, giving Cone a physical form of hypnotic suggestion. And it worked. Cone unconsciously mimicked the gesture, lowering his gun just enough to allow Ike's quick hands to knock it from his grasp. The revolver fell to the floor. Ike pounced on it. Cone stood frozen.

Ike pointed the gun. "Get your ass in the chair. No, wait. First, take your wallet out of your pocket and toss it over to me. Then get your ass in the chair."

"I'm not giving you shit," Cone said. "You probably don't know how to shoot a gun anyway."

"Why? Because I'm an educated guy in what you think is a soft profession? I wouldn't test me if I were you."

Cone laughed. "You're not going to shoot a federal agent."

"After what I've been through, I wouldn't be so sure if I were you."

Cone twitched forward. Ike pulled the trigger. The shot blew past the agent's head and ricocheted off the wall, smashing the two-way mirror. Shards of glass fell to the floor. Ike's ears rang.

"See. I'll shoot you if I have to and if there were witnesses in there they'd be in here by now shooting me."

"Okay. What do you want?"

"Your wallet and your cell phone."

Cone refused to move.

"Now!" Ike said, raising the gun on a plane with Cone's head.

Cone gave Ike what he asked for.

"I'm calling the police," Ike said.

Cone laughed. "You think the police will believe you? You'll be arrested for attacking a federal officer."

"We'll see about that." But as Ike started to dial 911, he heard a commotion coming from the other end of the hallway.

"My partner's here with his crew." Cone laughed.

Ike moved to the door and opened it enough to see a resurrected Frankie and what looked like a Middle Eastern man coming toward him. Ike looked for an escape to his right and found it. He jumped out of the room and fired Cone's gun in their direction. Both men dropped to the floor. Ike ran to the exit and down the stairs faster than he thought was possible in his current condition.

Ike looked out through the lobby doors. Frankie's mother sat in the driver's seat of a Land Rover pulled up to the curb. Helm was her passenger. They were talking animatedly to each other, and Ike was sure they hadn't seen him. He looked for an alternate way out and found stairs to a parking lot. Once outside, he saw a Dumpster next to a chain-link fence. He removed the cash from Cone's wallet and stuffed it into his pocket. He threw the wallet, gun, and cell phone into the bin. He looked behind him to see if anyone was following. No Cone. No Helm family.

He got in gear and moved with as much speed as his tortured knee would allow—out of the parking lot and into the dark Long Island night.

CHAPTER TWENTY-TWO

HAVE HOPE, MY BOY

Ike switched intermittently between a gimpy jog and a limping walk that took him to the Mineola, Long Island Railroad Station. His bare feet had encountered every piece of gravel, rock, and who knew what else along the way. It was just past 8:00 p.m. and he'd managed to get onto the station platform a few minutes before the train for Penn Station was due.

On the cold, concrete landing, Ike huddled his inadequately clad body in a shadowed corner with a clear view of the comings and goings of train riders. He studied each one and concluded they were hospital workers from the adjacent medical center. For the moment, everything around him seemed calm in the chill of the mid-October evening. Ike rubbed his hands together and blew into them to get some circulation and warmth going and tried to relax into the lull.

He looked out at the tracks and the opposite side platform and it sent him into a before-the-pain memory. The parallel landings became opposing bleachers that overflowed with screaming students, teachers, and administrators, all in attendance for the title game between Madison and Lincoln High Schools. The atmosphere in the gym was electric. The game was never close—Ike had been having one of those rare flow experiences. He'd been so in the moment, so one with the experience that his shot making was unconscious. Ike Miller couldn't miss even if he'd tried, and it was the first time the chants of *IKIE! IKIE! IKIE!* filled a gymnasium. The next day city tabloid sport pages trumpeted: *"Madison High wins PSAL Division One Championship. IKIE scores sixty."*

A city-bound slowed its way into the station. Its arrival interrupted Ike's flashback. Ike stood and stepped into an empty car, then moved to a seat in a rear corner. He desperately desired warmth and sleep, but even just closing his eyes was a luxury he couldn't afford. After the train pulled away a conductor came for tickets. With bruises and cuts on his face, and the look of homelessness that his naked feet and cut off pant-leg presented, he worried what the ticket-taker's response would be.

"Do you have money?" The conductor asked.

"How much to Jamaica Station?" Ike responded.

"Thirteen bucks."

Ike removed a twenty from his pocket. The conductor took the bill, gave Ike his change, and placed the punched ticket in the slot behind the seat. He looked at Ike more closely. Ike couldn't tell if his face showed suspicion or concern.

"You okay?" the conductor asked.

"Not really. But you can help me," Ike said.

"What do you want?"

"Do you have a cell phone? I need to make a fast call."

The conductor pulled his phone from his jacket pocket. "It's on. Go ahead."

"Thanks." Ike dialed Tony.

Thank God, Ike thought as Tony answered.

"I don't have a lot of time," Ike said. "Go to my office. In my desk are a set of keys, my company ID and a folder with some documents. In my closet you'll find a jacket, jeans, shirt, socks, and sneaks. Oh, and my Yankees hat. And a pair of shades. Put them in the backpack that's on the top shelf. Get in your car and meet me at Jamaica Station on the Manhattan-bound E train platform. Bring five hundred dollars. I'll pay you back as soon as I can."

Ike held his hand over the phone. "What time do we get into Jamaica?"

"Eight-fifty."

"Eight-fifty. I'll be waiting on the platform. I'll explain everything later."

The train bumped along, passing through Long Island villages that for the most part were just part of one big suburban sprawl. He tried to stay awake, but his efforts failed. His dreams were of Aja and Otto. "The answer is simple. What kept men alive at Auschwitz was hope. If even the slightest possibility existed that a loved one could be alive, a man would have courage to go on, to make the choice to persevere through his pain. Have hope, my boy. Have hope."

Aja was ministering to the wounds on his face, his feet, and his knee as they sat next to each other by his microphone. Tony played the Steely Dan classic, and Ike sang the Aja song with Donald Fagen. Tony, from the other side of the glass partition, spoke to Ike into his earpiece. "Her loving kindness is not an act. It is a holy gesture. Her soul will live forever in your heart."

"Mister, wake up." A man—a vague figure—stood between him and his love. He shook Ike's shoulders, but Ike refused to open his eyes.

"Wake up." This time said forcibly.

The conductor pushed at Ike's shoulders. Ike blinked his eyes open and gathered his body to an upright position.

"Jamaica Station," the conductor told him. "Time to get off."

CHAPTER TWENTY-THREE

THE KEY

Sitting in shadows was getting to be a habit. Ike tried to keep his head down, arms wrapped around his knees. He hoped that the look of homelessness would give him cover. From time to time he popped his head up, searching for Tony's arrival. The last train out had emptied the station populated now only by him and dark forms that in Ike's state of trauma and exhaustion moved in and out, above and below the track lights and into the blackness of the transit tunnel maze. Water dripped somwhere—a steady plink overwhelmed by the rush of a train from somewhere above. A digital clock hung from the curved ceiling. A half hour had passed. Tony should be here by now.

Footsteps.

A tall, plodding figure emerged from the shadows. Ike scrambled up into an alcove. He watched as the

distance between him and whoever grew smaller and he
thought about making a run for it. But fear or wisdom,
or perhaps both, kept him in place.

"Got word someone of your description jumped the
toll." A transit cop flashed a light toward Ike's face from
fifteen yards away.

Ike shielded his eyes with his arm. "Yes, officer."

"Was it you?" The cop was now standing close to Ike.

"No," Ike said.

"Now don't give me no crap. Just be honest and I'll
leave you alone. It's pouring out there. You don't want
me sending you into the rain now, do you?"

Ike was about to answer when a familiar voice said,
"Officer, I've got it."

"You from some agency?" the cop asked.

"Yeah, we're getting a few of these guys in out of the
weather."

"Well, take care of him. He needs a shower and some
clothes. And medical attention."

"I'll see to it," Tony said.

The cop nodded, turned, and headed to the opposite side of the platform.

As Ike watched him leave, he breathed a sigh of relief and turned to his friend. "I can't tell you how great
it is to see your bearded face."

"Tell me about it in the car," Tony said.

He wanted to avoid Manhattan. As difficult as it would
be for Cone to track him down in the vertical vastness of the Big Apple, Ike wasn't taking any chances.
He thought Cone would search for him in hotels, flop
houses, apartments of family, friends and their relatives.

He figured refuge in an outer borough would do for the night. He asked Tony to take him to a hotel across from La Guardia Airport. While Tony drove, Ike described his ordeal.

"You think that FBI guy is working with the Nazi?" Tony asked.

"Yeah. He even called Helm his partner."

"And Aja, she's really dead?" Tony asked, his tone incredulous.

"That's what Cone told me. She's in a morgue in lower Manhattan."

"I don't know what to say," Tony said, shaking his head. "When I met her and spent time with her driving back to Manhattan after the funeral, I knew she was someone with a deep and rich soul. I was happy the two of you met. I can't tell you how much pain I feel for her and you right now."

"Thanks," Ike said. He placed his hand on his friend's shoulder. "But I don't believe it."

"What don't you believe?" Tony asked.

"That she's dead," Ike said, looking outside through the passenger window. They were on the Grand Central Parkway. The airport was on the right. A plane descended along a nearby flight path. The highway exit for the hotel was a half-mile away. "Everything about Cone was a lie. So I think the story about her death was phony too."

"Why would he lie about that?" Tony said as he slowed the car onto the exit ramp.

"To scare me, but also to comfort me. To show me he was a friend. That he was on my side. That's what I think. But who knows? Hell, maybe it's true and she is dead. But I have to find out. If there's any chance she's still breathing, I have to find her."

They arrived at the Airport Marriott, a gray, concrete, ten-story edifice familiar to anyone who's ever traveled by air in North America. Tony parked. Ike grabbed the backpack.

Once inside his room, Ike tossed the bag onto the bed.

"Call the police. You can't do this alone," Tony said looking worried.

Ike didn't answer. He was debating whether to bring up something that might be painful to his friend.

"What's going on?" Tony asked.

"Remember all the legal crap you went through after your son died?" Tony's third child, six-year-old Aaron, had drowned in a pool accident. The death led to the destruction of Tony's marriage and family life and eventually, after horrible legal battles, put Tony on his spiritual path.

"Yeah." Tony nodded, his eyes closed.

"You told me you could never trust the cops, the legal system. You said they always had their own agenda and that it wasn't about the truth. Wasn't that what you said?"

Tony sat on the edge of one of the double beds. "I spoke with my guru about it many times. He told me that those in authority are fallible, especially if they don't have inner spiritual values, and lacking them they're not to be trusted. He taught me to trust my inner self instead, to believe in the essence of my soul."

"Right. That's what I mean," Ike said. "'Psyche' means the soul, right? Both of our gurus gave us similar instructions. Otto always told me to go inside myself to find the truth. My truth tells me I can't trust the police. That I have to find a way to do this on my own."

Ike noticed Tony had the look on his face he sometimes got during their "Name that Tune" lessons. It always meant that Ike was close, but still outside the bull's eye.

"Everything you said is true," Tony said. "You understand what's spiritual, or what, in your words, comes from the psyche. But there's also a physical dimension we have to live within, and there are aspects of it that are beyond our abilities. You can't—alone, at least—fight a depraved group of people who are better at their depravity than you are at your spiritual or your psychological knowledge. This is what evil is about: depravity that knows no bounds, no conscience or consciousness. You have to get experts, allies, to help you fight them. Isn't that how the Nazis were defeated in World War II?"

"I don't know, Tony," Ike said. "After what a cop, a Federal agent who was Jewish, of all things, did to me and my family, I think I'd better go it alone."

"I understand. But do this for me," Tony said. "Think about it tonight. Go deep inside yourself for the answer. If you don't want to go to the FBI or police but decide you need some kind of professional help, at least go to Hank. I trust him. He's got a tough-guy attitude, but I know he's always interested in doing the right thing. And we both know he's got the right connections."

Ike took a deep breath and nodded. "Okay."

"Good," Tony said. "By the way, I have the rest of your stuff."

"Did you find the keys?" Ike asked.

Tony reached into his pocket for the key ring and tossed it to Ike.

"I just don't pay attention sometimes," Ike said.

"What do you mean?"

"This key right here." Ike showed it to Tony. "It was given to me at the reading of Avram's will. I asked the lawyer what it was for, and he said it couldn't have been too important because Avram didn't stipulate the contents. I took it to the office and put it on my backup key ring and forgot about it. Guess what?"

Tony shook his head.

"Cone jarred my memory when he asked if I'd received a safe-deposit box key during the reading of Avram's will." Ike squinted to read the tiny print on it. "Have you ever heard of the Zurich International Bank?" He asked, looking up from the piece of metal.

Tony pursed his lips and shook his head.

"Damn. I wish I had a computer or a smart phone."

Tony flashed a knowing smile.

"What?" Ike said.

"I brought you your company iPhone with the rest of your care package. I thought you might need it, right?"

"Terrific. Didn't even think of it." Ike took it from Tony and turned it on. "Battery's low. You got the charger?"

Tony nodded. "It's in your backpack."

"Oh and the folder. Did you bring that too?"

"It's all in there," Tony said.

"Thanks." Ike retrieved it and looked quickly through the documents. "Got just what I need." He plugged the charger connected into a wall outlet, turned the phone on, and keyed in the search information. "Says here that the Zurich International Bank is a boutique outfit with offices in Zurich and Berne and a branch in Manhattan, in Chinatown on Bowery of all places." Ike nodded his head and had a determined look on his face. "That's where I'm going in the morning. Keep this close to the vest. For your sake as well as mine. I have to do this my way, first. No cops. No feds. One of the things Avram, told me was that he survived because he learned to rely on himself. Maybe in normal bad times, like hurricanes and earthquakes, that's a bad idea. But as a Jew during the Holocaust, it was sometimes a wise decision, at least he thought it was, and I'm going to rely on Avram Miller as my guru for this."

"Okay. Do what you have to. But think about our conversation," Tony said.

"I will. Now go. I'll be in touch."

CHAPTER TWENTY-FOUR

THE SAFETY BOX

Ike stood in the crowded subway car from Jackson Heights in Queens to Canal Street in lower Manhattan. Standing was made bearable by thoughts of embracing Aja again. They'd overcome the traumatic image of her splayed out on some cold floor with her throat slashed. He was grateful for whatever positive defenses he could muster.

When the train arrived at his stop, he maneuvered through the rush hour crowd and gingerly walked up the station stairs and onto the street. His knee was still painful, even after the ice he'd kept on it through a deep sleep of exhaustion. At shortly after 9:00 a.m. the crush of activity in this part of town was in its full chaotic swirl. He edged his way through the frenetic streams of morning New Yorkers.

Chinatown smelled of soy, sautéed onions, shellfish, and succulent meats. He passed groceries where window-front ducks and chickens hung in their dead-naked beckoning. It made him think of warmer, safer times with friends intent on a late-night food fix. A second memory followed: Christmas in a dim sum palace with his mother, Otto, and grandma Lainie. Grief rushed into awareness. There were very few places in this town that didn't remind him of his losses.

Automobile traffic on Canal Street was already gridlocked. The noise created by sirens, honking horns, and jackhammers drove through Ike's body, adding jitters to his already intense emotions.

On Bowery, the Zurich International Bank occupied the ground floor of a high-rise apartment house on the edge of restaurant row. Here, Chinatown melted into the button-down and black suit world of government buildings and courts. He looked over his shoulder. No one seemed to be following him, but how would he know?

He entered the bank.

A young woman with "Mae" on her nameplate was in charge of the safety deposit boxes. Ike handed her his key and his radio station ID with his picture and signature.

"I'll need a driver's license," she told him.

"I don't drive," Ike said.

She frowned. "I'll be back in a moment."

Ike took a seat. He noticed that a copy of the New York *Times* lay on the adjacent table. He reached for it. There, on the front page, was a story about Otto's death. The paper reported the murder as part of a larger investigation into the killings of Holocaust survivors, friends who'd survived the tortures of one Antonin Helm, infamous Nazi surgeon. Detective Romano was quoted: "It was as if the terror of the Nazi atrocities visited these men once again." That took Ike's breath away. Multiple columns that described Otto's contributions to the mental health field and his tireless work for the NYPD, Jewish causes, and peace organizations, followed the article about the murder. Ike felt himself choking up. *No tears in hoops*, he repeated again and again until he throttled the sadness.

The clerk returned. "My manager okayed your ID, but I need a copy of the alternative ownership document with your signature on it. We need to compare it to the form we have on file."

After Avram's lawyer read his grandfather's will, Ike had signed a number of official papers. This had been one of them. He found the form in the folder and handed it to Mae. She checked it against the one in her file and returned his copy to him before leading him into the vault. She found the box and slid it out from its slot. It weighed her down. Ike reached to help. He felt a mixture of excitement and fear at how heavy it was. He tried to cover up his anticipation by making a joke: "My grandfather collected rocks."

"Take as much time as you need," she said. "The private rooms are to the right."

Ike chose the first room. He closed the door behind him and placed the box on a table. A painting of a mountain climber hung above the desk. Despite the kitschy homage to Swiss alpine sports, something about the room gave off an austere yet mysterious aura, a sense that it was filled with secrets kept and truths revealed. It was as if he were in a confessional, or, as was his recent unpleasant experience, a viewing room in a funeral home.

Ike's heart pounded.

He lifted the safety deposit box cover. The container was packed. A manila envelope stared at him. Printed in bold letters was a command: *READ THIS FIRST.* Ike opened the envelope and removed a typed letter.

My dearest grandson,

We never wanted to burden you with what happened to us. But I feel you must know the story behind what you are about to find.

I was what the Germans called a Sonderkommando. It was my job to take the bodies from the gas chamber to the crematorium and after to take the ashes and bone to a disposal area in a stream by the woods.

Ike stopped reading and stared at the wall. This was precisely what Cone had told him. The word *Sonderkommando* by itself conjured ominous and frightening images. *Only the Nazis could have come up with that one,* Ike thought. He was about to get lost imagining what it was like to be one when he caught himself and turned his attention back to the letter.

As terrible as this job was, it allowed me to survive. Dr. Antonin Helm also used me to clean the surgery room after his horrible medical experiments. This dybbuk experimented with chemicals to learn how much should be used as anesthesia during surgery. He would operate on the men and they would die from the substance or wake up too soon in agony. They were already weak, and the stress alone would often kill them.

Some survived. You may know two of them, Hymie Safier and Baruch Gittlestein. They are part of our survivors group and have been to our home. Helm also forced Otto Sperber to be his assistant. It was how he managed to live, and I know it has always troubled him.

So now the story of what is in this box.

It was January of 1945 and I was colder than I have ever been in my life. The Russian army was advancing. There was tumult in the camp. The Germans were making last-minute preparations to leave Auschwitz. They burned documents and murdered the few remaining Jews they had not forced to go on the Death March. I became like a ghost, moving in shadows. I hid underneath one of the buildings with three other men, with rats, mice, and garbage that had accumulated in the last days. But I was afraid the SS guards would search for the few remaining prisoners precisely in places like this. So I ran for the crematorium. It was a place I knew the Nazis would not go. They would kill easily without conscience, without remorse, but they feared the face of death and always avoided that hellish place. The crematorium became my opportunity to escape.

I entered one of the ovens. I am sure you will find this hard to believe. To lie in such a place, to hide in ashes and grease from human bodies, and with such a terrible smell, oy veh is-mir, a place where I had placed many bodies of our people to have them burned after the Nazis murdered them with gas. The oven felt like my tomb. I felt a strange comfort, and I began to think that I did not want to live anymore. But I fought these feelings because I also thought that if I still lived after all I had been through, then it was God's will that I must survive.

Helm and one of his men entered the building. Helm asked his subordinate if the cellblock was empty of Jews. A voice I recognized as the cruelest of the guards said he had shot the last three under the infirmary. Helm wanted to know if Avram Miller was among them. The guard's reply was a military, "Yes, sir!" His answer confused me. In my mental condition, I wondered if I were already dead like the many murdered souls whose bodies I had been forced to burn here. Then Helm ordered the subordinate to hide a satchel. I heard footsteps approach the oven and I feared he would open the door and find me. Instead, I heard tapping and scraping nearby.

What was in the satchel? I did not know. But it was important because Helm told the guard that it must not be found by the camp commandant or other officers. An explosion shook the building. The Russians were getting close. Helm ordered the guard to hurry and finish. After he did, they left and closed the doors. I heard Helm saying, "Your family will remember you as a hero." Then, two shots, and then a car engine started and the car drove away. I pulled myself from the oven. I wanted to run because I did not know when Helm would be back. But I could not resist knowing what was hidden behind the wall.

What I found is here before you. You may wonder how it was that I could travel with these valuables. This too is something of a miracle. The satchel was very heavy but I was used to moving heavy objects even in my terrible condition. After I left the crematorium, I walked to a stream where the SS had made us dump the ash and bones of our people. I took what I could easily carry and easily liquidate and buried the rest by a tree I knew I would recognize. One year later, I returned. The satchel was still there. I traveled to Switzerland, where I divided its contents among several banks. After a few years in America, I began to take trips to Zurich to bring home small amounts until I placed everything in the vault you are now in. I have invested modest amounts in my business and to give our family a comfortable life.

Helm has never been brought to justice. I was always afraid he would come to America with some bulvan to track down the fortune. I lived constantly with this fear. If Feldstein is still alive, he will tell you the story of the search for this man and how the authorities have never found him. There were rumors he lived in Egypt and became a Muslim. Some say he died there, but no one has been able to confirm his death. You do not need to worry about him. If he still lives, he would be an old man, even older than I am.

Please use what is here to make a better life and to help others.

Your loving grandfather,

Avram.

As much as Ike detested and feared Helm, he had to acknowledge that the SS surgeon had sharp psychological or even psychic skills. To conclude what he had from his dream interpretation about Jews hiding in ovens combined with Otto's book dedication made Ike shake his head in macabre admiration.

Ike looked at the time on his phone. Forty-five minutes had passed. Was Mae wondering what took so long? Perhaps people had gone into these rooms and perished from the secrets they'd discovered.

Ike put the letter aside and dove into the box that held plastic cases filled with gold coins, velour bags, and envelopes of hundred dollar bills. He removed one of the bags and pulled open the string. Scores of diamonds, each larger than the next, fell into his palm and onto the desk like trick-or-treat candies. The size of the cache took his breath away. Ike pulled everything out to get to the final shelf. He banged on the box to make sure he hadn't left anything. But something heavy rattled against its walls. He pulled the shelf away to reveal a gun and a plastic container filled with bullets. Avram must have kept the weapon for his own protection and left it to Ike for the same reason. Ike wanted to curse Avram for his secretiveness. But another one of Coach's sayings was, "You can only play the game you're in."

"Coach," Ike said aloud. "I'll need my best shot and superior 'D' to win this one."

He opened the gun's cylinder and slid bullets into the chambers. He hadn't made it up when he told Cone he knew how to use it. He thought for a moment about what he should do with it. Just as he was about to place it back in the box, he heard Avram's voice in his head, *"what is wrong with you? You must take it to protect yourself. That is the reason I left it here for you."* Ike nodded—feeling the heat of shame he always felt when Avram spoke to him this way—and pocketed the gun inside his jacket. He removed cash from an envelope, folded the money and slid it inside a front pocket of his jeans. He deposited the rest of the treasure back into the box and took it back to Mae who locked it up again.

As he headed for the bank's exit, Ike had a sensation he'd only had on the hardwood during the stiffest of competition. Everything stood out in sharp detail: the bank's marble floors, the tellers and customers doing business, the large arched windows, and the armed security guard stationed a few steps in front of the revolving doors. Ike noticed the shadows and where the light came in. He had a sensation of being watched. He glanced around, but saw no one he recognized.

He couldn't do any of this he realized when he was out on the street again – find Aja, get justice, settle scores – without, as Tony had described it, getting allies to help him. He thought about what he would say as he pulled out his phone and put in a call to Hank Grimm.

CHAPTER TWENTY-FIVE

IF ONLY

He set up a meeting with Hank at The Golden Mike. In the meantime, Ike decided to put his pummeled body into a cab and have it deliver him directly to the saloon's door. From where he was in Manhattan, the uptown trip by taxi would use up a good chunk of the sixty minutes he had to get there. It gave him time to think.

His father had abandoned him, but his family had shielded him from that loss and from horrors suffered in a world that had exploded in hatred and destruction. Ike had always felt this as deprivation, but now he began to see their protection as a loving act. He needed to "man up," as Coach would say, give up his resentments, and give credit to them for their kind intentions.

When the taxi arrived at Columbus Circle, traffic was frozen. Sirens screamed. Police cars and fire trucks dodged stopped vehicles. Smoke was pouring from a window some blocks to the north.

"Driver, let me out. I'll walk the rest of the way," Ike said.

The driver pulled off to the side of the street. Ike gave him a fifty and told him to keep the change. The driver smiled broadly, got out of the cab, and opened the door for him.

To get to Mike's, Ike decided to cut through Central Park. Passers-by walked their dogs, skaters bobbed and weaved along the blacktop path. Autumn colors and midday sunlight made him feel that in a city where chaos theory and Murphy's Law ruled, he'd arrived in an oasis. He wondered if it might be the last time.

Ike exited the park and crossed Fifty-Ninth Street.

What am I going to tell Hank? He thought.

Some of it would be too hard to swallow, especially the story about a Jewish FBI agent, a hunter of war criminals, in partnership with Antonin Helm. Ike wondered how Hank would respond.

A flat screen television in an electronics store window displayed a cable sports network replay of an NBA last second game-winner. Slow motion shots showed the ball leaving the player's hand from mid-court, referees stabbing their three-point signal into the air, ecstatic teammates and delighted fans jumping, hugging, and high-fiving. Okay, that was never going to be him. But Coach had always thought that Ike had what it took to get the job done.

To do what this job was going to take meant something alien to how he'd lived the past few years, cocooned in a comfortable chair, dispensing advice in an air-conditioned radio station, grooving with Tony, playing rock 'n' roll shrink. He had to take his shot with confidence. Why speak with Hank at all? He could find Aja, rescue her, and bring justice to Cone and Helm without the station cop's help. Couldn't he?

No, Tony had this one right. He couldn't.

Yeah, but what am I going to tell Hank?

Ike continued on. He walked past a strip of tourist shops and the Duane Reade drugstore where he'd bought the basketball he and Aja played with the night they met. He shook his head and sighed. This time he said it out loud: "What the hell am I going to tell Hank?"

"You're not going to tell him shit," Cone said and shoved a revolver into Ike's back. "Get in the car."

Cone drove onto the West Side Highway toward the southern tip of Manhattan and around to the east side of the island onto the FDR Drive. Ike sat cuffed with his hands just above the base of his spine, searing pain radiating through his arms and lower back.

"Where you going?" Ike asked. He could feel his heart racing.

"You know," Cone said, his eyes focused intently on the road. He continued along the highway and got off at an exit adjacent to the Manhattan Bridge. They sat at a light. Cone turned slightly toward Ike.

"Was Helm right?" He asked.

Ike was silent.

"Tell me now. Was Helm right?"

Ike stared straight ahead.

"You fucking better tell me or I'll shoot you in the knee. Then if you still won't talk, I'll shoot the good one. "Was Helm right?"

Ike didn't want to give him the satisfaction of an answer. But this wasn't the time or place to take a stand. "Yeah. Helm was right."

"How much is in there?"

"I don't know how to value it. But let's just say it's an amount beyond your wildest dreams."

Cone nodded his head slowly and showed a tiny smile that Ike read as restrained excitement.

"If we're going to the bank why are we in this part of town?" Ike asked.

"You'll see," the agent said.

Cone drove west, cutting through Lower East Side residential streets. Ike braced for a surprise. After a stop at another light, Cone pulled into an empty parking lot.

"What are you doing?" Ike asked.

His first thought was that Cone was going to kill him, but Cone needed Ike to get to the box. Ike was safe until Cone got his hands on the treasure. It wasn't going to happen here.

The agent drove around to the back of the lot. He stopped the car and turned off the engine. He pushed his seat back, turned to Ike, and slammed his fist into Ike's temple. The force pushed his head into the passenger side window. Cone got out, walked around to Ike's door and opened it.

"Get out," Cone said as he pulled Ike by the scruff of his collar. "You're going to drive."

Cone unlocked the cuffs and rough-handled Ike into the driver's seat. "Get in. And don't try anything stupid. As fucked up as you are right now, I know you know I have a gun."

I have one too. Ike thought, praying Cone wouldn't check.

Ike did what he was told and crumbled into the driver's seat. Cone walked behind the car and into the passenger side.

Cone, pointed his gun at Ike. "Drive—carefully and slowly. Don't fuck with me. You've done enough of that."

Were there any parts of his body that didn't hurt? *You're alive. Stop complaining.* The thought was followed by a burst of adrenaline. What Cone had inflicted with his fist was no worse than an elbow to the head on the way to the hoop. Whenever that had happened, he'd gotten up from the hardwood and played with even more awareness and intensity than before the insult.

"You gotta realize something," Cone said. "You can't fool me. You thought you got over on me, didn't you? Let me tell you something. The meeting you had with that Keys fellow put your friend in big trouble. If you don't want him to have a fatal accident, you better do everything I tell you from now on. That's the *emmis.*"

Ike was pissed. First Cone had threatened Tony, and then he'd used Yiddish, which Ike had always associated with grandparents' love for him.

Cone pushed the revolver into Ike's ribs. "I *let* you get away. I watched every move you made. Going north was a good touch. But I wanted you to lead me to the bank. And you did. You did everything just right."

"Yeah, you're a great detective—so smart, so devious. But you're a fucking sociopath."

Just drive to the bank," Cone said.

Ike did what he was told.

At a traffic light Cone turned to him. "You lied to me. You knew all along about the safety-deposit box."

"I didn't."

"Quit giving me shit," Cone shouted. He cocked his gun and pointed it at Ike's leg.

Ike knew it was all bravado with Cone now. Later would be something else. "When Avram died six months ago his attorney gave me the key and a document transferring ownership to me. I only remembered the box when you asked about it."

"You never went to the vault before?"

"No. I asked the attorney what was in it. He said likely small items and old documents because if there'd been something of value, Avram would have listed it. As time passed, I just forgot about it."

"What a bunch of crap," Cone said.

"Believe what you want."

"Whatever. It doesn't matter now," Cone said. He reached into the back seat and pulled out a leather satchel. "You're going to go to the vault and fill this up with everything that's in that box. You're going to come outside and hand it to me. After that, we'll see."

"I could make a scene and tell the clerk to call the police," Ike said.

"Yeah, you do that. Then I get on my cell, call Helm and have the Arab kill Aja. Oh, I forgot to tell you. She's alive. So if you want her to continue living you won't do that," Cone said.

"I knew it." Ike let out a sigh of relief.

"Yeah. But the Arab guy, Tarek, had his way with her, if you get my drift. I thought it important to share that with you." Cone flashed a nasty smile.

Ike burned.

Cone pushed his revolver into Ike's side again. "Park. We're here."

"Good," Ike said. "Let's get this over with."

CHAPTER TWENTY-SIX

SHOCK AND AWE

It was near closing time at the bank. Lines were twice as long as they'd been earlier in the day. Cone seemed to vent impatience by trying to be funny. "I wonder if they've got enough toasters." When Ike didn't respond to the joke, Cone put his hand on Ike's back and pushed him forward. "Move it."

They headed for the vault.

Mae approached. "Mr. Miller! Back so soon?"

Ike nodded.

"What happened to the side of your head?" she asked.

"Played a rough game of basketball in the park."

"Hmm, that looks nasty," she said. "Do you need something for it?"

Ike shook his head. "Thanks for asking."

Mae retrieved the ledger from a file cabinet. Ike signed it and Mae led the way to the vault.

"Don't forget this," Cone said and tossed him the satchel.

Mae brought the heavy box into the private room with the kitschy Alpine scene. She put it on the table and left, closing the door. Ike pulled out the desk chair and sat. He needed to think through what he was about to do. He glanced at the cheesy artwork. He felt a certain kinship with the mountain climber, scaling what looked like treacherous terrain. Would the climber make it to the top or would his bones lie bleaching in a ravine somewhere? *And for that matter, what about me?* He felt for Avram's gun and shook his head. Cone had underestimated him again and this time he was going to pay.

His hands trembled as he opened the box. "One breath at a time," he told himself. He opened the first sack of gems and poured the rocks onto the desktop. There were dozens of diamonds sprinkled in front of him. He lifted the largest stone, rolled it between his fingers, and held it up to the light. Tiny streaks of color reflected into his eyes. *Bling,* he thought. He poured the diamonds back inside their velvet home and deposited the sacks in the leather case. He removed two envelopes of cash, but left the gold coins and the rest of the currency in the box. He patted the loaded pistol inside his jacket again.

He gathered the box and satchel and left the room.

Mae rose from her desk and walked to meet him. Ike followed her into the vault, placed the container into its slip, and with his and the bank's matching keys locked it. He thanked her for her help. He hefted the leather case—now home to an incredible collection of World War II spoils–and handed it to Cone. They walked together at a moderate pace toward the bank exit, where a security guard stood by the door. As they came within a few yards of him, Ike dropped to one knee.

"What are you doing?" Cone said.

"My knee locked. Shit, that hurts."

"Okay. Take it easy. Get up and let's get out of here."

The guard approached Ike. "You okay, sir?"

Ike nodded and rose. In one swift motion he stepped into the guard and pushed him down with his left arm. With his right hand he removed the gun from his pocket and pointed it at Cone.

"Kill me and you'll destroy the nice little life you have," Cone said. His right hand moved to his suit jacket. Ike wasn't going to wait to see the gun. He pulled the trigger twice. The gunshots startled him, reverberating from the stone walls of the bank. Cone fell holding his gut as blood oozed from his body onto the cold marble. Alarm bells rang. Patrons ran, or dropped to the floor, or took cover behind desks. Ike pivoted and pointed the gun at the security guard who was reaching into his holster.

"Don't. I'm not a threat to anyone else." He kept his gun fixed on the guard as he grabbed the satchel and backed out of the bank.

Outside, he moved through the Chinatown backstreets as fast as the weight of his cache and his hurting knee would allow. Breathless after a couple of blocks, he stopped a taxi and jumped in. He collapsed into the back seat, ears ringing, breath ragged.

After a moment of silence, the cabbie turned to him. "The way it works is you have to tell me where you're going."

Ike didn't know where to go. He needed time to think but couldn't come up with a safe place. He realized the longer he neglected to respond, the more this fare would stick out in the driver's mind. Now that the driver had gotten a good look at his passenger, Ike needed to make the cab ride a normal one.

"Fifty-Second Street and Eleventh Avenue," Ike said.

"Okay," the cabbie said.

Ike tried to relax. He leaned back into his seat. He heard sirens and looked out the window. He saw a caravan of police cars, unmarked sedans with flashing red emergency lights, and EMS vehicles headed in the opposite way. From overhead he heard the rotors of a helicopter. Ike was certain he was now wanted for killing a federal agent.

"You're a warrior. Never forget that."

"Okay, Coach," Ike said.

"What's that, mister?" the driver asked.

"Nothing. Sorry. Just thinking out loud," Ike said, surprised he'd spoken his thoughts. He resolved to keep his mouth shut the rest of the ride.

Hell's Kitchen Playground.

Ike's good leg shook as he sat on a park bench. On the court he'd played on just a few days ago, four junior high kids were in a two-on-two game—both awkward and graceful as they played their version of Kobe's or Lebron's moves and shots. He'd been their age. He remembered the carefree twists and turns and jumps and drives he'd practiced as he tried to emulate Michael Jordan or John Stockton. But the word "carefree" was not something he might ever use to describe his life again. His family was gone. He'd just killed a federal agent. A fugitive Nazi wanted very much to have access to the fortune in the leather satchel at his feet. And the woman he loved was in danger—but alive, he reminded himself.

He had killed a man. As the fog of action cleared away he realized how complicated his emotions were. Guilt—a hard remorse in the center of his gut—came first. But he could reason himself out of that. It was self-defense. No it was something else. The act he had performed, of pulling a trigger and sending lead projectiles into another human being with the intention of taking his life, made him weak and lightheaded. It reminded him of how he felt when he learned the cops had shot his father.

If I had to could I do it again?

He thought about Jamal's time in the marines. He'd been a sniper. Snipers didn't just kill one person, as Ike had in self-defense. Snipers were trained to take out many enemies. Maybe that was part of the answer. The greater the number and the farther away the more emotionally disconnected the act, the easier (if easy could ever be used as a description) it was to do. The intimacy of killing—at point-blank range—a person with a name you knew, was different, unless of course you were pathological, like Cone. Like Helm and the rest. He wanted to ask Jamal about it—about how he did it, and how it made him feel.

"Any of you boys know Coach Jamal and the Devils?"

"Yeah. I'm gonna play for him when I'm older," one of them said.

"Great. Do you know if they'll be practicing here today?"

Headshakes and shrugs gave Ike the answer.

"Okay," Ike smiled. "Just want to tell you how great you're playing."

"Thanks mister," the same kid said. The boys got back to their game.

Then it came to him.

Jamal had twice invited Ike to the Garden. That's where he had to go next. First, he had to secure the diamonds.

With one hand Ike held on tightly to the subway pole, and with the other he gripped the satchel. The subway car was packed. He was sardined in with students, Wall Street guys, hardhats, midtown workers, the homeless, and cops. He was sure every cop he saw was zeroing in on him, trying to match his face to some wanted photo that was already making the rounds. Ike put his shades back on, pulled his baseball cap lower, and bowed his head.

Two officers got on at the Times Square stop. They looked at a sheet of paper then scanned the car. One cop maneuvered his way through the straphangers and toward him. He was a couple of bodies away when a voice loud enough to overcome the rumbling and screeching of the moving train shouted, "I'm a veteran. "I lost my arm fighting for you!"

The man raised his stump high. His face was twisted and flushed. "Won't you help me, please? Five dollars is all, and you can have my CD. It's called 'Shock and Awe.'"

The cops altered their focus from their printout to the vet. "Hey, buddy, you can't solicit here," one of them told him. Ike shuffled nearer the doors an inch at a time.

The train stopped at the Thirty-Fourth Street Station. Ike, holding the case tightly against his chest, hustled from the subway car and up onto the street.

Midtown Storage was on Thirty-Fourth Street between Fifth and Sixth Avenue. Its home, the Excelsior office building, was undergoing a face-lift. Ike navigated through the dark, labyrinthine tunnels, over wood planks, and under scaffolds to reach the front door of the building.

A security man directed him to the elevator and the Midtown Storage office on the second floor.

The office had the look and feel of a professional operation, very much like a bank vault in an international money center. A buttoned-down guy named Alex, about Ike's age, gave him a brochure and an application form. To lease a box required Ike's signature and a passport or driver's license. Ike called over to the clerk.

"I don't have a license. Will you accept this?" Ike asked and showed him his radio station ID.

Alex frowned. "I'm sorry, sir. Since 9/11 we have strict rules about what is considered identification. We only accept a license or passport."

"I understand," Ike said. "But I hardly look like a terrorist."

Alex ruefully chuckled. "Neither did Mohammed Atta, and you know the outcome there."

Ike had never been in a position to offer a bribe. His grandparents and their friends must have used every means of financial influence they had to get themselves out of impossible situations before and during the war. Certainly Avram wouldn't have shied away from offering diamonds or cash whenever it had been necessary.

Ike signaled Alex to come closer.

"I need to store important items and I want to insure what I have for your limit. What is it?"

"Two million."

Two million? The diamonds alone were worth two hundred million according to Helm. *This isn't good risk-reward,* Ike thought. But in the end, Ike didn't give a flying hook shot from center court about the diamonds and what they were worth. He just wanted a place for safe storage and easy access.

"You get a commission, right?"

"Yes."

"Okay. What if I gave you this?" Ike looked all around the office, then removed the roll from his pocket. He handed it to Alex.

Alex palmed the money. "Sir, I really can't. I could lose my job," he whispered.

"That's over five grand. How long does it take you to make that kind of money from commissions?"

Alex's face communicated moral dilemma. He glanced in all directions, quickly pocketed the cash inside his jacket, and picked up the application. "Do you at least remember a credit card number and expiration date?" Alex asked.

Ike did, and Alex entered his Master Card information into the form.

"References. I need two," Alex said.

He gave him Tony and Hank's phone numbers.

"Good. Let me get you a key, and I'll take you to the vault." Alex stepped into a back office. After about a minute, Ike began to worry that Alex was having a fit of conscience. He thought about bolting. But just as his anxiety approached the border of panic, the clerk returned.

"Here's your key. Just a verbal follow-up to what you've signed. You have rented the box for thirty days. Each day after, if you don't renew your subscription, you will be fined fifty dollars. If the box is unclaimed after six months we have the right to open it only after a faithful attempt is made to contact you or your references. The content of the box is insured for two million dollars. But I can assure you it is as safe, if not safer, than a vault at the Federal Reserve Bank. Our reputation is on the line, and we only have satisfied customers."

Ike followed Alex into the vault. The clerk removed the empty box and handed it to Ike. He entered a private room similar to the one in the Zurich International Bank minus the cheesy painting of a hiker. Instead, a glossy color photo of the Knicks' Walt "Clyde" Frazier stealing the ball from Jerry West in the 1970 NBA finals hung near a window. Ike took that as a good omen. He put one sack of diamonds in his jacket pocket, stuffed the satchel into the storage locker. He patted everything down—the sack of gems, the envelope of cash, and the gun. He locked the storage door and walked out from the vault.

He thanked Alex and left Midtown Storage for the offices of Madison Square Garden.

CHAPTER TWENTY-SEVEN

CRITICAL CONDITION

Helm and his bodyguard sat in the main office of the abandoned hospital. It was Bremer's hangout, a workspace that had devolved into a clutterer's paradise or nightmare depending on one's point of view, with vodka bottles, newspapers, magazines, and office papers strewn everywhere. Tarek had cleared the desk. Bremer had rigged a satellite device to the TV. When Helm was tired and stressed he enjoyed the international news programs from al-Jazeera and CNN.

Cone hadn't returned Tarek's calls. Either he was betraying him, or he was another miserable incompetent. If Cone had been in the Gestapo, they'd have sent him to Dachau for this kind of behavior. It was hard enough to trust him just for the fact that he was a Jew. It would have once been inconceivable that Helm would do business with a Jew. But one thing he'd learned in a world with so many upside-down alliances was that anything was possible, and in the end wealth trumped religion, race, and ideology. Helm had to remind himself that without Cone he would not have had a chance to enter the U.S. Tarek, through his connections in the Brotherhood and other fundamentalist organizations, had vetted the agent and pronounced him reliable because, like all Jews, money was what mattered most and Cone, who'd have to live on a modest government retirement, had been looking for the big score to make his golden years not only golden, but diamond studded as well.

Time was running out. At ninety-three, Helm's aged body needed many medications for his joints, his heart, and even a cancer of the blood that doctors had reassured him would progress slowly. He knew he would die soon. How much longer could he live under the best of circumstance? To think he had survived all these years when Mengele and Eichmann and the higher-ups were all long since dead. It made time even more precious. With his fortune intact he would live the rest of his short life in luxury, then die a natural death in his Egyptian villa with all debts paid.

Helm checked his watch again and his cell phone. He picked up the remote control and found CNN. The anchor was reporting news about a terrorist attack in Yemen. The reporter said that more than fifty Muslims were killed in a suicide bombing. *Terror*, thought Helm, *is a necessary and useful political tool, the loss of life a terrible collateral of war, and in the end it is the fault of the Jews, the Zionist occupiers.*

The door opened. His daughter entered. Tarek rose to usher her in. Helm gestured grandly that Maria should sit in the chair next to him at the desk. Tarek shut the door and stood against it with his arms folded against his chest. "Since I have arrived," Helm began. "I'm afraid that none of our discussions have revealed honesty on your part."

"But father—"

"I want no if, ands, or buts. What I want is that you answer this question. Do you realize how much jeopardy you have put us in?" He pointed to himself and Tarek.

"Father," she said, her voice strident with anxiety. "We thought you had died. We were trying—"

"Yes, yes, trying to steal my valuables. You have murdered a number of Jews. I do not care about them. What I am worried about is how these killings could harm us. I want to hear the details."

"I always thought you'd be concerned for my welfare. I'm getting old too and have nothing to fall back on in my old age."

"Details. I asked for details!" Helm shouted and banged his fist on the desk.

"We have more details now. The CNN anchor adopted a somber tone. *"We'll be showing the bank security tape in slow motion. Please use discretion upon viewing, as you will see scenes of terrible violence. The men you are watching now are FBI agent Simon Cone, the man in the suit, and popular radio psychologist, Dr Ike Miller–known to his listeners as Dr. Ike— wearing a baseball cap and a denim jacket. As you can see, Miller drops to the floor. The security guard approaches. Miller removes a gun from his jacket, pushes the security guard down and points the handgun, identified as a forty-four-caliber revolver, at Agent Cone. Some words are exchanged between Cone and Miller. Cone appears to be attempting to retrieve something*

from inside of his coat, but before he is able Miller shoots the agent twice in rapid succession.

At first the words lurked outside the old man's consciousness like an annoying fly buzzing near his ear. But as the impact of the anchorman's words traveled into his body and up through the nerve endings of his spine to his brain, he turned to the TV. Maria whose back was to the screen, looked over her shoulder, then faced the TV. Tarek moved away from the door and walked closer. *Agent Cone was taken to a local hospital, where he is listed in critical condition. Dr. Miller's whereabouts are unknown. We will update you as new information becomes available."*

Helm pointed the remote and clicked off the television. Stunned, he stared at the dark screen. Tarek shook his head. Maria's ruddy complexion grew even redder.

"This is all because of your meddling and your greed!" Helm shouted at Maria. "Where is your son?"

"I don't know," she said, and began to sob.

"Stop your display of emotions. I will not have it. We must stay strong to complete the task. Tarek, can you answer?"

"Yes, Dr. Helm. Franz Paul is in the Laundry building. He is watching over the woman."

"Yes, yes, the Jew lover. Call him now, and tell him to bring her here at once. We need to have a serious chat."

CHAPTER TWENTY-EIGHT

JAMAL

Ike felt as if he were on defense, compelled to pen-
etrate triple screens formed by rush hour humanity
that blocked his way in every direction along Seventh
Avenue. Strong gusts blew blasts of winter through and
across the street. Commuters rushed for cabs and were
pushed off balance as they adjusted their coats to brace
against the turbulence. A woman struggled to maneuver
a baby carriage a few yards away. The sharp cry of her
child cut through the other noise. Crossing the wide
avenue, Ike dodged the congestion of taxis, tourist and
city buses, passenger cars, and delivery boys on bikes,
one going against the traffic. A gaggle of nuns, in a half
jog, nearly crashed into him as they tried to beat the
light. Ike lifted the collar of his jacket and pulled the
bill of his hat lower and tighter on his head. Despite

the grayness of the day he made sure to keep his shades securely on.

Ike had looked up Jamal's office in a web listing but the Garden web page— for security reasons, Ike presumed—gave nothing specific about departments and office locations. All he learned was that headquarters were at 2 Pennsylvania Plaza. He found his way to the MSG corporate building and asked a uniformed man at the reception desk for Jamal's office.

"Who should I say is here?" the guard asked.

"Tell him Ike."

"That's it. Just Ike. You don't have a last name?" the guard asked.

"Just say Ike. He'll know."

The security guard picked up his phone and relayed the message. "Mr. Jamison says to wait here. He'll be down in a few minutes."

Ike wondered why he wasn't asked to go up. He began to worry it had something to do with his face being broadcast throughout the world, and that Jamal already knew what had happened. Ike scanned the area around him. There were no television monitors in the lobby. A streaming billboard announced upcoming events. The Knicks were playing a preseason game against the Nets tonight. Steely Dan was in concert at the Beacon Theater. He felt a dull pain of sadness. *If things were normal I'd take Aja to hear Donald Fagen sing her song.* He lost himself in the fantasy of a real date with dinner before the show, a long hand-holding walk afterward, and lovemaking in his apartment—the pre-murder apartment, of course. Just as he started to feel the cruel heaviness of his here-and-now, a voice called out from behind him.

"What are you doing here?" Jamal asked him.

Ike turned, startled by the harshness of Jamal's tone.

"I know I invited you to give me a visit. But not after what you just did."

Ike approached, keeping his voice low. "I'm not going to hurt you. I came here because I was hoping you could help me."

Jamal flashed a look of disgust. "You've got to be kidding. What help do you think I could possibly offer you? You killed a federal officer and it's all over the tube. The only help I'd give is to tell you to give yourself up."

"I know this looks real bad. But you know the kind of guy I am—"

"You think I know you after all these years, and a couple of meetings on a basketball court? Are you nuts or something?" Jamal asked.

"I need you to hear me out, that's all," Ike said.

"I'm not sure I should be alone with you, let alone talking with you now," Jamal said.

"Then why'd you come down? You could have told the security guard over there to call the police or just to say you weren't available. So why—"

"Curiosity, maybe, and…I don't know for sure."

"Curiosity. Good. At least give me the opportunity to tell you what this is about and to listen to a proposal."

"I don't know" Jamal paused, as if a thought intruded. "No. You need to leave."

Ike approached him. "Please. You're my last hope," he said, close to tears.

Jamal looked away, shook his head, and then eyed Ike. "Okay. What's your story?" Jamal asked.

"We need to go somewhere private so I can tell you," Ike said.

Jamal's look turned into a stare. "I hope I'm not going to regret this. Follow me."

They rode the elevator up to the fourth floor, and walked down a corridor lined with administrative offices. Jamal led the way to a door with "Jamal Jamison, Director, Community Relations" posted on it. They entered into an open space with a secretary seated at a desk. Jamal told her to hold his calls and led Ike into his private office. He pointed to a chair alongside a desk, pivoted around it, and settled into his own seat. Ike's playground teammate stared at him with a face that could only be described as severe.

"You're in a load of trouble. Do you know how bad this is?" Jamal said.

"Yeah," Ike said, looking away. "I know I'm fucked. In ways you can't possibly imagine."

"Shooting a federal officer isn't enough?" Jamal asked.

"That's bad," Ike said, shaking his head. "But the bigger story is much worse." He paused to catch his breath. He removed his sunglasses.

"Your eye still looks messed up—" Jamal said, looking at Ike's shiner.

"When you asked me about it at the playground I didn't know the whole story. Now I do and I need you to listen to it."

Jamal shook his head. "Okay, you've got five minutes, and then I'll do the judging whether you stay or not."

"I need more. Give me twenty minutes. If you won't help me after that then you can call the cops or just let me go and that'll be that. If you think what I have to say is credible, and you agree to help me, then there really is something in it for you. And it's big."

"You're not in a position to negotiate, man. Five minutes—"

"Please, Jamal." The tears were closer this time. But Ike choked them back. "Okay, if what I say in five minutes doesn't have your attention, I'll stop."

Even though Jamal looked wary, Ike saw an opening. He knew his time-limited pitch had better be a good one. He started with Otto, because Jamal knew about the murder, and gave him the whole story from Frankie's attack to Aja to Cone to Helm and his family. Ike could tell that he'd piqued not only Jamal's interest, but also his sympathy. Five minutes morphed into ten and ten into the original request of twenty. When Ike told him about the discovery of diamonds in the safe-deposit box and that he'd make a substantial donation of the gems to the Devils if Jamal agreed to help, Jamal's attention was as rapt as if his old friend was on "D" in the last minute of a tight game. After Ike finished his story, they sat silently.

Ike studied Jamal's face. He seemed to be engaging in serious mental calculations, hand across his mouth, head back, and eyes moving side-to-side.

"I know I must be crazy to even ask this," Jamal finally said. "But what is it you want from me?"

"You have skills I don't have. You're an expert with a rifle, a sniper, and as a marine I figure you may have been trained in rescue missions. I want your help finding

Aja and getting her out. Then I want the people who killed Otto—the Nazi doctor and his family—brought to justice."

Jamal shook his head. "Why don't you just call the police, the feds? Tell them what you just told me."

"Right. After I shot one of their guys. Don't think that'll work. There's so much money involved, who knows who's straight and who's crooked? And besides, it's past all of that now."

"Speaking of money, you said something about diamonds—a donation to the team," Jamal said.

"Yeah. I did and I mean it. You want to see them?"

"You brought them with you?"

Ike nodded. He reached inside his jacket, pulled out the felt sack, and placed it on the desk.

At first Jamal just stared at the package in front of him. He shook his head. "No, Ike. Sorry. I can't put my life in jeopardy again. Two tours in Iraq were enough. Not to mention I have my boys—my team."

"I hear you, I really do," Ike said nodding his head. "But there's one extra piece of information you need to know."

"What's that?"

"Aja's a marine. She served in Iraq as an MP." Ike paused to let that sink in. "She's also an all-American hoopster from UConn."

Jamal leaned back in his seat. He laughed his deep "ha-ha." It was like he was taking pleasure in the dilemma that Ike had presented him. He sat quietly for a moment. He rocked backed and forth, then bent forward. "I don't give a damn about her basketball *bona fides*. But marines don't abandon marines. That's the code. We have to get her out, Ike. There's no two ways about that."

"Thanks," Ike said and paused. "And the diamonds, you want to see them?"

"Damn straight I do."

Ike poured a few onto the table. He picked one up and handed it to Jamal, who raised it to the light, then scratched it across the glass top of his desk. He held it up to the light again.

"Goddammit, this is real!" he declared. He sat back in his chair and made eye contact with Ike. "It's real! We'll be the best dressed damn team in the league."

"With the best of everything to help the boys and other kids too."

Jamal started to get up, but sat back down. "The fed killed your granddaddy?"

"He was in on it," Ike said.

"And the Nazi twisted your bad knee and cut you?" Jamal's seemed to feel Ike's pain.

"He twisted my knee more than once, but he didn't get to cut me because of Cone's fake rescue. It was a confidence game. Scare the shit out of me first. Then rescue me and gain my confidence, get me to show him the stones, and then he was going to kill me. But, yeah, my knee's a little sore. I've played with worse."

"That's good to know," Jamal said. "Because I think you're going to need your legs for what's coming next."

Ike nodded solemnly.

Jamal had an important meeting that was going to take the first quarter of the game. Ike found a dark corner near the exit behind the end court as the Knicks and

Nets went through their pre-season paces. The crowd made a low-level buzz as if they were half paying attention to a particularly boring sermon. Ike looked at his watch. His stomach cramped with anxiety.

An acrobatic dunk by one of the Knicks rookies woke up the crowd, and they responded with a communal blast of cheers. Ike felt the urge to check in with Tony. It had been a close call for his friend, something he'd never tell him. Nevertheless, with Helm still on the loose, he just wanted to make sure his bearded wonder was safe.

Ike waited for the noise to calm down. He rang up his producer.

"Ike, it's you, thank God. Are you okay?"

"Yeah. How about you?"

"Man, I can't believe you shot Cone," Tony said. "Some FBI guys were here with Hank earlier. He said you were supposed to meet him at Mike's."

"Yeah. But Cone got to me before I got to Hank. Anyway, you know the rest of the story."

Tony fell silent. Ike's guard went up. Maybe Hank was listening, or the Feds had put a bug on the line. "I don't think it's a good idea talking about this now. It's not why I called," Ike said.

"Where are you?"

"Can't tell you," Ike said. But at that moment the crowd's roar and the PA announcer's voice told Tony where Ike was. Ike wondered if he'd made a mistake by calling the station.

"You sure you're okay?" Tony asked.

Ike wanted to thank Tony for helping him when he had no one else. But what if someone was listening? His gesture of gratitude could incriminate his friend. "Yeah, I'm okay."

"That's good," Tony said. "The callers really care, Ike. They're asking if we know where you are. Everyone's worried, afraid for you."

Ike felt a chill. "Look, I have to go."

Ike and Jamal hopped a cab to a car rental office. Jamal used his license and credit card to secure an SUV with a GPS system. Their first stop was his apartment building in Astoria, Queens. Ike waited in the car while Jamal gathered weapons and supplies that would be "appropriate for the operation." When Jamal used the word "operation," Ike jumped like a combat soldier might upon hearing a car backfire. The trauma response was likely as permanent to his psyche as Frankie's broken swastika tattoo was to his hand. Ike figured using the word "operation" was Jamal's way of psyching himself up for combat. That raised the scary and all-too-real proposition that there'd be more killings.

Jamal came out dressed in desert camouflage fatigues and carrying a large duffel bag. He gestured to Ike to get out and follow him to the cargo door.

"Let me show you what I've got in here," Jamal said, as he pressed the hatch button. He placed the duffel in the back and unzipped it. "One fifty caliber Barrett sniper rifle with a target scope, my M-16, and two semi-automatic service revolvers—one for me and one for you—and plenty of ammo clips."

"I've got the gun I used in the bank, and it's loaded."

"You had it on you the whole time?"

"Yeah."

"Okay, look, its okay to use that old thing. But these weapons are easier to fire and load. So keep this with you." Jamal handed him one of the semi-automatics.

"What else you got in there?" Ike gestured to the canvas bag.

"Flashlights, knives, duct tape, gloves, night vision goggles and some other crap I didn't have the time to rummage through," Jamal said as he zipped up the duffel. "You ready?"

Ike exhaled hard and nodded.

"Okay, then, let's get going."

Ike programmed the GPS while Jamal drove.

"Turn right," was the first direction they heard from the calm female voice of the GPS as they made their way out of Queens for the Metro State Psychiatric Center.

CHAPTER TWENTY-NINE

A TERRIBLE PROBLEM

He could barely contain his rage. But despite the shock and humiliation that he initially felt now that his fortune was taken from him a second time and by the grandson of the original perpetrator, he had to—like the chess master he once was— maintain his composure and think about the moves to come.

"I have a safe haven," Tarek said, removing his cell phone from his shirt pocket as if he were about to organize arrangements.

"No." Helm shook his head vigorously.

"But how can we stay? When the FBI takes him into custody he will tell them about us and about this place."

"Perhaps," Helm said as he rose from behind Bremer's desk. "But you said, 'when they take him into custody.' That will not happen. He is free, and his next move will be to come here for the woman."

"In matters such as this you have always relied on my advice. And I advise—"

"I do not need your advice. You are my bodyguard and my subordinate. It is an order. We will stay here. He will come and he will demand a hostage exchange: the federal agent for the jewels. I will not leave this place until I retrieve what is mine."

Tarek nodded and stepped back.

Helm looked at his wristwatch. "Where is Franz Paul?"

"He should have arrived with her by now," Tarek said.

"Yes. Call him again."

Tarek punched the number into his phone and waited. "I have his voice mail."

For the moment Helm was lost in thought. "I do not like this. Go check on him."

A concrete path of more than a hundred yards led from the main building to the Laundry. The FBI agent was a formidable opponent. The pain from Tarek's broken nose and the scratches and bruises on his body attested to that. Franz Paul was tough and vicious and very strong. But he didn't have Aja Connolly's military fighting skills.

The night temperature was dropping rapidly. He removed the AK-47 from his shoulder, and made sure the magazine was loaded and set for firing. He entered the building, turned on his flashlight, and headed down a flight of stairs to the receiving area, and to the abandoned office that served as Aja's prison. At the entrance, he stopped to listen. It was quiet. Tarek shielded himself against the wall and kicked in the door. He darted inside, rifle raised, and scanned the room. In the far right-hand corner was a crumpled form. He stepped toward it and turned it over.

Tarek shook his head and pulled out his cell phone.

"We have a terrible problem. Have Fisher and Bremer join you and make sure both you and your daughter are armed. I will be there in less than two minutes."

CHAPTER THIRTY

BROKEN TOMBSTONES

After an hour on the Long Island Expressway followed by a short drive through a residential area, Jamal and Ike came to a swath of blackness with woods on both sides of the road. Jamal snapped on the SUV's high beams, then turned the headlights off as they crept closer to the center of the campus. The silhouette of the main hospital building loomed in the dark like a mountain range over a valley.

Jamal drove north of the main building, stopped in a spot sheltered by a line of trees, and turned off the car's engine. He got out of the vehicle first. Ike followed. The afternoon winds he'd fought through near the Garden had turned into a nor'easter with bitter gusts blowing in from Long Island Sound. The white vapor of their exhaled breaths billowed into the space between them.

Racing clouds alternately hid and revealed a moon sliver high above the main building.

"Before we do anything, Ike Miller, we're going to do what my team always does before a game, and what me and my buddies did when we went into combat. We're going to pray." They locked arms and bowed their heads.

Ike prayed he'd find Aja in one piece and asked for strength to face whatever came his way.

Jamal pulled Ike into a hug.

"Jamal, I'm really grateful for this. I want you to know just in case—"

"No doubts. Visualize a successful shot, like I tell my boys. Then if you need to thank me, you do it when we've executed the op and all is well. You know what I'm saying?"

"Yeah."

"You said you know where they're keeping her," Jamal said.

"I think so. When Cone told me she was dead, he said they found her in the Laundry building, and I re-member it from a graduate school field trip. You see that crumbling bubble that looks like an old indoor ten-nis court?" Ike pointed. "That's it. That's the Laundry."

"All right then. Let's go," Jamal said.

They hooked around the building through a rocky field hoping to come upon a back entrance. The only light was from the flashlights they held low. The only sound came from the wind that whipped at them in increas-ingly more powerful waves. After about fifty yards, Ike tripped over what felt like a large stone. He tried to prevent his fall with his hands and landed on his side. His hip crashed into something hard.

"Ah, shit."

"You okay?" Jamal asked.

"Yeah, just give me a sec to catch my breath," he said and rubbed at the bruise.

Jamal pointed his flashlight to Ike's spot on the ground and then in a circle around him. "You'll never guess where we are," he said.

"Where?"

"Turn around."

Ike twisted his torso in the direction of the beam. Rows of tombstones–some broken and fallen over, receded in the flashlight's beam. "A cemetery," Ike said. "Fitting, isn't it?"

"Let's get out of here," Jamal said. "I'll feel a lot more comfortable if we get our behinds moving. You catch your breath yet?"

"Yeah."

Jamal pulled Ike to his feet. They moved carefully through the field of stones and wood crosses and found a concrete walkway and a brick structure with an iron grate on one wall.

Ike stopped to examine it.

"What you got there?" Jamal asked.

"Looks like a furnace," Ike said. He pointed at embers aglow in the gray ash. "And someone's burned something in here very recently."

Jamal joined him and placed his flashlight on Ike's discovery. "Probably an incinerator."

Ike stepped away from the furnace, and shook his head. "What if..."

"What if what?" Jamal asked.

Ike's body went cold. Frightening scenarios too horrible to name raced through his mind. "I couldn't help but think about Avram and the job he had in Auschwitz," Ike said.

"He was in a crematorium, Ike. This is just some old trash furnace," Jamal said."

Ike was in a panic. Like the proverbial chicken without a head, he began a mindless search for a tree branch, a stick, a metal pole—anything that could help him poke around what was inside the furnace.

"What are you doing?" Jamal asked.

"What if—"

Jamal caught up to his friend and grabbed his arm. "You're letting your imagination run wild."

"They're Nazi murderers. I wouldn't put anything past them," Ike said.

Jamal got into Ike's face. "Listen to me. Didn't you tell me she was too valuable to them? That killing Aja would destroy any chance of getting their loot?"

Ike nodded.

"Okay. Then this is only what it is. Let's not jump to conclusions. We're going to find out what really happened soon enough, right?"

"Okay. You're right. Let's get out of here," Ike said.

"Good."

They walked down the ramp into an underground garage. Dumpsters and hazardous material vehicles waited near an entrance. They walked through, into a hallway with three doors on each side. Ike checked the right. Jamal checked the left. Except for mice and cockroaches, they found no signs of life. They turned a corner to another hallway and came upon a single door halfway down the corridor.

"Someone's been here," Jamal said.

"How do you know?"

"I learned to sniff these things out in Iraq. Smells of body odor."

"I don't smell it."

"I've had lots of experience."

Ike nodded.

"Hug the walls," Jamal said.

They slid against a wood railing to a partially opened door. Ike remembered Greg and Sarah's bodies behind Otto's door. Sweat slicked his palms.

Jamal placed his index finger to his lips. "Take it real slow. I'll lead," he whispered. He raised his sniper rifle. Ike held the flashlight and they entered. They carefully scanned the room. A crumpled shape darkened one corner of the floor.

"What do we have over there?" Jamal asked.

Ike stopped and shook his head. "I'm afraid it's her."

"Calm down. We can't know that from here. Remember, they don't want her dead."

They crossed to the corner, and Jamal used his rifle to roll the body over.

"I can't believe it," Ike said.

"What?"

"This time Frankie's really dead."

"One down," Jamal said. "Don't see any gunshot wounds." He crouched to get a closer look. "His neck's broken. Someone knows how to kill with their hands."

Ike thought, *Could Aja have done this?* His second thought was, *Why not?* She of the quick, strong hands that blocked his shot, a trained marine and a federal agent. "I think Aja did it."

Jamal chuckled. "You got one hell of a gal there."

"Let's check the main building. That's where they kept me, in a basement. It's also where the surgical theater is," Ike said.

Outside, they hugged the brick walls and came upon a line of windows above a concrete ledge at one side of the building.

Ike remembered his so-called escape with Cone, and compared their path to the buildings around him. "Let's go in through here. I think it's shorter," he said.

Sounds. Leaves rustling. Twigs breaking.

They froze and pressed their backs against the wall. Jamal pointed to his ears. The rustling sound was getting closer. Whoever was coming their way didn't seem concerned about concealment. Ike pulled out the pistol Jamal had given him, held it close to his chest, and waited.

"Turn your flashlight on," Jamal whispered. He pointed to Ike's left.

Ike pointed the beam down and moved it in a line. There, beneath the ledge, was a large raccoon. The animal looked at Jamal, then Ike, and then toward the corner of the building. Ike followed with his flashlight to a nest of baby raccoons. It looked like mom was just making sure nothing would disturb her cubs.

Relieved, Ike put the gun back into his jacket. Jamal pushed one window up just enough to get through. He sat on the ledge with his back against the window, then turned his hips and slid his legs beneath the partially opened casement. He squirreled his body underneath, pushed off, and disappeared inside. Ike mimicked Jamal's movements and followed. He landed on his feet, jarring his knee. He rubbed it and dropped into a crouch, scanning the area with his flashlight. It was an empty square room that might not have seen human life for decades. Jamal signaled Ike forward. They advanced to the door. Ike opened it slowly, and Jamal shone his light into the corridor. Ike felt like he was standing in a vacuum-packed container. The absence of sound and circulating air triggered feelings of suffocation. His skin went clammy and cold. *No time for a panic attack,* he told himself. *Breathe.*

Jamal looked over at him. "Focused and positive," he whispered.

"Let's move," Ike said. Movement helped. It always did.

They continued on.

They followed the corridor, checked rooms on each side of a passageway that was curved like a gym track. But after nearly completing the circle, they hadn't found the cell Ike had woke up in. Two doors remained. Jamal opened the one on the right. Ike snapped on his flashlight. Concrete steps led down. "This is it. They tied me to that chair."

Jamal found the light switch and flipped it. The fluorescent fixtures buzzed and glowed a muted yellow.

A table stood in the corner. Ike pointed to the shoes under the table.

"What is it?"

"It's her sneakers and socks," Ike said.

Streaks of blood ran across the tops and sides of the shoes. It was the pair Aja had worn on the playground.

"They've taken her to the surgical theater," Ike said.

"How do you know that?"

"Trust me on this. It's what he does."

"Where is it?" Jamal said.

"It's got to be the next one."

In the hallway, Jamal signaled Ike to be careful and quiet. Light spilled through the center crack of the double doors.

"They're in there," Jamal said.

"How we doing this?" Ike asked.

Jamal hesitated. "Not this way. We'd be too exposed, too vulnerable." He paused again. "This is an amphitheater, right?"

Ike nodded.

"Okay, we need to find where the audience comes in up top," Jamal said.

"Let's go."

They found it on the second floor. A brass plate announced, "Doctors and Interns only." A graffiti vandal had defaced the sign, and "Fuckors and Retards" had become their new designations.

"Some kind of payback, huh?" Jamal wondered.

"Probably for good reason," Ike said.

"All right, let's have a peek." Jamal said. He inched the door open. "It's dark up here. Good."

Jamal opened the door just enough to slide through. Ike followed. They crawled their way to the back of the last row and leaned their shoulders against the seats. Aja lay on the operating table. Helm's crew had restrained her with the same wide rubber straps they'd used to secure Ike.

"I'm not sorry for what I did, you piece of shit!" she yelled, then spit in Helm's face.

"Now, now, that is not the way a lady is supposed to act." He moved behind her and stroked her hair. Ike cringed.

A lean, muscular man came into view in the spaces between the seats. He approached Aja, closed his fist and punched her in the face.

"You see," Helm said, continuing to fondle her hair. "You will have to tolerate a great deal of pain. What Tarek just gave you is a love tap compared to what I will do to you."

Maria approached the table. "Thank you, Father."

"It is justice. She killed my grandson and your only child. We will avenge him by doing away with her in a manner historically fitting for this marvelous medical facility."

Historically fitting? A chill ran though Ike's body.

Jamal got his attention. "Listen to me." He spoke low to avoid the echoing acoustics in the amphitheatre. "I've got it figured out what to do. Get yourself down there, slow and careful. You'll have darkness to about the third row. Don't worry. I've got you covered. Once you're there, all hell is going to break loose. But what-ever happens, don't leave that spot."

"Why?"

"I don't want you getting captured or shot. You got it?"

Ike nodded.

"Good. Besides, one of them may try to make a run for it up the stairs, because I'm not going to let them get out the door down there." He raised his rifle. "I want you to be ready to stop them."

"Okay," Ike said.

"Ike, I mean it. Don't try to be a hero."

"All right." It burned, even though he knew Jamal was right.

"Go."

Ike cautiously maneuvered down the auditorium. Somewhere in the middle of his descent, he flashed to the cheering crowd again: *IKIE! IKIE! IKIE!* For a moment the surgical theater was a basketball arena, and every seat was filled with adoring fans exhorting him to make the big play.

IKIE! IKIE! IKIE!

He came to the third row and squatted behind the aisle seat. He looked back at Jamal, only to see a small red dot in the darkness. On the surgical stage the man whose face he'd ironed rolled a wheeled cart toward the operating table and next to Aja's head.

"Thank you, Fisher. You see, my dear, humane ECT, or electro-convulsive therapy, is practiced with sedatives and anesthesia. To guard against tongue biting, or the horrific possibility of swallowing one's tongue a rubber guard is placed in the patient's mouth. We will do none of those things because I want you to feel every excruciating sensation. You will suffer convulsions, and with nothing to protect your mouth, you might just swallow your tongue. Choking is a horrible death. A fitting penalty for what you have done to my grandson."

Fisher handed him two sets of wires.

"I will place the electrodes on your temples. It won't hurt a bit, not yet," Helm said.

"Fuck you," Aja yelled, as she squirmed and struggled against her bindings.

Ike wanted to rush down to her and blast all of them. But Jamal's words restrained him from starring in this game.

Just as Helm put the electrodes to Aja's head, a loud crack reverberated through the amphitheater, then a second one. Aja's restraints, like overstretched rubber bands, snapped and flew across her body. For a moment everything froze. Then Aja blinked her eyes, shook her head, and rolled from the surgical table, taking cover underneath. Helm and his cohorts dropped to the floor. Ike waited, gun raised.

Jamal shouted, "Put the guns down."

Bremer fired wild. The bullet crashed into a seat somewhere between Ike and the last row. Jamal returned fire. Gouts of blood and pieces of Bremer's brain splashed across the operating room floor and walls. As the caretaker's body fell, his revolver dropped from his hand and bounced on the floor much the way the gun had in Ike's basketball dream. Aja belly-crawled to the gun and secured it. She rolled back under the table and turned toward Helm's bodyguard. Ike watched as she steadied her shooting hand to line him up. She fired two shots. Tarek howled and crumbled to his knees. Despite his horrific wounds, he still maintained shaky control of his revolver. He pointed it in Aja's direction. But before he could get off a shot, Jamal's rifle blasts found Tarek's chest and blew him into the next world.

Maria and Fisher ran toward the door, but flattened themselves on the floor after Jamal put a bullet into the wall inches from their heads. Ike jumped up from his hiding spot and rushed the surgical stage.

"Ike!" Aja cried out. "Thank God you're okay."

He touched his heart and turned his hand toward her. He kept his eyes and his gun on Maria and Fisher.

Where was Helm? Hiding in a corner or behind a seat in the darkness, armed and aiming at him?

"Aja, did you see where Helm went?" Ike shouted.

"No." She lowered herself into a crouch and scanned the auditorium for the old Nazi.

The amphitheater doors burst open.

"Federal agents! Put down your weapons." Five men in navy blue windbreakers stormed inside. The agent in the lead looked around then focused on Ike. "I said put it down."

Ike complied.

"Who's Ike Miller?" the agent asked.

"I'm Ike Miller."

"And who are you?" he asked, addressing Aja.

"FBI. Special Agent Aja Connolly."

The agent nodded. "Are the both of you okay?"

"Yes," they said in unison.

"Where's the Nazi?"

"I don't know," Ike said.

Aja shrugged. "We lost track of him."

The lead agent waved his hand to his men. "Look around."

"Jamal, where's Helm?" Ike's shout echoed through the amphitheater.

No answer.

"Jamal, did you track him?" Ike shouted again.

"Who the fuck is Jamal?" the agent yelled.

Ike took off up the stairs.

"Stop!" The Fed headed after him.

Ike's fear for his friend propelled him up the stairs. "Stop!"

But by that time Ike was standing behind the top row of seats. The only sign that someone had been here were four spent shells on the concrete walkway. Jamal must have seen Helm slip away and was headed after him.

Ike ran for the door.

Aja cried out, "Don't. Ike, please!"

It didn't matter. It was time and timing. Time to settle the score, to finish his family's unfinished business. And the timing couldn't be more perfect. He was the one who had to do it. He needed to find Helm before anyone else did.

He ran hard, like on the wing of a fast break, no longer feeling pain or restriction from his knee. He took the corridor to the first exit sign, headed down the stairs and out the front of the hospital. It had gotten colder — not as cold as Auschwitz must have been on the fateful day Avram discovered Helm's loot — but cold enough. He was headed to the left of the main building, toward the woods behind the Laundry. Two men leaned against the rental SUV. They shouted at him, but they were too far away to catch him. He just kept going toward the goal.

At the back of the Laundry lay the shortest path to the thicket of trees that bordered the hospital. Helm was headed there. That had to be his plan. It was his only way out, and once out, he could slip away. The old

Nazi had mastered it a long time ago—the art of slipping away.

Ike ran past the incinerator and into the burial grounds. The wind was howling, and a wintry mix of rain and snow began to knife sideways across the cemetery. Ike switched on his flashlight and looked for a clear lane that would take him to the border of the woods. Ahead of him, less than fifty yards away, Helm stumbled frantically. Ike saw his opportunity to close the distance. Helm turned and took a wild shot that ricocheted off of something to Ike's right.

Ike lowered himself behind a tombstone, than crept along the most direct route to intercept Helm.

Sleet turned into a downpour.

"Drop it and get down on the ground, you son of a bitch." No more than fifteen feet away, Aja, drenched from the rain, mud swallowing her bare feet, pointed her gun at Helm. "Drop the fucking gun and get down."

But Helm kept the gun pointed at her. It was a standoff. Either Helm or Aja, or both, were going to be killed. Ike couldn't let Aja die. And killing Helm on some sloppy desecrated field of the dead may have had some poetry to it, but it wasn't the right way. It wasn't justice. It wasn't the way to settle the score, to finish the lingering pain that his family and all the other families had suffered at the hands of this *dybbuk*, as Grandpa Avram had called him. In a nano-second, Ike's decision turned into reaction. He flung himself toward the old Nazi.

But he was a tick off—time and timing gone awfully wrong.

Airborne in the space between the woman he was in love with and the Nazi who'd tormented his family,

Helm fired twice and the two bullets smashed into Ike's body.

Ike heard Jamal's voice shout from somewhere nearby, "Oh shit!" and Aja's scream.

Ike Miller dropped down into the cold mire of the violated graveyard. He knew he was in trouble as nothing could stop what was rapidly overtaking him. Sound, sight, and sensation left him one by one. And just as his waning consciousness merged into the darkness of the burial ground around him, Ike heard the words of her song again.

This time he didn't get to the ending.

CHAPTER THIRTY-ONE

THE EYES OF TRUTH

One Week Later

In darkness, he felt the vibrations of a steady beat. Professor Keyes, in his white robes and turban asked Ike to play "Name That Tune." Ike listened closely and heard: *Beep...Beep...Beep...Beep.* The song, what was it? *Beep, beep. Beep, beep.* The Playmates' "Beep, Beep," about a little Nash Rambler that outperforms a Cadillac. An automotive David and Goliath tale. Tony looked proud that Ike knew it.

No. It was Antwanne bouncing a basketball next to his bed." *Beep...beep...beep...beep...*

Or was it a heartbeat?

Darkness.

"One-twenty to one-oh-four, Knicks over the Suns, Melo with thirty-two, Amar'e with fourteen," Jamal said, reading the box score from the sports section of the New York *Post*.

"*IKIE! IKIE! IKIE!*" the crowd chanted and roared.

Coach, who looked like Jamal, led them in the huddle. "Here's the play. Antwanne, when you bring up the ball I want you to throw it to Bull who'll be set on the right block. Now, Bull, you get in front of your man, hands ready for Antwanne's pass. Benny–hey boy, you sure are looking real good. How much you lose? Twenty pounds, huh? You're a different young man. Okay, now, Benny your job is to cut off of Bull this way."

Beep…Beep…Beep…Beep

"Bull, you're going to make that bounce pass to him when he cuts to the hoop. Got that?"

Darkness. Stillness. Tumbleweeds rolling across a desecrated burial ground.

"We're sending a shout-out to our dear friend and creator of *Psych 'n' Roll*, Dr. Ike. Buddy, I know you can hear us, cause we put that fine stereo radio by your bed, and Jamal has made sure it's on. So this is for you, Ike Miller. Our theme today is "Recovery:" Ike's recovery, my recovery, and you the callers—your recovery, or that of anyone close to you. If you have a recovery story and want to share it with us, call us at 800-555-5454. Before we take your calls, let's kick off this segment with Van Morrison's, "Start All Over Again," from his album *Enlightenment*. Van will be followed by the Stones' recording of 'Soul Survivor.'"

"I say 'Phil Jackson,' you say…?" Jamal asked.

"Eleven NBA titles," Rabbit said.

"Damn right. And you know what he told Michael and Scottie, Kobe and Shaq, and all the rest of his boys?"

The breeze caused by their shaking heads cooled Ike's face.

"He told them that every game is played one breath at a time. You boys know what that means, don't you? Ike here knows what it means. If you're hearing me, my friend, that's all it takes."

Beep…Beep…Beep…Beep

Why is Tony playing that silly song again? I need to turn that damn thing off and get some rest, Ike thought.

"Jamal, Jamal, look," Junior said. "Ike's opening his eyes. He's trying to move."

Jamal jumped quickly to his friend's bedside. "Thank God. We thought… Antwanne, run to the nurses' desk, and get somebody here."

Antwanne took off, but in his haste dropped the basketball that was in the crook of his arm. Jamal gathered it up. "Go. Get someone here fast."

Ike couldn't speak, but his confused eyes asked the question.

"You're in Mount Sinai Hospital," Jamal said.

Ike nodded. It was followed by another questioning look.

"There's a lot to tell you. We'll talk about it soon. First, let's have the doctors examine you."

Ike was out of his coma, and he was going to be okay. But getting to okay was not going to be as easy as a game of horse. Most of his blood had been replaced.

One bullet had collapsed a lung and another had lacerated his diaphragm. The doctors had intubated him after the surgery to keep him breathing. Rehab, which started a few weeks after the tubes were removed, was a particularly grueling time. None of the challenges he'd ever faced as a basketball player—workouts, weight room, yoga, strategy sessions, working on moves and shots hour after hour–had prepared him for the tough exercises and the almost constant pain, both physical and mental. At first he thought he'd never get through the regimen, but slowly everything came together. His wind improved. The muscles of his arms and legs grew stronger. His knee was free of pain for the first time in years.

The show's crew visited often. The new station announcer, Samantha Bernstein, a petite dark-haired beauty, was particularly thoughtful and attentive. She brought him homemade pie, Danish pastries from a West Side bakery, and loaded a half dozen mysteries and the New York *Times* onto a Kindle. Once he could think straight, he read everything as voraciously as he inhaled Samantha's goodies.

The *Times*, in a series entitled, "The Last of the Sadistic Nazi Doctors," kept Ike abreast of the ongoing investigation against Helm and his ties to the Muslim Brotherhood. Of particular interest was Cone's story. Cone had survived the shooting and was in a high-security lockup awaiting trial.

Hank came every day. He felt terrible, responsible for not having protected Ike despite the fact he'd called the FBI after listening to Ike's call to Tony from the Garden. An assistant US attorney general occasionally accompanied Hank along with the station's attorney. They briefed Ike about the case against Helm, who was locked-up in solitary confinement, and began to prepare him for his future testimony. A Justice Department decision was pending on whether Helm would be tried in the States for multiple murders or if extradited for war crimes. The news of his arrest had ignited a storm of competing interests. The Israelis wanted him, so did The Hague, and so did Germany. Ike couldn't care less who meted out justice, just that someone would.

Helm's daughter, Maria Jordan, and James "Fisher" Morgan, the guy whose face Ike had ironed, were the only survivors of the crew that had frightened poor Baruch Gittlestein to death, murdered Hymie Safier and his girlfriend, Stephanie, Feldstein and Yossi, Greg and Sarah, and Otto. They were also awaiting trial for multiple counts of conspiracy and first-degree murder.

"Good morning everyone. Welcome to a special edition of *Psych 'n' Roll*, coming to you from the Big Apple on WNYT," Samantha spoke into her announcer's microphone. "Our theme today is 'Never Again,' and we begin with a warm welcome back to the airways to our show's creator and host, Dr. Ike Miller."

Ike had shed thirty pounds during the month he'd spent in the hospital and the three in a rehab facility. It was the least he'd weighed since high school, and his thinness made him look and feel vulnerable and unsure. Was he ready to get back on the horse?

Now he obsessed over his intro—so absorbed in trying to get it perfect that he hadn't noticed the station crew had gathered for a group hug and ovation, as Tony cut his mike and the show's theme song began to play.

"Take in the love, Ikie boy. Take it in and enjoy," Tony said, coming from the production booth to join them.

And he tried.

Ike tried to feel his friends' support after Otto's death, and after Aja's disappearance that night in the graveyard after the ambulance drove away with Ike in it. He rationalized that she likely had to go undercover again, but it didn't make him feel less abandoned or angry. But ultimately his ruling emotion was deep sadness. Her vanishing act had made it difficult for him to feel everyone else's love during the last four months.

"Rollover Siggie Freud Gonna Tell Dr. ke the News" went into its outro, the crew left the broadcast stage, and Tony retreated to his position on the opposite side of the glass partition. He got Ike's attention, held up his hand, and counted down. "You're on, my man."

Ike placed his trembling lips close to the microphone and spoke: "I want to thank everyone for staying with *Psych 'n' Roll.* Tony's been terrific in my absence and I'm forever indebted to him. Also, I'm deeply touched by your cards, emails, and get well gifts. It made bearable what was a difficult rehab and recovery.

"We're going to kick off our program with a recording from the New Age rock group, Enigma. Enigma performs with deep emotions and their songs are about important subjects. You'll enjoy their other-worldly, evocative sound." Ike cued Tony to play the song.

"You okay buddy?" Tony said into Ike's earpiece.

"Yeah, a little shaky. But at least I'm getting on the bike again. There was a time I didn't think I'd make it. Even today when I got out of bed, I wondered if could really do this thing again. But I'm here, and ready or not, here I go."

"I'll get you through. But if you need to go home, don't worry about it. I got pretty good at this."

"I know. For a while there, I worried I'd be out of a job," Ike said, smiling.

"No way that's ever going to happen," Tony said and winked at him.

As much as Ike tried not to he couldn't stop thinking about Aja. Did she long for him as well? What did she feel, really? The complete blackout, without a note, an email, or even a word passed along to him from an FBI official, put Ike in a universe of sadness and loss. His heart hurt as much as his aching body.

"Damn her," he blurted out.

"Still haven't heard anything, huh?" Tony said.

"Let's get to the callers. Talking about her gives me a headache."

The Enigma recording was in its fade.

"Okay. Watch me now. Three, two, one, you're on." Tony pointed.

"That was "The Eyes of Truth," by Enigma," Ike said. "I want everyone out there to remember "The Eyes of Truth." Here's why I chose that recording to open up today's show:

"In my family the eyes of truth were closed. God knows my folks' denial, avoidance, whatever, were for the purpose of protecting me. I've come to understand that their philosophy wasn't 'Eyes of Truth' and 'Never

Again,' but more like 'who the hell wants to remember this' and 'let's not burden our innocent child.' For a time during my recent ordeal, I was angry about their omissions. But I came to realize that they did the best they could do and that I needed to take responsibility for my own knowledge and my own preparedness in life. I've resolved to have my eyes of truth wide open, and with what I've seen, to say 'Never Again.'

"For those of you who don't know the backstory, my grandfather, Avram Miller, discovered a cache of jewels at the end of World War II. Those gems were the reason for the trouble I recently found myself in. They were stolen or extorted from Jewish families and Jewish businessmen by the war criminal Antonin Helm. My grandfather happened upon this treasure as he was escaping Auschwitz. Jewish agencies I've consulted say there's no possible way to locate the rightful owners. With no legitimate claim, they remain in my possession. Because the treasure is tainted by war, murder, and torture, I don't want any part of it for myself. So I'm announcing today that that I've formed a foundation, The Miller-Sperber Eyes of Truth Trust Fund. A percentage of the trust will be used for families of Holocaust survivors, to help survivors and their children and grandchildren cope with psychological trauma. Some will go to help disadvantaged youngsters through sports and education. It's my way of saying "never again!"

"Okay, enough about me. Let's hear what your eyes of truth tell you. What do you see that guides you to say never again? That's the topic. To give you some time to reflect on the question, Tony will play the rap recording, "Never Again" by Remedy, a member of the

Wu-Tang Killa Bees. You'll be listening to lyrics that pull no punches."

Tony sent "Never Again" into the broadcast ether.

Ike leaned back in his chair and noticed his partner was on the phone.

"A call on your personal line," Tony said into Ike's headset.

"Who is it?"

"Don't know. You want to take it or should I get the number?"

"Male or female?"

"It's not your missing girlfriend," Tony said.

"Thanks for not saying her name. Let me see who it is."

Ike removed the studio phone from its cradle. "Hello. Who's this?"

No answer.

"Hello," he repeated.

Tinny, echoing silence.

"Aja, if it's you, it's okay. We can talk. I mean, I want to talk with you," Ike said. A dial tone followed. His mind flew into that reverberating emptiness and emerged with the old question he'd grappled with during his ordeal: instinct or paranoia? But that was for later. He had a show to do.

"You okay?" Tony asked, a concerned look on his face.

"Yeah. Just a prankster, I guess," Ike said.

"Really?"

"Really. At first I thought it was something. But... no."

"Okay. You ready for the first caller?" Tony asked.

Ike nodded.

"You're on."

"We have Steve on the line from Biloxi, Mississippi," Ike said. "Steve, your eyes of truth. What do they tell you?"

"I'm an alcoholic," Steve said. "And I will never again deny that I have a drinking problem. I made that commitment to myself and my family."

"Thanks for that, and I'm so glad to hear your resolution, Steve. Tony and I wish you the best in your recovery."

More than half a dozen callers followed Steve. Their eyes of truth led them to say never again to war, prejudice, child abuse, bullying, hunger, greed, and homelessness. So engaging were the discussions that Ike promised to continue the topic in the next show.

Tony played "In Your Eyes," by Peter Gabriel.

It was time to go home.

CHAPTER THIRTY-TWO

FINAL SHOT

February 2011

Ike walked toward the subway station on Columbus Circle. He raised the collar of his navy woolen overcoat against the late February winds. The cold got to him now in a way it never had before.

Now that his grandfather was gone, Ike was the only Miller-Sperber family member left standing. He resolved not only to keep standing and walking and breathing, but also to have a family to stand with him. *Maybe,* he thought, *it's time to find someone normal, someone who wants children, maybe lots of them, and create the family I never had.* Love without the insanity of whatever it was with Aja would be a great thing. He wondered if Samantha would have dinner with him. He pulled out his phone and called her.

"Ike? Everything okay?" she asked.

"Yeah. Just want to talk to you about a couple of things," he said. Even this baby step of connecting with a woman was nerve-wracking. He wondered if his voice betrayed his feelings.

"Am I doing a good job for the show?" she asked.

"Absolutely. You've got a lively personality, know psychology, and sound great. You're precisely what we need. But that's not the reason I called. I want to thank you for visiting me and bringing me all those wonderful things. You hardly know me, and that was so considerate of you."

"You're welcome," she said. "It was my pleasure."

"I'd love to take you to dinner."

"Oh, you don't have to do that."

"It's the least I can do. The only dining out I've done the last four months was to eat the gruel they brought me in the hospital. I'd appreciate it if you'd join me at a real restaurant."

She laughed softly. "I'd love that."

Ike felt his spirits rise.

"Good. I'm going into the subway now. How about if I call you when I get home and we'll figure out a time for tonight? Is that okay?"

"Yeah. That sounds great."

"Good. Talk to you later."

Ike entered the station. The lunchtime commuter traffic was maybe sixty percent of what it would be during rush hour, but there was enough of a crowd to make getting a seat on the "1" train a low-level competition—one no longer impeded by a knee worked over by a crazed Nazi surgeon. When a wave of straphangers pushed out as he pushed in, a seat opened next to the car doors and

Ike plopped himself onto it. He still had trouble believing how winded such a simple act could make him. The doctors said a year for full recovery, and then he could start a program of aerobic exercise and weight training. When he was strong enough he could return to hoops, but it would be without the weekend obsession he'd had for so many years, the obsession fueled by his inability to transcend that final game of that NCAA Finals weekend.

Two stations, a short walk, and he'd be home.

Ike closed his eyes.

Images of Aja ran through his thoughts. Was she the one who'd called the station? No. She wouldn't play that kind of game. Then who? Aja floated back into his thoughts. Snippets of their time together both horrifying and sublime might have made other riders wonder about the changes his face was going through, but as a psychologist and as an anonymous person on a train, Ike knew people didn't care what he was thinking. And as a New Yorker, he knew no one was really paying attention to him anyway.

Ike opened his eyes and scanned the crowded subway. He began to skip through the advertisements that lined the cabin's walls above the windows. There it was again: "If you see something, say something." It was a good message to New Yorkers, citizens of a great city who too often just walked past any mischief or mayhem they happened upon. He scanned the crowded car. Across from him sat a college-aged student playing a video game as she leaned her elbows on a textbook. Next to her, a guy in a suit was reading the New York *Times*, and scrunched next to him was a bearded Orthodox Jew reading a prayer book. Something about the man was

familiar. Ike wondered if he was someone Avram had
done business with. Ike closed his eyes again. He realized how relaxed he was about the warning ad compared
to the last time he'd pondered its words. He didn't see
anything, and he had nothing to say. The train stopped
at 71st Street. The bearded Hasid and the video game
college student got off.

The train came into the Seventy-Ninth Street Station.
Ike hustled–the unencumbered movement felt great —
up the exit stairs and out to the street. On his way to
the Towers, he called Samantha. They would meet at
a gourmet health food restaurant at six-thirty. He felt
excited by the possibilities.

He was already exhausted from the little he'd done
today and wanted the elevator to come and get him to
the thirtieth floor now if not sooner. He pushed the up
button twice, as if somehow repeated pokes of his index
finger would make the machinery run faster. He looked
up at the floor number indicator and saw the elevator
stop at thirty. He wondered if he'd just missed his neigh-
bor, Brian, a Wall Street guy, who'd been nice enough to
check in on him a few times since Ike came home.

Damn, Ike thought. *What a pain waiting is.*

The second elevator, too, had just arrived on his
floor, as if it were a runner-up in some bizarre elevator race. *Must be a delivery, or someone visiting Brian,* Ike
thought. It all added up to a longer delay and his fatigue
and physical discomfort spawned increased irritation.
He dropped onto one of the small loveseats manage-
ment had placed opposite the elevator and kept his eyes
on the indicator.

Finally, the first elevator headed down. When the display light flashed "18," Ike revisited the tragedy that was his grandfather's murder. There were just too many reminders of Otto in this neighborhood. Maybe a move downtown, or to the East Side, or closer to the radio station would be a good idea. Or, with increased success, he could broadcast from anywhere: LA, the Caribbean, Europe, Hawaii. *Yeah, how about a gig in Maui?* Ike heard Otto in his head tell him: *"Maybe you should only take a vacation to Maui. You would be miserable in such a place so far from everyone."*

The sliding sound of the elevator doors got him back into the present. Ike stood and wearily walked in. *"Oy,* I feel like such an old Jewish man," he said aloud and laughed. Destination: thirty. In a Big Apple minute, he was walking down the hallway. *A nap would be heaven.*

Ike opened his apartment door and ambled into the kitchen. He was about to get a glass and fill it from the dispenser on the fridge when he noticed a smell. A barely perceptible odor reminded him of how Jamal was able to sniff out a presence. Was that it? Someone was, or had been, in the apartment. Ike sniffed again. He checked the calendar on his I-Phone. Monday. The cleaning service wasn't due today.

"Hello," Ike called out toward the back of the apartment.

Silence.

But he listened more intently now. The wind rattled the building. There was always rattling thirty stories up. He walked cautiously toward the back of his place. He checked his bedroom and the master bath that was forever off-limits. He entered the guest bathroom with its frightening reminder of violence, the atoms and molecules of that horror still infiltrating the room's atmosphere. The only place left was the second bedroom, a room he'd converted into a home office. If an intruder was there, Ike needed to be prepared. He bent down to a trash basket under the vanity and pulled out the .44 he'd used to shoot Cone. He kept it underneath his other two weapons: the iron and hair-dryer.

"Put it down, Ike, and come out of there," a familiar voice said.

Ike put the gun on the top of the sink and turned around.

It was the religious Jew who'd exited the subway car one stop before his. As he'd left the car, the Hasid's plodding gait hadn't registered. Now there was no mistaking Simon Cone.

"Keep moving," Cone ordered.

"Where?"

"Just keep going. I'll tell you when to stop."

Cone used his gun to push him into the kitchen and dining room area.

"You thirsty or something? I was just about to get a glass of water," Ike said.

"Very funny."

"I'm not making a joke. Ever since your partners busted me up, I need to drink a lot of water. Mind if I get a glass?"

"Knock yourself out."

Ike removed a glass from the dry rack next to his sink and put it under the fridge dispenser. For some reason he wasn't afraid. Perhaps it was some numbing benefit of spending so much time being chased, tied up, and shot.

"I'm here to finish business with you," Cone said.

"Really." Ike stared at him. "Before finishing business, can you tell me how you got out of jail?"

"They say cops are fucked in prison. Not me. So many people owe me. A get out of jail card was easy. But it came at a cost. I had to negotiate a ten percent freedom fee with the guys who got me out of there," he said, smirking.

"How are you going to do that?" Ike asked.

"When you give me what I deserve," he said. His eyes narrowed, and his facial muscles tensed.

"That's interesting," Ike said. "As far as I'm concerned, you deserve the chair, lethal injection, gas, or the firing squad. I don't care how you get what you deserve, just that you get it. The same goes for your Nazi partner. But I'm just saying."

Cone took two steps forward and grabbed Ike by the collar of his coat. He dug the muzzle of his gun into Ike's temple. "Fucking with me deserves a never again. I know you know what that means. Get the jewels for me now and I'll leave you alone."

"The diamonds are gone," Ike said. He waited for fear to set in, but it wasn't happening.

"Bullshit," Cone said.

"No bullshit. You know Cone, they were worth close to two hundred and three hundred million dollars. Helm was probably lowballing. Anyway, you're late to the party unless you've got a good charity or foundation we can support. The jewels were liquidated and the value placed in a trust, The Miller-Sperber Eyes of

Truth Trust Fund. Terrific name, don't you think? It was created to clean up all that blood money and do some good. You have to apply first."

Cone's face was inches from Ike's and his skin was turning a shade best described as mauve. He had broken out in a sweat. He kept the gun hard against Ike's temple.

"I'm done with you," Cone said.

The apartment door burst open, and Ike heard the sharp snap of a gunshot. Ike wondered if he were dead. But then the bullet hole in Cone's forehead spurted blood onto Ike's face and clothing. He dropped to the floor at Ike's feet.

Aja ran to him. "You okay?"

Ike was in some fuzzy, disconnected place. "I guess," he said.

Aja's eyes were full of tears. She pulled him close and kissed him on the lips. "Thank you for coming to get me. I'll always be grateful. I love you," she said. "And I'm sorry for what happened. But darling, I have to go."

Ike wanted to hold onto her. But she pulled away and walked out the door. He shook his head to bring himself into focus. *But darling, I have to go.* He ran after her. An envelope lay on the floor just inside the apartment door. His name was written on the front. He ran past it and out into the hallway. The elevator door closed. Ike ran to the exit and down the stairs, knowing full well that even if he were in his best shape he'd never get down in time to catch up to her. He had to try. He labored down the thirty flights of stairs, winded and feeling the pain of lungs not fully healed. He burst into the main lobby.

Wagner held open the door, eyes widening at the sight of Ike's bloody face.

There were no signs of Aja on the street. A cab idled at the light on the corner of Riverside Drive. The passenger could have been her. Wagner tapped him on the shoulder. "You looking for the woman who just ran out?"

"Yeah," Ike panted.

"She told me to tell you not to. She said to read the letter."

"That's it?"

"That's it."

Ike nodded. The light changed and the cab accelerated through the intersection and down the street and out of sight. He was letting her go. So much of what had happened and what was still happening to him had that as the lesson.

He had to let go.

"Wagner, I need you to do something."

"Sure. What is it?"

"Call the police and send them up to my apartment."

Final Shot Discography
(In Order of Appearance)

"Roll Over Siggie Freud Gonna Tell Dr. Ike the News" (original music and lyrics by Chuck Berry, parody lyrics by Ira Kalina, performed by Scott Barber.)

"Monday, Monday" (John Phillips, performed by The Mamas & the Papas)

"Hate It Here" (Jeff Tweedy, performed by Wilco)

"I Can't Quit Her" (Al Kooper, performed by Blood, Sweat & Tears)

"Our House" (Graham Nash, performed by Crosby, Stills, Nash, & Young)

"What's New Pussycat?" (Burt Bacharach and Hal David, performed by Tom Jones)

"How Much is That Doggie in the Window?" (Bob Merrill, performed by Patti Page)

"Respect Yourself" (Luther Ingram, performed by The Staple Singers)

"Respect" (Otis Redding, performed by Aretha Franklin)

"Take Away My Pain" (John Petrucci, performed by Dream Theater)

"So Central Rain" (Bill Berry, Peter Buck, Mike Mills, and Michael Stipe, performed by REM)

"Walk On By" (Burt Bacharach and Hal David, performed by Dionne Warwick)

"Mockingbird" (Inez Foxx and Charlie Foxx, performed by James Taylor)

"Aja" (Donald Fagen and Walter Becker, performed by Steely Dan)

"Rikki Don't Lose that Number" (Donald Fagen and Walter Becker, performed by Steely Dan)

"Love and Vengeance," (Ira Kalina and Scott Barber, performed by Scott Barber)

"Rawhide" (Ned Washington and Dimitri Tiomkin, performed by Frankie Laine)

"The Goodbye Look" (Donald Fagen, performed by Donald Fagen)

"Blinded by Love" (Mick Jagger and Keith Richards, performed by The Rolling Stones)

"Dream" (Felice Bryant and Bordleaux Bryant, performed by The Everly Brothers)

"Caravan" (Van Morrison, performed by Van Morrison)

"Is That All There Is?" (Jerry Leiber and Mike Stoller, performed by Peggy Lee)

"I Only Have Eyes for You" (Harry Warren and Al Dubin, performed by The Flamingos)

"Love Stinks" (Peter Wolf and Seth Justman, performed by J. Geils Band)

"All You Need Is Love" (John Lennon and Paul McCartney, performed by The Beatles)

"Empire State of Mind" (Jay-Z, performed by Jay-Z and Alicia Keys)

"Proud Mary" (John Fogerty, performed by Ike & Tina Turner)

"A Hard Rain's A-Gonna Fall" (Bob Dylan, performed by Bob Dylan)

"Missing" (Bruce Springsteen, performed by Bruce Springsteen and The E Street Band)

"All Over" (Phoebe Snow, performed by Phoebe Snow)

"Ramblin' Man" (Dickey Betts, performed by The Allman Brothers Band)

Beep Beep, (The Playmates, performed by The Playmates)

"Start All Over Again" (Van Morrison, performed by Van Morrison)

"Soul Survivor" (Mick Jagger and Keith Richards, performed by The Rolling Stones)

"The Eyes of Truth" (Enigma, performed by Enigma)

"Never Again" (Remedy, performed by Remedy)

"In Your Eyes" (Peter Gabriel, performed by Peter Gabriel)

About the Author

Having had a forty-year distinguished career in psycho-therapy and marriage and family therapy as a diagnostician, therapist, supervisor, and professor, Ira Kalina, Ph. D. turned to his other passion, writing fiction, for the next phase of his life. "Final Shot" is Dr. Kalina's first novel, and the first in a series of mysteries he has dubbed *The Psych 'n' Roll Mystery Series*.

In addition to his writing, Dr. Kalina is the moderator of the simulated online radio advice and music show located at www.psychnrollradio.com. This unique program, now in blog and podcast format, provides advice, coaching, and personal support using Dr. Kalina's expertise. Each program is based on a topic of the day (emotional, relationship, problems of daily life, music for the soul, spirituality, and more) of his choice, and occasionally the choice of participants. Each subject begins with a musical set related to the theme. Songs or musical productions from various genres follow each individual interaction as well. A new show and topic is presented every Wednesday.

Dr. Kalina lives on Long Island. He is married and has two adult sons.

70615713R00188

Made in the USA
Columbia, SC
10 May 2017